John Jenkins, Evan Evans

Some Specimens of the Poetry of the Ancient Welsh Bards

John Jenkins, Evan Evans

Some Specimens of the Poetry of the Ancient Welsh Bards

ISBN/EAN: 9783337328023

Printed in Europe, USA, Canada, Australia, Japan

Cover: Foto ©Andreas Hilbeck / pixelio.de

SPECIMENS OF THE POETRY

OF

THE ANCIENT WELSH BARDS.

Translated into English,

WITH EXPLANATORY NOTES ON THE HISTORICAL PASSAGES, AND A SHORT ACCOUNT OF MEN AND PLACES MENTIONED BY THE BARDS.

BY THE

REV. EVAN EVANS, (IEUAN PRYDYDD HIR.)

"Vos quoque, qui fortes animas belloque peremptas
"Laudibus in longum, Vates, dimittitis ævum,
"Plurima securi fudistis carmina Bardi."
LUCANUS.

——— "Si quid mea carmina possunt
"Aonio statuam sublimes vertice Bardos,
"Bardos Pieridum cultores atque canentis
"Phœbi delicias, quibus est data cura perennis
"Dicere nobilium clarissima facta virorum,
"Aureaque excelsam famam super astra locare."
LELANDUS in Assertione Arturii.

REPRINTED FROM DODSLEY'S EDITION OF 1764.

PUBLISHED BY JOHN PRYSE, LLANIDLOES, MONTGOMERY;
AND SOLD BY ALL BOOKSELLERS.

TO

SIR ROGER MOSTYN,

OF

MOSTYN AND GLODDAITH, BART.,

Representative of the County, Lord Lieutenant, and Lieutenant Colonel of the Militia of Flintshire.

SIR,

I HOPE you will pardon my presumption in prefixing your name to the following small collection of British poems, to which you have a just claim, as being lineally descended from those heroes they celebrate, and retain in an eminent manner the worth and generous principles of your renowned ancestors. The British Bards were received by the nobility and gentry with distinguished marks of esteem, in every part of Wales, and particularly at Gloddaith and Mostyn, where their works are still preserved in your curious libraries. I hope, therefore, an attempt to give the public a small specimen of their works will not fail of your approbation, which the editor flatters himself with, from the generous manner with which you treated him, particularly by lending him some of your valuable books and manuscripts.

That you may long continue to be an ornament to your country, and a pattern of virtuous actions, and a generous patron of learning, is the sincere wish, of,

Sir,

Your obliged

Humble Servant,

EVAN EVANS.

PREFACE.

AS there is a natural curiosity in most people to be brought acquainted with the works of men, whose names have been conveyed down to us with applause from very early antiquity, I have been induced to think, that a translation of some of the Welsh Bards would be no unacceptable present to the public. It is true they lived in times when all Europe was enveloped with the dark cloud of bigotry and ignorance; yet, even under these disadvantageous circumstances, a late instance may convince us, that poetry shone forth with a light, that seems astonishing to many readers. They who have perused the works of Ossian, as translated by Mr. Macpherson, will, I believe, be of my opinion.

I mean not to set the following poems in competition with those just mentioned; nor did the success which they have met with from the world, put me upon this undertaking. It was first thought of, and encouraged some years before the name of Ossian was known in England. I had long been convinced, that no nation in Europe possesses greater remains of ancient and gennine pieces of this kind than the Welsh; and therefore was inclined, in honour to my country, to give a specimen of them in the English language.

As to the genuineness of these poems, I think there can be no doubt; but though we may vie with the Scottish nation in this particular, yet there is another point, in which we must yield to them undoubtedly. The language of their oldest poets, it seems, is still perfectly intelligible, which is by no means our case.

The works of Taliesin, Llywarch Hên, Aneurin Gwawdrydd, Myrddin Wyllt, Avan-Verddig, who all flourished about the year 560, a considerable time after Ossian, are hardly understood by the best critics and antiquarians in Wales, though our language has not undergone more changes than the Erse. Nay, the Bards that wrote a long while after, from the time of William the Conquerer to the death of Prince Llewelyn, are not so easy to be understood; but that whoever goes about to translate them, will find numerous obsolete words, not to be found in any Dictionary or Glossary, either in print or manuscript.

What this difference is owing to, I leave to be determined by others, who are better acquainted, than I am, with such circumstances of the Scottish Highlands, as might prove more favourable towards keeping up the perfect knowledge of their language for so many generations. But, be that as it may, it is not my intent to enter into the dispute, which has arisen in relation to the antiquity of Ossian's poems. My concern is only about the opinion the world may entertain of the intrinsic value of those which I offer. They seem to me, though not so methodical and regular in their composition as many poems of other nations, yet not to be wanting in poetical merit; and if I am not totally deceived in my judgment, I shall have no reason to repent of the pains I have taken to draw them out of that state of obscurity, in which they have hitherto been buried, and in which they run great risk of mouldering away.

It might perhaps be expected, that I should say something of the Bards in general on this occasion; but as I have treated that subject in my Latin Dissertation, which I shall annex to these translations, it will be sufficient to observe here, that the usual subjects of their poems were the brave feats of their warriors in the field, their hospitality and generosity, with other commendable qualities in domestic life, and elegies upon their great men, which were sung to the harp at their feasts, before a numerous audience of their friends and relations. This is the account that the Greek and Roman writers have given of them, as I have shown at large in the above-mentioned treatise, which I intend to publish.

The following poems, from among many others of greater length, and of equal merit, were taken from a manuscript of the learned Dr. Davies, author of the Dictionary, which he had transcribed from an ancient vellom MS. which was wrote, partly in Edward the Second and Third's time, and partly in Henry the Fifth's, containing the works of all the Bards from the Conquest to the death of Llewelyn, the last prince of the British line. This is a noble treasure, and very rare to be met with; for Edward the First ordered all our Bards, and their works, to be destroyed, as is attested by Sir John Wynne of Gwydir, in the history he compiled of his ancestors at Carnarvon. What remained of their works were conveyed in his time to the Exchequer, where he complains they lay in great confusion, when he had occasion to consult them.

As to the translation, I have endeavoured to render the sense of the Bards faithfully, without confining myself to too servile a version; nor have I, on the other hand, taken liberty to wander much from the originals; unless where I saw it absolutely necessary, on account of the different phraseology and idiom of language.

If this small collection has the good fortune to merit the attention of the public, I may, in some future time, if God permit me life and health, proceed to translate other select pieces from the same manuscript. The poems, in the original, have great merit; and if there is none in the translation of this specimen, it must be owing entirely to my inability to do the Bards justice. I am not the only person who admires them: men of the greatest sense and learning in Wales do the same.

It must be owned, that it is an arduous task to bring them to make any tolerable figure in a prose translation; but those who have any candour, will make allowances. What was said of poetry in general by one of the wits, that *it is but Prose run mad*, may very justly be applied to our Bards in particular: for there are not such extravagant flights in any poetic compositions, except it be in the Eastern, to which, as far as I can judge by the few translated specimens I have seen, they bear a great resemblance.

I have added a few Notes, to illustrate some historical facts alluded to in the poems, and a short account of each poem, and the occasion it was written upon, as far as it could be traced from our ancient manuscripts.

I have been obliged to leave blanks in some places, where I did not understand the meaning in the original, as I had but one copy by me, which might be faulty. When I have an opportunity to collate it with other copies, I may clear these obscure passages.

SPECIMENS OF ANCIENT WELSH POETRY.

A POEM *composed by Owain Cyveiliog, prince of Powys, entitled by him* HIRLAS, *from a large drinking horn so called, used at feasts in his palace. He was driven out of his country by Owain Gwynedd, prince of North Wales, and Rhys-ap-Griffydd-ap-Rhys-ap-Tewdwr, prince of South Wales, A.D.* 1167, *and recovered it, by the help of the Normans and English, under Henry the second. He flourished about A. D.* 1160, *in the time of Owain Gwynedd and his son David. This poem was composed on account of a battle fought with the English at Maelor, which is a part of the counties of Denbigh and Flint, according to the modern division.*

WHEN the dawn arose, the shout was given; the enemy gave an ominous presage; our men were stained with blood, after a hard contest; and the borders of Maelor Drefred were beheld with wonder and astonishment. Strangers have I driven away undaunted from the field with bloody arms. He that provokes the brave man, ought to dread his resentment.

Fill, cup-bearer, fill with alacrity the horn of Rhys, in the generous prince's hall; for Owain's hall was ever supported by spoils taken from the enemy; and in it thou hearest of the relief of thousands. There the gates are ever open.

O cup-bearer, who, with patience, mindest thy duty, forsake us not; fetch the horn, that we may drink together, whose gloss is like the wave of the sea; whose green handles shew the skill of the artist, and are tipped with gold. Bring the best meath, and put it in Gwgan Draws's hand, for the noble feats which he hath achieved: the offspring of Grònwy, who valiantly fought in the midst of dangers; a race of heroes for worthy acts renowned: and men, who, in every hardship they undergo, deserve a reward; who are in the battle foremost: the guardians of Sabrina. Their friends exult, when they hear their voice. The festal shout will cease when they are gone.

Fill thou the yellow-tipped horn, badge of honóur and mirth, full of frothing meath; and if thou art desirous to have thy life prolonged to the year's end, stop not the reward due to his virtue, for it is unjust; and bring it to Griffydd, with the crimson lance. Bring wine in the transparent horn; for he is the guardian of Arwystli,[1] the defence of its borders; a dragon of Owain the generous, whose descent is from Cynvyn; a dragon he was from the beginning, that never was terrified in the battle; his brave actions shall follow him. The warriors went to purchase renown, flushed with liquor, and armed like Edwin; they paid for their mead, like Belyn's[2] men, in the days of yore. And as long as men exist, their valour shall be the common theme of Bards.

Fill thou the horn; for it is my inclination, that we may converse in mirth and festivity with our brave general; put it in the hand of the worthy Ednyfed, with his spear broken to pieces, and his shield pierced through. Like the bursting of a hurricane upon the smooth sea . . . . in the conflict of battle, they

1 Arwystli, the name of one of the cantreds of Powys. 2 Belyn, a great man from Lleyn in Carnarvonshire, mentioned in the Triades, and is said there to have fought with Edwin, king of the Northumbrians, in Bryn Cenau in Rhos, in the county of Denbigh; probably he was one of Cadwallon's generals; it is well known, and confessed by Beda himself, that that prince was a terrible scourge to the Saxons.

would soon break in pieces the sides of a golden-bordered shield: their lances were besmeared with gore, after piercing the heads of their enemies; they were vigorous and active in the defence of delightful Garthan.[1] Heard ye in Maelor the noise of war, the horrid din of arms, their furious onset, loud as in the battle of Bangor,[2] where fire flashed out of their spears? There two princes engaged, when the carousing of Morach Vorvran[3] happened.

Fill thou the horn; for it is my delight, in the place where the defenders of our country drink mead, and give it to Selyf the fearless, the defence of Gwygyr;[4] woe to the wretch that offends him, eagle-hearted hero: and to the son of Madoc, the famous and generous Tudur, like a wolf when he seizes his prey, is his assault in the onset. Two heroes, who were sage in their counsels, but active in the field, the two sons of Ynyr, who, on the day of battle, were ready for the attack, heedless of danger, famous for their exploits; their assault was like that of strong lions, and they pierced their enemies like brave warriors; they were lords of the battle, and rushed fore-

1 Garthan, the name of a fort or castle somewhere near the Severn.

2 This was the famous battle of Bangor-is-y-coed in Flintshire, after the murder of the monks, at the instigation of Austin, the first converter of the Saxons to Christianity. This is the account Humphrey Lloyd gives of that affair: "Ille vero [Augustinus S.] ob hanc contumeliam, & quod archiepiscopo Cantuariæ a se constituto, & quod cum Romana ecclesia in quibusdam non convenirent, Anglorum odium ita in eos concivit, ut paulo post (ut dixi) ab Ethelfredo, Ethelberti, Cantiæ regis, ob Augustino incitati, opera & auxiliis, monachi pacem petentes, crudeliter occisi; & postea Britanni duce Brochwelo Powisiæ Rege, victi sunt, donec tandem Bletrusii Cornaviæ ducis, Cadvanni Northwalliæ, Mereduci Suthwalliæ regum copiis adjuti, & Dunoti abbatis viri doctissimi concione animati, quique jussit (ut nostri annales referunt) ut unusquisque terram oscularetur, in memoriam communionis corporis Dominici, aquamque ex Deva fluvio manu haustam biberet, in memoriam sacratissim isanguinis Christi pro eis effusis, & ita communicati, memorabili prœlio Saxones, occisis (ut Huntingtonensis refert) ex eis MLXVI. Cadvanumque in civitate Legionis regem creavere." Britan. Descript. Commentariolum, p. 90, & 91, Moses Williams's Edition. This battle is called in our annals sometimes Gwaith Caerlleon, that is, the battle of Chester, and is said to have been fought, A. D. 633.

3 We have no account at present, that I know of, who this Morach Vorvran was, nor the occasion of his joy and festivity, alluded to in this poem; probably it was upon the defeat of the Saxons at Bangor.

4 The name of a place, but where situated, I know not.

most with their crimson lances; the weight of their attack was not to be withstood; their shields were broke asunder with much force, as the high-sounding wind on the beach of the green sea, and the encroaching of the furious waves on the coast of Talgarth.[1]

Fill, cup-bearer, as thou regardest thy life; fill the horn, badge of honour at feasts, the hirlas[2] drinking-horn, which is a token of distinction, whose tip is adorned with silver, and it's cover of the same metal; and bring it to Tudur, the eagle of battles, filled with the best wine; and if thou dost not bring us the best of all, thy head shall fly off: give it in the hand of Moreiddig, encourager of songs, whose praise in battle is celebrated; they were brethren of a distant clime, of an undaunted heart, and their valour was observable in their countenance. Can I forget their services? . . . . . Impetuous warriors, wolves of the battle, their lances are besmeared with gore; they were the heroes of the chief of Mochnant,[3] in the region of Powys. Their honour was soon purchased by them both; they seized every occasion to defend their country, in the time of need, with their bloody arms, and they kept their borders from hostile invasion. Their lot is praise; it is like a mournful elegy to me to lose them both! O Christ! how pensive am I for the loss of Moreiddig, which is irreparable.

Pour thou out the horn, though they desire it not, the drinking horn, hirlas, with cheerfulness, and deliver it into the hand of Morgant, one who deserves to be celebrated with distinguished praise. It was like poison to me, to be deprived of him, and that he was pierced - - - - - - - - by the keen sword.

1 Talgarth, the name of many places in Wales; but this must be somewhere near the sea.

2 Hirlas, the epithet of the horn, from *hir*, long; and *glâs*, blue, or azure.

3 Mochnannwys, in the original, he calls himself prince of the Mochnannwys, or inhabitants of Mochnant.

Pour, cup-bearer, from a silver vessel, an honourable gift, badge of distinction. On the large plains of [1]Gwestun I have seen a miracle; to stop the impetuosity of Gronwy, was more than a task for an hundred men. The warriors pointed their lances, courted the battle, and were profuse of life; they met their enemies in the conflict, and their chieftain was consumed by fire near the surges of the sea.[2] They rescued a noble prisoner, Meurig the son of Griffydd, of renowned valour; they were all of them covered with blood when they returned, and the high hills and the dales enjoyed the sun equally.[3]

Pour the horn to the warriors, Owain's noble heroes, who were equally active and brave. They assembled in that renowned place, where the shining steel glittered. Madoc and Meilir were men accustomed to violence, and maintained each other in the injuries they did to their enemies; they were the shields of our army, and the teachers of warlike attack. Hear ye, by drinking mead, how the lord of Cattraeth went with his warriors in defence of his just cause, the guards of Mynyddawc[4] about their distinguished chief. They have been celebrated for their bravery, and their speedy march. But nobody has ever performed so noble an exploit as my warriors, in the tough land of Maelor, in rescuing the captive.

Pour out, cup-bearer, sweet and well strained mead, (the thrust of the spear is red in the time of need,) from the horns of wild oxen, covered with gold, for the honour,

1 Gwestun, the name of a place somewhere in Powys.

2 By this circumstance, it seems they rescued the prisoner from some maritime town.

3 Sun equally, that is, at noon day, which added much to the merit of the action.

4 The guards of Mynyddawc Eiddin, or of Edinborough, in the battle of Cattraeth, which is celebrated by Aneurin Gwawdrydd, in his heroic poem entitled the Gododin. Mynyddawc was a prince of the North: he is mentioned in the Triades of Britain; and his guards, who were famous for their loyalty and bravery, were reckoned among the three noble guards of the kingdom of Britain; the other two being the guards, or, as the word Gosgordd may be translated, the clans of Melyn, the son of Cynvelyn, and the guards of Drywon, the son of Nudd, in the battle of Rhodwydd Arderydd.

and the reward of the souls of those departed heroes. Of the numerous cares that surround princes, no one is conscious here but God and myself. The man who neither gives nor takes quarter, and cannot be forced by his enemies to abide to his word, Daniel the valiant and beautiful: O cup-bearer, great is the task to entreat him; his men will not cease dealing death around them, till he is mollified. Cup-bearer, our shares of mead are to be given us equally before the bright shining tapers. Cup-bearer, hadst thou seen the action in the land of Llidwm,[1] the men whom I honour have but what is their just reward. Cup-bearer, hadst thou seen the armed chiefs, encompassing Owain, who were his shield against the violence of his foes, when Cawres[2] was invaded with great fury. Cup-bearer, slight not my commands: may we all be admitted into Paradise by the King of kings; and long may the liberty and happiness of my heroes continue, where the truth is to be discerned distinctly.

1 Llidwm, the name of a place somewhere in Maelor.
2 I do not recollect what country this place is in.

A POEM

To Myfanwy Fechan[1] *of Castell Dinas Bran,*[2] *composed by Howel-ap-Einion Lygliw,*[3] *a Bard who flourished about A.D.* 1390.

I AM without spirit, O thou that hast enchanted me, as Creirwy[4] enchanted Garwy.[5] In whatever part of the world I am, I lament my absence from the marble castle of Myfanwy. Love is the heaviest burden, O thou that shinest like the heavens, and a greater punishment cannot be inflicted than thy displeasure, O beautiful Myfanwy. I who am plunged deeper and deeper in love, can expect no other ease, O gentle fair Myfanwy with the jet eyebrows, than to lose my life upon thy account. I sung in golden verse thy praises, O Myfanwy; this is the happiness of thy lover, but the happiness is a misfortune. The well-fed steed carried me pensive like Trystan,[6] and great was his speed to reach the golden summit of Bran. Daily I turn my eyes, and see thee, O thou that shinest like the waves of Caswennan.[7] Charming sight to gaze on thee in the spacious royal palace of Bran. I have rode hard,

1 I cannot recollect who Myfanwy Fechan, the subject of the poem, is, but guess her to be descended from the princes of Powys.

2 Castell Dinas Bran, or Bran's Castle, is situated on a high hill near Llangollen in Denbighshire. Mr. Humphrey Llwyd, the antiquarian, thinks it took its name from Brennus; but Llwyd of the Museum, more probably, from Bran, the name of a river that runs thereabout. Bran signifies a crow, and is the name of several rivers in Wales. I suppose on account of their black streams issuing from turfaries. There are still remains of the ruins of this castle.

3 Howel-ap-Einion Lygliw was a man of note in his time, and a celebrated Bard. Dr. Davies thinks he was uncle to Griffydd Llwyd-ap-Dafydd-ap-Einion Lygliw, another famous bard, who flourished A.D. 1400.

4 Creirwy, a lady of great beauty often mentioned by the bards.

5 Garwy, one of king Arthur's knights.

6 Trystan-ap-Tallwch, another of king Arthur's knights.

7 Caswennan, the name of one of king Arthur's ships, which was wrecked in a place denominated from her Goffrydau Caswennan.

mounted on a fine high-bred steed, upon thy account, O thou with the countenance of cherry-flower bloom. The speed was with eagerness, and the strong long-ham'd steed of Alban[1] reached the summit of the highland of Bran. I have composed, with great study and pains, thy praise, O thou that shinest like the new-fallen snow on the brow of Aran.[2] O thou beautiful flower descended from Trefor.[3] Hear my sorrowful complaint. I am wounded, and the great love I bear thee will not suffer me to sleep, unless thou givest me a kind answer. I, thy pensive Bard, am in as woeful plight as Rhun[4] by thy palace, beautiful maid. I recite, without either flattery or guile, thy praise, O thou that shinest like the meridian sun, with thy stately steps. Should'st thou, who art the luminary of many countries, demand my two eyes, I would part with them on thy account, such is the pain I suffer. They pain me while I look on the glossy walls of thy fine habitation, and see thee beautiful as the morning sun. I have meditated thy praise, and made all countries resound with it, and every singer was pleased in chanting it. So affecting are the subjects of my mournful tale, O Myfanwy,[5] that lookest like flakes of driven snow. My loving heart sinks with grief without thy support, O thou that hast the whiteness of the curling waves. Heaven has decreed, that I should suffer tormenting pain, and wisdom and reason were given in vain to guard against love. When I saw thy fine shape in scarlet robes, thou daughter of a generous chief, I was so affected, that life and death were equal to me. I sunk away, and scarce had

1 Alban, Scotland. It seems the Bard rode upon a Scotch steed.

2 Aran, the name of two high mountains in Merionethshire.

3 Some of the Trefor-family (and perhaps descendants) now live near Castell Dinas Bran.

4 Rhun, son of Maelgwn Gwynedd king of Britain, A.D. 570. I do not remember the story alluded to here by the Bard.

5 I suppose Myfanwy Fechan was descended from Tudur Trefor earl of Hereford, of one side. The worthy family of the Mostyns of Mostyn and Gloddaith, are descended from Tudur Trefor.

time to make my confession. Alas! my labour in celebrating thy praises, O thou that shinest like the fine spider's webs on the grass in a summer's day, is vain. It would be a hard task for any man to guess how great my pain is. It is so afflicting, thou bright luminary of maids, that my colour is gone. I know that this pain will avail me nothing towards obtaining thy love, O thou whose countenance is as bright as the flowers of the haw-thorn. O how well didst thou succeed in making me to languish, and despair. For heaven's sake, pity my distressed condition, and soften the penance of thy Bard. I am a Bard, who, though wounded by thee, sing thy praises in well sounding verse, thou gentle maid of slender shape, who hinderest me to sleep by thy charms. I bring thy praises, bright maid, to thy neat palace at Dinbrain;[1] many are the songs that I rehearse to celebrate thy beautiful form.

1 Dinbrain, the same as Dinas Bran.

AN ODE

Of David Benvras, to Llewelyn the Great, Prince of Wales, A.D. 1240.

HE who created the glorious sun, and that cold pale luminary the moon, grant that I attain the heights of poetry, and be inspired with the genius of Myrddin;[1] that I may extol the praise of heroes, like Aneurin,[2] in the day he sung his celebrated Gododin; that I may set forth the happiness of the inhabitants of Venedotia, the noble and prosperous prince of Gwynedd, the stay and prop of his fair and pleasant country. He is manly and heroic in the battle, his fame overspreadeth the country about the mountain of Breiddin.[3] Since God created the first man, there never was his equal in the front of battle. Llewelyn the generous, of the race of princes, has struck terror and astonishment in the heart of kings. When he strove for superiority with Loegria's king, when he was wasting the country of Erbin,[4] his troops were valiant and numerous. Great was the confusion when the shout was given, his sword was bathed in blood; proud were his nobles to see his army; when they heard the clashing of swords, then was felt the agony of wounds[5] - - - - - - - - - - - - - - - - -

1 There were two Myrddins, or Merlins, as they are wrongly written by the English, viz. Myrddin Emrys and Myrddin Wyllt; the last was a noted poet, and there is a poem of his extant, entitled Avallennau, or the Apple-trees.

2 Aneurin Gwawdrydd Mychdeyrn Beirdd, i. e. Aneurin the monarch of Bards, was a celebrated poet of North Britain. His poem, the Gododin, upon the battle of Cattraeth, is extant; but by reason of its great antiquity, is not easily understood at this distance of time, being upwards of twelve hundred years old: however, it appears, from what is understood of it, to have been a very spirited performance.

3 Craig Vreiddin, is a high hill in Montgomeryshire.

4 I know not where this country is.

5 Some lines are wanting in the original.

Many were the gashes in the conflict of war. Great was the confusion of the Saxons about the ditch of Knocking.[1] The sword was broke in the hand of the warrior. Heads were covered with wounds, and the flood of human gore gushed in streams down the knees.

Llewelyn's empire is wide extended, he is renowned as far as Porth Ysgewin.[2] Constantine was not his equal in undergoing hardships. Had I arrived to the height of prophecy, and the great gift of ancient poesy, I could not relate his prowess in action; no, Taliesin[3] himself was unequal to the task. Before he finishes his course in this world, after he has lived a long life on earth, ere he goes to the deep and bone-bestrewed grave, ere the green herb grows over his tomb, may He that turned the water into wine, grant that he may have the Almighty's protection, and that for every sin, with which he hath been stained, he may receive remission. May Llewelyn, the noble and generous, never be confounded or ashamed when he arrives at that period; and may he be under the protection of the saints.

1 Knocking, I suppose, is somewhere near Offa's ditch.

2 Porth Ysgewin is near Chepstow, in Monmouthshire or Glamorganshire.

3 Taliesin Ben Beirdd, or the chief of Bards, flourished about the year 560, or thereabout, under Maelgwn Gwynedd king of Britain, called by Gildas Maglocunus. Many of Taliesin's poems are extant, but on account of their great antiquity are very obscure, as the work of his cotemporaries are. There is a great deal of the Druidical Cabbala intermixed in his works, especially about the transmigration of souls.

A POEM

To Llewelyn the Great, composed by Einion the son of Gwgan, about 1244.

I INVOKE the assistance of the God of Heaven, Christ our Saviour, whom to neglect is impious. That gift is true which descendeth from above. The gifts that are given me are immortal, to discern, according to the great apostle, *what is right and decent;* and, among other grand subjects, to celebrate my prince, who avoids not the battle nor its danger; Llewelyn the generous, the maintainer of Bards. He is the dispenser of happiness to his subjects, his noble deeds cannot be sufficiently extolled. His spear flashes in a hand accustomed to martial deeds. It kills and puts its enemies to flight by the palace of Rheidiol.[1] I have seen, and it was my heart's delight, the guards of Lleision[2] about its grand buildings; numberless troops of warriors mounted on white steeds. They encompassed our eagle: Llewelyn the magnanimous hero, whose armour glistened; the maintainer of his rights. He defended the borders of Powys, a country renowned for its bravery; he defended its steep passes, and supported the privileges of its prince. Obstinate was his resistance to the treacherous English. In Rhuddlan he was like the ruddy fire flaming with destructive light. There have I seen Llewelyn the brave gaining immortal glory. I have seen him gallantly ploughing the waves of Deva, when the tide was at its height. I have seen

1 Rheidol is the name of a large river in Cardiganshire, and Glasgrug, one of the palaces of the princes of South Wales, is very near it, about a measured mile from Aberystwith, and at present the property of the Rev. Mr. William Powel, of Nanteos.

2 Lleision was one of the palaces of the princes of Powys, corruptly now called Llysin; and the park about it is called Llysin-park, the patrimony of Lord Powys.

him furious in the conflict of Chester, where he doubly repaid his enemies the injuries he suffered from them. It is but just that he should enjoy the praise due to his valour. I will extol thee, and the task is delightful. Thou art like the eagle amougst the nobles of Britain. Thy form is majestic and terrible, when thou pursuest thy foes. When thou invadest thy enemies, where Owain thy predecessor invaded them in former times; full proud was thy heart in dividing the spoils, it happened as in the battles of Kulwydd and Llwyvein.[1] Thy beautiful steeds were fatigued with the labour of the day, where the troops wallowed in gore, and were thrown in confusion. The bow was full bent before the mangled corse, the spear aimed at the breast in the country of Eurgain.[2] The army at Offa's Dike panted for glory, the troops of Venedotia, and the men of London, were as the alternate motion of the waves on the sea-shore, where the sea-mew screams; great was our happiness to put the Normans to fear and consternation. Llewelyn the terrible with his brave warriors effected it; the prince of glorious and happy Mona. He is its ornament and distinguished chief.

The lord of Demetia[3] mustered his troops, and out of envy met his prince in the field. The inhabitants of Stone-walled Carmarthen were hewn to pieces in the conflict. Nor fort, nor castle, could withstand him: and before the gates the English were trampled under foot. Its chief was sad, the unsheathed sword shone bright, and hundreds of hands were engaged in the onset at Llan

1 The battle of Llwyvein was fought by Urien Reged and his son Owain, against Ida king of the Northumbrians. It is celebrated by Taliesin in a poem, entitled Gwaith Argoed Llwyvein, i. e. the battle of Argoed Llwyvein.

2 Eurgain, Northop in Flintshire, so called from Eurgain, the daughter of Maelgwn Gwynedd.

3 Demetia. This expedition of Llewelyn-ap-Iorwerth was against the Flemings and Normans, of which there is an account in Powel's History of Wales, p. 277, 278.

Huadain.[1] In Cilgeran[2] they purchased glory and honour . . . . In Aber Teivi the hovering crows were numberless . . . thick were the spears besmeared with gore. The ravens croaked, they were greedy to suck the prostrate carcases. Llewelyn, may such fate attend thy foes. Mayest thou be more prosperous than the noble Llywarch[3] with his bloody lance. Thy glory shall not be obscured. There is none that exceedeth thee in bestowing gifts on the days of solemnity. In battle thy sword is conspicuous. Wherever thou goest to war, to whatever distant clime, glory follows thee from the rising to the setting sun. I have a generous and noble prince, the lord of a large territory. He is renowned for his coolness and conduct. Whole troops fall before him; he defendeth his men like an eagle. My prince's brave actions will be celebrated in the country by Tanad.[4] He is valorous as a lion, who can resist his lance? He is charitable to the needy, and his relief is not sought in vain. My prince is dressed in fine purple robes. He is like generous Nudd[5] in bestowing presents. Like valiant Huail[6] in defying his enemy. He is like Rhydderch[7] in distributing his gold. Let his praise resound in every country. He possesses a large territory and immense

1 Llan Huadain, the name of a place in Pembrokeshire.

2 Cilgeran, the name of another place in the same county, near the river Teivi.

3 Llywarch Hen, the son of Elidir Lydanwyn a nobleman of North Britain, and cousin german to Urien Reged king of Cumbria; he was a great warrior, and fought successful against the Saxons; but fortune at last favouring the Saxons, he was obliged in his old age to retire to Wales. He had twenty-four sons, who wore golden chains, and were all killed in battles against the Saxons. Llywarch Hen was a noted Bard, his works are extant, wherein he celebrates the noble feats of his sons, and bewails his misfortunes, and the troubles of old age, especially in distress.

4 Tanad is the name of a river in Montgomeryshire, which emptieth itself into the Severn.

5 Nudd Hael, or the Generous, was a nobleman of North Britain remarkable for his liberality.

6 Huail was a brother of Gildas, the son of Caw, and a noted warrior. His brother Gildas was the author of the Epistle De excidio Britanniæ.

7 Rhydderch Hael, or the Generous, was another nobleman of the North, noted for his liberality.

riches, wherever you turn your eyes. In wealth he is equal to Mordaf; like him he opens his liberal hand to the Bard. He is like warlike Rhun[1] in bestowing his favours. He is the subject of my meditation. I am to him as an hand or an eye.[2] He is not descended from a base degenerate stock; and I myself am descended from his father's courtiers. His fury in battle is like lightning when he attacks the foe: his heart glows with ardour in the field like magnanimous Gwriad.[3] His enemies are scattered as leaves on the side of hills drove by tempestuous hurricanes. He is the honourable support and owner of Hunydd.[4] He is the grace, the ornament of Arvon.[5] Llewelyn, terror of thy enemy, death issued out of thy hand in the South. Thou art to us like an anchor in the time of storm. Protector of our country, may the shield of God protect thee. Britain, fearless of her enemies, glories in being ruled by him, by a chief who has numerous troops to defend her; by Llewelyn, who defies his enemies from shore to shore. He is the joy of armies, and like a lion in danger. He is the emperor and sovereign of sea and land. He is a warrior that may be compared to a deluge, to the surge on the beach that covereth the wild salmons. His noise is like the roaring wave that rusheth to the shore, that can neither be stopped or appeased. He puts numerous troops of his enemies to flight like a mighty wind. Warriors crowded about him, zealous to defend his just cause; their shields shone bright

1 Rhun, the son of Maelgwn Gwynedd king of Britain, a great warrior.

2 As an hand, &c., i. e. I am as necessary to him as one of those members to the body, to celebrate his martial feats.

3 Gwriad is the name of a hero mentioned in the Gododin.

4 Hunydd, the name of a woman, probably the prince's mistress. The Bards had no great affection for Joan the princess, daughter of king John, because she was an Englishwoman, and not faithful to the prince's bed.

5 Arvon, the county of Carnarvon, so called, because situated opposite to Môn, or Anglesea. Arvon, literally Supra Monam, from the particle Ar, super, and Môn, Mona.

on their arms. His Bards make the vales resound with his praises; the justice of his cause, and his bravery in maintaining it, are deservedly celebrated. His valour is the theme of every tongue. The glory of his victories is heard in distant climes. His men exult about their eagle. To yield or die is the fate of his enemies—they have experienced his force by the shivering of his lance. In the day of battle no danger can turn him from his purpose. He is conspicuous above the rest, with a large, strong, crimson lance. He is the honour of his country, great is his generosity, and a suit is not made to him in vain. Llewelyn is a tender-hearted prince. He can nobly spread the feast, yet is he not enervated by luxury. May he that bestowed on us a share of his heavenly revelation, grant him the blessed habitation of the saints above the stars.

A PANEGYRIC

Upon Owain Gwynedd, Prince of North Wales, by Gwalchmai, the son of Meilir, in the year 1157.

I WILL extol the generous hero descended from the race of Roderic,[1] the bulwark of his country, a prince eminent for his good qualities, the glory of Britain, Owain the brave and expert in arms, a prince that neither hoardeth nor coveteth riches.—Three fleets arrived, vessels of the main, three powerful fleets of the first rate, furiously to attack him on a sudden. One from Iwerddon,[2] the other full of well-armed Lochlynians,[3] making a grand appearance on the floods, the third from the transmarine Normans,[4] which was attended with an immense, though successless toil.

1 Owain Gwynedd, prince of North Wales, was descended in a direct line from Roderic the Great, prince of all Wales, who divided his principality amongst his three sons.

2 Iwerddon, the British name of Ireland, hence the Hibernia of the Latins, and 'Ιέρνη and 'Ιουέρνια of the Greeks, probably called from the British Y Werdd Ynys, i. e. the Green Island.

3 Lochlynians, the Danes, so called from the Baltic, which our ancestors called Llychlyn. Llychlyn is the name of Denmark and Norway, and all those northern regions mentioned in the works of our bards.

4 Normans. Moses Williams, in his notes on the Æræ Cambro Brittanicæ, gives the following account of this battle.

"Normanni, qui in hoc loco Frainc appellantur, erant copiæ quas Henricus Secundus in Monam misit A.D. MCLVII. duce Madoco filio Maredudii Powisiæ principe. Hi ecclesias SS. Mariæ et Petri (ut annales nostri referunt) spoliavere. Istæ vero ecclesiæ in orientali Monæ plaga sunt, unde liquet locum Tal Moelvre dictum alicubi in Mona esse, fortasse etiam haud procul ab ecclesiis prædictis: omnes vero qui navibus egrediebantur a Monæ incolis interfecti sunt." Vide Annales a Powelo editos, p. 206, 207.

It seems by Gwalchmai's poem to have been a very large fleet, which came partly from Ireland, partly from the Baltic, and the rest from Normandy, to invade the principality. It is plain that its forces were numerous, as they came from so many countries; but it seems they met with a very warm reception from the prince and his sons, and that they were glad to sail away as soon as possible.

The Dragon of Mona's sons[1] were so brave in action, that there was a great tumult on their furious attack, and before the prince himself, there was vast confusion, havoc, conflict, honourable death, bloody battle, horrible consternation, and upon Tal Moelvre a thousand banners. There was an outrageous carnage,[2] and the rage of spears, and hasty signs of violent indignation. Blood raised the tide of the Menai, and the crimson of human gore stained the brine. There were glittering cuirasses, and the agony of gashing wounds, and mangled warriors prostrate before the chief, distinguished by his crimson lance. Lloegria was put into confusion, the contest and confusion was great, and the glory of our prince's wide-wasting sword shall be celebrated in an hundred languages to give him his merited praise.

1 Owain Gwynedd had many sons noted for their valour, especially Howel, who was born of Finnog, an Irish lady. He was one of his father's generals in his wars against the English, Flemings, and Normans, in South Wales, and was a noted Bard, as several of his poems, now extant, testify.

2 It seems that tne fleet landed in some part of the firth of Menai, and that it was a kind of a mixed engagement, some fighting on shore, others from the ships. And probably the great slaughter was owing to its being low water, and that they could not set sail: otherwise I see no reason why, when they were worsted on land, they should continue the fight in their ships. It is very plain that they were in great distress, and that there was a great havoc made of them, as appears from the remainder of this very spirited poem.

AN ELEGY

To Nest,[1] *the daughter of Howel, by Einion, the son of Gwalchmai, about the year* 1240.

THE spring returns, the trees are in their bloom, and the forest in its beauty, the birds chaunt, the sea is smooth, the gently-rising tide sounds hollow, the wind is still. The best armour against misfortune is prayer. But I cannot hide nor conceal my grief, nor can I be still and silent. I have heard the waves raging furiously towards the confines of the land of the sons of Beli.[2] The sea flowed with force, and conveyed a hoarse complaining noise, on account of a gentle maiden. I have passed the deep waters of the Teivi[3] with slow steps. I sung the praise of Nest ere she died. Thousands have resounded her name, like that of Elivri.[4] But now I must with a pensive and sorrowful heart compose her elegy, a subject fraught with misery. The bright luminary of Cadvan[5] was arrayed in silk, how beautiful did she shine on the banks of Dysynni,[6] how great was her innocence and simplicity, joined with consummate prudence: she was above the base arts of dissimulation. Now the ruddy earth covers her in silence. How great was our grief, when she was laid in her stony habitation. The burying of Nest was an irreparable loss. Her eye was as sharp as the hawk, which argued her descended from noble ancestors. She added to her native beauty by her goodness and virtue.

1 Who this lady was is not known at present.
2 What country this is I cannot recollect.
3 Teivi, the name of a large river in Cardiganshire.
4 Elivri, the name of a woman; but who she was, or when she lived, is not clear.
5 Cadvan is the saint of Towyn Meirionydd.
6 Dysynni is the name of a river that runs by Towyn.

She was the ornament of Venedotia, and her pride. She rewarded the Bard generously. Never was pain equal to what I suffer for her loss. Oh death, I feel thy sting, thou hast undone me. No man upon earth regreteth her loss like me; but hard fate regardeth not the importunity of prayers, whenever mankind are destined to undergo its power. O generous Nest, thou liest in thy safe retreat, I am pensive and melancholy like Pryderi.[1] I store my sorrow in my breast, and cannot discharge the heavy burden. The dark, lonesome, dreary veil, which covereth thy face, is ever before me, which covereth a face that shone like the pearly dew on Eryri.[2] I make my humble petition to the great Creator of heaven and earth, and my petition will not be denied, that he grant, that this beautiful maid, who glittered like pearls, may, through the intercession of Holy Dewi,[3] be received to his mercy, that she may converse with the prophets, that she may come into the inheritance of the All-wise God, with Mary and the Martyrs. And in her behalf I will profer my prayer, which will fly to the throne of Heaven. My love and affection knew no bounds. May she never suffer. Saint Peter be her protector. God himself will not suffer her to be an exile from the mansions of bliss. Heaven be her lot.

1 I cannot recollect at present who this person is, nor the occasion of his grief, though it is mentioned in some of our manuscripts.

2 Eryri, Snowdon, called Creigiau Eryri and Mynydd Eryri, i. e. the rocks and mountains of snow, from Eiry, which signifies snow. As Niphates, the name of a mountain, from a word of the same signification in Greek.

3 Dewi, St. David, a bishop in the time of king Arthur, and the patron saint of Wales.

A POEM

To Llewelyn-ap-Iorwerth, or Llewelyn the Great; in which many of his victories are celebrated.

Composed by Llywarch Brydydd y Moch, a Bard, who, according to Mr. Edward Llwyd of the Museum's Catalogue of the British writers, flourished about the year 1240; but this poem is certainly of more ancient date, for prince Llewelyn died in the year 1240. However that be, the original was taken from Llyfr Coch o Hergest, or the Red book of Hergest, kept in the Archives of Jesus College, Oxon. I have no apology to make for the Bards' method of beginning or concluding their poems, but that it was their general custom ever since the introduction of Christianity to this island, which was very early. We have no poems that I know of before that period, but some few remains of the Druids in that kind of verse called Englyn Milwr. It was the custom of the heathen poets themselves to begin their poems with an invocation of the Supreme Being. As for instance, Theocritus in the beginning of his Idyllium in praise of Ptolemæus Philadelphus,

Ἐκ Διὸς ἀρχώμεσθα, ϗ εἰς Δία λήγετε, Μοῖσαι.

But I shall not here enter into a critical dissertation of their merits or defects; my business, as a translator, being to give as faithful a version from the original as I possibly could at this distance of time; when many of the matters of fact, the manners of the age, and other circumstances, alluded to in their poems, must remain obscure to those that are best versed in the records of antiquity.

MAY Christ, the Creator and Governor of the hosts of heaven and earth, defend me from all disasters; may I, through his assistance, be prudent and discreet ere I come to my narrow habitation in the grave. Christ, the son of God, will give me the gift of song to extol my prince, who giveth the warlike shout with joy. Christ who hath formed me of the four elements, and hath endowed me with the deep and wonderful gift of poetry—Llewelyn is the ruler of Britain and her armour. He is a lion-like brave prince, unmoved in action, the son of Iorwerth,[1] our strength and true friend, a descendant of Owain[2] the destroyer, whose abilities appeared in his youth. He came to be a leader of forces, dressed in blue, neat and handsome. In the conflicts of battle, in the clang of arms, he was an heroic youth. When ten years old he successfully attacked his kinsman.[3] In Aber Conwy, ere my prince, the brave Llewelyn, got his right, he contested with David,[4] who was a bloody chief, like Julius Cæsar. A chief without blemish, not insulting his foes in distress, but in war impetuous and fierce, like the points of flaming fire burning in their rage. It is a general loss to the Bards, that he is covered with earth. We grieve for him.—Llewelyn was our prince ere the furious contest happened, and the spoils were amassed with eagerness.[5] The purple gore ran over the snow-white breasts of the warriors, and there was an universal havoc and carnage after the shout. The parti-coloured waves flowed over the broken spear, and the warriors were silent. The briny wave came with force, and another met it mixed

1 Iorwerth, surnamed Drwyndwn, or with the broken nose, the father of Llewelyn, was the eldest son of Owain Gwynedd, but was not suffered to enjoy his right on account of that blemish.

2 Owain Gwynedd, prince of North Wales.

3 Llewelyn was the lawful heir of the principality of North Wales, in right of his father Iorwerth, and accordingly put in his claim for it, and got it from his uncles David and Rodri, when he was very young.

4 David, the son of Owain Gwynedd, who succeeded his father as prince of Wales.

5 This battle is not mentioned by any of our historians. The description is very animated in the original, and very expressive of such a scene. It was fought near Porth Aethwy. The steeds of the main is a poetical expression for ships.

with blood, when we went to Porth Aethwy on the steeds of the main over the great roaring of the floods. The spear raged with relentless fury, and the tide of blood rushed with force. Our attack was sudden and fierce. Death displayed itself in all its horrors: so that it was a doubt whether any of us should die of old age. Noble troops, in the fatal hour, trampled on the dead like prancing steeds. Before Rhodri was brought to submission, the church-yards were like fallow grounds. When Llewelyn the successful prince overcame near the Alun[1] with his warriors of the bright arms, ten thousand were killed, and the crows made a noise, and a thousand were taken prisoners. Llewelyn, though in battle he killed with fury, though he burnt like outrageous fire, yet he was a mild prince when the mead-horns were distributed - - - - - - - - he gave generously under his waving banners to his numerous Bards gold and silver, which he regardeth not, and Gasgony prancing steeds, with rich trappings, and great scarlet cloaks, shining like the ruddy flame: warlike, strong, well-made destroying steeds, with streams of foam issuing out of their mouths. He generously bestoweth, like brave Arthur, snow-white steeds by hundreds, whose speed is fleeter than birds.

Thou that feedest the fowls of the air like Caeawg[2] the hero, the valiant ruler of all Britain, the numerous forces of England tumble and wallow in the field before thee. He bravely achieved above Deudraeth Dryfan,[3] the feats of the renowned Ogrfan.[4] Men fall silently in the field, and are deprived of the rites of sepulture. Thou hast

1 Alun, the name of a river in Flintshire, where there was a battle fought by Llewelyn against the English.

2 Caeawg Cynnorawg is the name of a hero celebrated by Ancurin Gwawdrydd in the Gododin.

3 Deudraeth Dryfan is the name of some place near the sea. There are many places in Wales called Deudraeth; but where this in particular is situated I cannot guess.

4 Ogrfan Gawr, an ancient British prince, cotemporary with king Aurthur.

defeated two numerous armies, one on the banks of Alun of the rich soil, where the Normans were destroyed, as the adversaries of Arthur in the battle of Camlan.[1] The second in Arfon, near the sea shore - - - - - - -
And two ruling chiefs, flushed with success, encouraged us like lions, and one superior to them both, a stern hero, the ravage of battles, like a man that conquers in all places. Llewelyn with the broken blade of the gilt sword, the waster of Lloegr, a wolf covered with red, with his warriors about Rhuddlan. His forces carry the standard before him waving in the air. Thou art possessed of the valour of Cadwallon,[2] the son of Cadfan. He is for recovering the government of all Britain. He kindly stretched his hand to us, while his enemies fled to the sea shore, to embark to avoid the imminent destruction, with despair in their looks, and no place of refuge remained, and the crimson lance whizzed dreadfully over their brows. We the Bards of Britain, whom our prince entertaineth on the first of January, shall every one of us, in our rank and station, enjoy mirth and jollity, and receive gold and silver for our reward - - - - - - - - -
- - - - - - - - - - - - - -
- - - - - - - - - - - - - -
- - - - - - - - - - - - - -

Caer Lleon,[3] the chief of Môn, has brought thee to a low

1 Camlan, the name of a place somewhere in Cornwall, where the decisive battle between king Arthur, and his treacherous nephew Medrod happened, who had usurped the sovereignty while he was absent on a foreign expedition. King Arthur, according to our ancient historians, slew Medrod with his own hand; but received his death-wound himself, and retired to Ynys Afallon or Glastenbury, where he soon afterwards died. His death was politically concealed, lest it should dispirit the Britons. Hence arose so many fabulous stories about it.

2 Cadwallon, the son of Cadfan, is that victorious king of Britain, who was a terrible scourge to the Saxons. Beda, in his ecclesiastical history, calls him tyrannum sævientem, an outrageous tyrant.

3 Caer Lleon, Chester, so called, as our historians relate, from Lleon Gawr, or king Lleon, and not from Castra legionum, as modern writers will have it. Cawr anciently signified a king, as Benlli Gawr, is called by Nennius, cap. 30, Rex Benlli; but now it signifies a giant, or a man of an extraordinary strength and stature. It is not improbable but that the Ancient Britons chose such for their kings.

condition. Llewelyn has wasted thy land, thy men are killed by the sea - - - - - - - - -

He has entirely subdued Gwyddgrug,[1] where the English ran away, with a precipitate flight, full of horror and consternation. Thy fields are miserably wasted, thy cloister, and thy neat houses, are ashes. The palace of Elsmere[2] was with rage and fury burnt by fire. Ye all now enjoy peace by submitting to our prince, for wherever he goeth with his forces, whether it be hill or dale, it is the possession of one sole proprietor. Our lion has brought to Trallwng three armies that will never turn their backs, the residence of our enemies ever to be abhorred. The numerous Bards receive divers favours from him. He took Gwyddgrug. See you who succeeds in Mochnant[3] when he victoriously marches through your country. On its borders the enemy were routed, and the Argoedwys[4] were furiously attacked, and covered with blood. We have two palaces now in our possession. Let Powys[5] see who is the valiant king of her people, whether it argueth prudence to act treacherously. Whether a Norman chief be preferable to a conquering Cymro. We have a prince, consider it, who, though silent about his own merit, putteth Lloegr to flight, and is fully bent to conquer the land that was formerly in the possession of Cadwallon, the son of Cadfan, the son of Iago - - - - - -

- - - - - - - - - - -

A noble lion, the governor of Britain, and her defence, Llewelyn, numerous are thy battles, thou brave prince of

1 Gwyddgrug, Mold, in Flintshire, so called from Gwydd, high, and Crug, a hill. Mold is a corruption of Mons altus.

2 Elsmere, the name of a town in Shropshire.

3 Mochnant is a part of Powys.

4 Argoedwys, the men of Powys, from Ar, above, Coed, wood. The Powysians are called by Llywarch Hen, gwyr Argoed. As, "Gwyr Argoed erioed a'm porthant," i. e. I was ever maintained by the men of Argoed.

5 The princes of Powys adhered to the kings of England, and the lords Marchers, against their natural Prince, to whom they were to pay homage and obedience, according to the division made by Rhodri Mawr, as appears from the Welsh History.

the mighty, that puttest the enemy to flight. Mayest thou my friend and benefactor overcome in every hardship. He is a prince with terrible looks who will conquer in foreign countries, as well as in Môn the mother of all Wales. His army has made its way broad thro' the ocean, and filled the hills, promontories, and dales. The blood flowed about their feet when the maimed warriors fought. In the battle of Coed Aneu,[1] thou supporter of Bards, didst overthrow thy enemies. The other hard battle was fought at Dygen Ddyfnant,[2] where thousands behaved themselves with manly valour. The next contest, where noble feats were achieved, was on the hill of Bryn yr Erw,[3] where they saw thee like a lion foremost in piercing thy enemies, like a strong eagle, a safeguard to thy people. Upon this account they will no longer dispute with thee. They vanish before thee like the ghosts of Celyddon.[4] Thou hast taken Gwyddgrug and Dyfnant by force, and Rhuddlan with its red borders, and thousands of thy men overthrew Dinbych,[5] Foelas,[6] and Gronant;[7] and the men of Carnarvon, thy friends, were busy in action, and Dinas Emreis[8] strove bravely in thy cause, and they vanquished with the renowned Morgant[9] at their head all that stood before them. Thy pledges know not where to turn their faces, they cannot enjoy mirth or rest. Thou wert honourably covered with blood, and thy wound is a glory

1 Coed Aneu, the name of a place near Llanerchymedd, in Anglesea.

2 Dygen Ddyfnant, another place whose situation I am ignorant of, where another battle was fought.

3 Bryn yr Erw, another place unknown.

4 Celyddon, the British name of that part of North Britain, called Caledonia by the Romans.

5 Dinbych, Denbigh.

6 Foelas, or Y Foel las, i. e. the green summit, which is the name of a place in Denbighshire, where there is an old fort, now in the possession of Watkyn Wynn, Esq., colonel of the Denbighshire militia, whose seat is near it.

7 Gronant, the name of a fort or castle in Flintshire.

8 Dinas Emreis or Emrys, the name of a place in Snowdon, near Bedd Gelert, where Gwrtheyrn, or Vortigern, attempted to build a castle.

9 Morgant, the name of one of Llewelyn's generals.

to thee. When thou didst resist manfully the attack of the enemy, thou wert honoured by thy sword, with thy buckler on thy shoulders. Thou didst bravely lead thy forces, the astonishment of Lloegr, to the borders of Mechain[1] and Mochnant. Happy was the mother who bore thee, who art wise and noble, and freely distributest rich suits of garments, thy gold and silver. And thy Bards celebrate thee for presenting them thy bred steeds, when they sit at thy tables. And I myself am rewarded for my gift of poetry, with gold and distinguished respect. And should I desire of my prince the moon as a present, he would certainly bestow it on me. Thy praise reacheth as far as Lliwelydd,[2] and Llywarch is the man who celebrates with his songs - - - - - -
My praises are not extravagant to thee the prodigy of our age, thou art a prince firm in battle like an elephant. When thou arrivest at the period of thy glory, when thy praises cease to be celebrated by the Bard and the harp, my brave prince, ere thou comest, before thy last hour approaches, to confess thy sins, after thou hast through thy prowess vanquished thy enemies, mayest thou at last become a glorious saint.

1 Mechain, a part of Powys. 2 Caer Liwelydd, Carlisle.

AN ODE

To Llewelyn, the son of Griffydd, last prince of Wales of the British line, composed by Llygad Gwr, about the year 1270.

IN FIVE PARTS.

I.

I ADDRESS myself to God, the source of joy, the fountain of all good gifts, of transcendent majesty. Let the song proceed to pay its tribute of praise, to extol my hero, the prince of Arllechwedd,[1] who is stained with blood, a prince descended from renowned kings. Like Julius Cæsar is the rapid progress of the arms of Griffydd's heir. His valour and bravery are matchless, his crimson lance is stained with gore. It is natural to him to invade the lands of his enemies. He is generous, the pillar of princes. I never return empty-handed from the North. My successful and glorious prince, I would not exchange on any conditions. I have a renowned prince, who lays England waste, descended from noble ancestors. Llewelyn the destroyer of thy foes, the mild and prosperous governor of Gwynedd, Britain's honour in the field, with thy sceptered hand extended on the throne, and thy gilt sword by thy side. The lion of Cemmaes,[2] fierce in the onset, when the army rusheth to be covered with red. Our defence who slighteth alliance with strangers, who with violence maketh his way through the midst of his enemy's country. His just cause will be prosperous at

1 Arllechwedd, a part of Carnarvonshire.

2 Cemmaes, the name of several places in Wales. The Bard means here a cantred of that name in Anglesea.

last. About Tyganwy[1] he has extended his dominion, and his enemies fly from him with maimed limbs, and the blood flows over the soles of men's feet. Thou dragon of Arfon[2] of resistless fury, with thy beautiful well-made steeds, no Englishman shall get one foot of thy country. There is no Cymro thy equal.

II.

There is none equal to my prince with his numerous troops in the conflict of war. He is a generous Cymro descended from Beli Hir,[3] if you enquire about his lineage. He generously distributeth gold and riches. An heroic wolf from Eryri.[4] An eagle among his nobles of matchless prowess; it is our duty to extol him. He is clad in a golden vest in the army, and setteth castles on fire. He is the bulwark of the battle with Greidiawl's[5] courage. He is a hero that with fury breaketh whole ranks, and fighteth manfully. His violence is rapid, his generosity overflowing. He is the strength of armies arrayed in gold. He is a brave prince whose territories extend as far as the Teivi,[6] whom nobody dares to punish. Llewelyn the vanquisher of England is a noble lion descended from the race of kings. Thou art the king of the mighty, the entertainer and encourager of Bards. Thou makest the

1 Tyganwy, the name of an old castle near the mouth of the river Conway to the east; it was formerly one of the royal palaces of Maelgwn Gwynedd, king of Britain, and was, as our annals relate, burnt by lightning, ann. 811, but was afterwards rebuilt, and won by the Earls of Chester, who held it for a considerable time, but was at last retaken by the princes of North Wales.

2 Arfon, the country now called Carnarvonshire.

3 Beli. This was probably Beli Mawr, to whom our Bards generally trace the pedigree of great men.

4 Eryri, Snowdon, which some suppose derived from mynydd eryrod, the hill of eagles, but more probably from mynydd yr eiry, the hill of snow. Snowdon, in English, signifies literally the hill of snow, from Snow and Down, that being still a commom name for a hill in England, as Barham Downs, Oxford Downs, Burford Downs, &c.

5 Greidiawl, the name of a hero mentioned by Aneurin Gwawdrydd in his Gododin.

6 Teivi, the name of a large river in Cardiganshire.

crows rejoice, and the Bryneich[1] to vomit blood, they feasted on their carcases. He never avoided danger in the storm of battle, he was undaunted in the midst of hardships. The Bards[2] prophecy that he shall have the government and sovereign power; every prediction is at last to be fulfilled. The shields of his men were stained with red in brave actions from Pwlffordd[3] to the farthest bounds of Cydweli.[4] May he find endless joys, and be reconciled to the Son of God, and enjoy Heaven by his side.

III.

We have a prudent prince, his lance is crimson, his shield is shivered to pieces; a prince furious in action, his palace is open to his friends, but woe is the lot of his enemies. Llewelyn the vanquisher of his adversaries is furious in battle like an outrageous dragon; to be guarded against him availeth not, when he cometh hand to hand to dispute the hardy contest. May he that made him the happy governor of Gwynedd and its towns, strengthen him for length of years to defend his country from hostile invasion. It is our joy and happiness that we have a brave warrior with prancing steeds, that we have a noble Cymro, descended from Cambrian ancestors, to rule our country and its borders. He is the best prince that the Almighty made of the four elements. He is the

1 Bryneich, the men of Bernicia, a province of the Old Saxons in the North of England. The inhabitants of Deira and Bernicia are called by our ancient historians, Gwyr Deifr a Bryneich.

2 It was the policy of the British princes to make the Bards foretell their success in war, in order to spirit up their people to brave actions. Upon which account the vulgar supposed them to be real prophets. Hence the great veneration they had for the prophetical Bards, Myrddin Emrys, Taliesin, and Myrddin Wyllt. This accounts for what the English writers say of the Welsh relying so much upon the prophecies of Myrddin. There are many of these pretended prophecies still extant. The custom of prophecying did not cease till Henry the Seventh's time, and the reason is obvious.

3 Pwlffordd, is the name of a place in Shropshire. There is a bridge of that name still in that county.

4 Cydweli, the name of a town, and Comot, in Carmarthenshire.

best of governors, and the most generous. The eagle of Snowdon, and the bulwark of battle. He pitched a battle where there was a furious contest to obtain his patrimony on Cefn Gelorwydd;[1] such a battle never happened since the celebrated action of Arderydd.[2]

He is the brave lion of Mona, the kind-hearted Venedotian, the valiant supporter of his troops in Bryn Derwen. He did not repent of the day in which he assaulted his adversaries: it was like the assault of a hero descended from undaunted ancestors. I saw a hero disputing with hosts of men like a man of honour in avoiding disgrace. He that saw Llewelyn like an ardent dragon in the conflict of Arfon and Eiddionydd,[3] would have observed that it was a difficult task to withstand his furious attack by Drws Daufynydd.[4] No man has ever compelled him to submit: may the Son of God never put him to confusion.

IV.

Like the roaring of a furious lion in the search of prey, is thy thirst of praise, like the sound of a mighty hurricane over the desert main, thou warlike prince of Aberffraw.[5] Thy ravage is furious, thy impetuosity irresistible, thy troops are enterprising in brave actions, they are fierce and furious like a conflagration. Thou art the

1 Cefn Gelorwydd, is the name of some mountain, but where it is situated I know not.

2 Arderydd, is the name of a place somewhere in Scotland; perhaps, Atterith, about six miles from Solway Frith. This battle is mentioned in the Triads, and was fought by Gwenddolau ap Ceidiaw and Aeddan Fradawg, petty princes of the North, against Rhydderch Hael, king of Cumbria, who got the battle. Myrddin Wyllt, or Merlin, the Caledonian, was severely handled by Rhydderch Hael, for siding with Gwenddolau, his patron, which he complains of in his poem entitled Afallenau, or Apple-trees.

3 Eiddionydd, now Eifionydd, the name of a Comot, or district, in Carnarvonshire.

4 Drws Daufynydd, is the name of a pass between two hills, but where it lies I know not. Drws Daufynydd signifies, literally, the door of the two hills. There are many passes in Wales denominated from Drws, as Drws Ardudwy, Drws y Coed, Bwlch Oerddrws, &c.

5 Aberffraw, the name of the prince's chief palace in Anglesea.

warlike prince of Dinefwr,[1] the defence of thy people, the divider of spoils. Thy forces are comely and neat, and of one language. Thy proud Toledo sword is gilt with gold and its edge broke in war. Thou prince of Mathrafal,[2] extensive are the bounds of thy dominions, thou rulest people of four languages. He staid undaunted in battle against a foreign nation, and its strange language. May the great King of heaven defend the just cause of the warlike prince of the three provinces.

V.

I make my address to God, the source of praise, in the best manner I am able, that I may extol with suitable words the chief of men, who rageth like fire from the flashes of lightning, who exchangeth thrusts with the burnished steel. I stand in armour by the side of my prince with the red spear in the conflict of war, he is a brave fighter, and the foremost in action. Llewelyn, thy qualities are noble, I will valiantly make my path broad with the edge of my sword. May the prints of the hoofs of my prince's steeds be seen as far as Cornwall. Numerous are the persons that congratulate him upon this success, for he is a sure friend. The lion of Gwynedd, and its extensive territories, the governor of the men of Powys, and the South, who hath a general assembly of his armed troops at Chester, who ravageth Lloegr to amass spoils. In battle his success is certain, in killing, burning, and in overthrowing castles. In Rhos, and Penfro,[3] and in contests with the Normans, his impetuosity prevaileth. The offspring of Griffydd, of worthy

1 Dinefwr, the name of the prince of South Wales's palace, pleasantly situated upon a hill above the river Towy, in Carmarthenshire, now in the possession of George Rice, of Newton, Esquire, member of parliament for that county.

2 Mathrafal, the seat of the prince of Powys, not far from Pool, in Montgomeryshire, now in the possession of the earl of Powys.

3 Rhos and Penfro, the names of two Cantreds in Pembrokeshire.

qualities, generous in distributing rewards for songs. His shield shines, and the strong lances quickly meet the streams of gushing gore. He extorteth taxes from his enemies, and claimeth another country as a sovereign prince. His noble birth is an ornament to him. He besiegeth fortified towns, and his furious attacks like those of Fflamddwyn[1] reach far. He is a prosperous chief with princely qualities, his Bards are comely about his tables. I have seen him generously distributing his wealth, and his mead-horns filled with generous liquors. Long may he live to defend his borders with the sharp sword, like Arthur with the lance of steel. May he who is lawful king of Cymru, endued with princely qualities, have his share of happiness at the right hand of God.

1 Fflamddwyn, the name of a Saxon prince, against whom Urien, king of Cumbria, and his son Owain, fought the battle of Argoed Llwyfein.

A POEM

Entitled the Ode of the Months, composed by Gwilym Ddu of Arfon, to Sir John Griffydd Llwyd, of Tregarnedd and Dinorwig.

Why the Bard called this piece the "Ode of the Months" I cannot guess; but by what he intimates in the poem, which is, that when all nature revives, and the whole animal and vegetable creation are in their full bloom and vigour, he mourned and pined for the decayed state of his country. The hero he celebrates made a brave but successless attempt to rescue it from slavery. It will not be amiss to give a short account of the inhuman massacre of the Bards made by that cruel tyrant Edward the first, which gave occasion to a very fine Ode by Mr. Gray. Sir John Wynne, of Gwydir, a descendant in a direct line from Owain Gwynedd, mentions this particular, and says he searched all the records in the Exchequer at Carnarvon, and in the Tower of London, for the antiquities of his country in general, and of his own family in particular. I shall set down his own words, as I find them in a very fair copy of that history lent me by Sir Roger Mostyn, of Gloddaeth and Mostyn, Bart., a person no less eminent for his generous communicative temper, than for many other public and private virtues.

"This is the most ancient song (i. e. one of Rhys Goch of Eryri's, a Bard who flourished A. D. 1400) I can find extant of my ancestors since the reign of Edward the first, who caused our Bards all to be hanged by martial law, as stirrers of the people to sedition; whose example being followed by the governors of Wales until

Henry the Fourth's time, was the utter destruction of that sort of men; and since then that kind of people were at some further liberty to sing, and to keep pedigrees, as in ancient time they were wont; since which time we have some light of antiquity by their songs and writings," &c.

The following is taken from an old British grammar, written in English, by William Salesbury, printed at London, 1567. I have transcribed it faithfully according to the old orthography. "Howbeit when the whole Isle was commonlye called Brytayne, the dwellers Brytons, and accordingly their language Brytishe, I will not refell nor greatly deny; neither can I justly gainsaye, but their tongue then was as copious of syt woordes, and all manner of proper vocables, and as well adornated with woorshipful sciences and honourable knowledge as any other of the barbarous tongues were. And so still continued (though their sceptre declined, and their kingdom decayed, and they also by God's hand were driven into the most unfertyl region, barenest country, and most desart province of all the isle) untyll the conquest of Wales. For then, as they say, the nobles and the greatest men beyng captives and brought prysoners to the tower of London, there to remayne during their lyves, desired of a common request, that they might have with them all such bokes of their tongue, as they most delited in, and so their petition was heard, and for the lightness soon granted, and thus brought with them all the principallest and chiefest books, as well of their own as of other their friends, of whom they could obtain anye to serve for their purpose. Whose mind was none other but to pass the time, and their predestinate perpetual captivitie in the amenous varietie of over reading and revoluting many volumes and sundry books of divers sciences and strange matters.

"And that is the common answer of the Welshe Bardes (for so they call their country poets) when a man shall object or cast in their teeth the foolysh uncertainty and the phantasticall vanities of their prophecies (which they call BRUTS) or the doubtful race and kinde of their uncanonized saynctes: whom that notwithstanding they both invocate and worship wyth the most hyghe honoure and lowliest reverence. Adding and allegying in excuse thereof, that the reliques and residue of the books and monuments, as well as the saynctes lyves, as of their Brutysh prophecies and other sciences (which perished not in the tower, for there, they say, certain were burned) at the commotion of OWAIN GLYNDWR, were in like manner destroyed, and utterly devastat, or at the least wyse that there escaped not one, that was not uncurablye maymed, and irrecuperably torn and mangled.

"'Llyfrau Cymru au llofrudd
Ir twr Gwyn aethant ar gudd
Ysceler oedd Yscolan
Fwrw'r twrr lyfrau ir tan.'
Gutto'r Glyn. A.D. 1450.

"The books of Cymru and their remains went to the White Tower, where they were hid. Cursed was Ysgolan's act in throwing them in heaps into the fire."

It is not improbable that our Bard might have been one of those who suffered in the cause of his country, though he had the good luck to escape Edward's fury. I wish I may be so happy as to convey some faint idea of his merit to the English reader. The original has such touches, as none but a person in the Bard's condition could have expressed so naturally. However not to anticipate the judicious reader's opinion, to which I submit mine with all deference, I shall now produce some account of this great man, taken from that skilful and candid antiquary Mr. Robert Vaughan of Hengwrt's notes on Dr. Powel's history of Wales, printed at Oxford, 1663.

"Sir John Griffydd Llwyd, knight, the son of Rhys ap Griffydd ap Ednyfed Fychan, was a valiant gentleman, but unfortunate, 'magnæ quidem, sed calamitosæ virtutis,' as Lucius Florus saith of Sertorius. He was knighted by king Edward, when he brought him the first news of his queen's safe delivery of a son at Carnarvon Castle; the king was then at Rhuddlan, at his parliament held there. This Sir Griffydd afterwards taking notice of the extreme oppression and tyranny exercised by the English officers, especially Sir Roger Mortimer, lord of Chirk, and justice of North Wales, towards his countrymen the Welsh, became so far discontented, that he broke into open rebellion, verifying that saying of Solomon, 'Oppression maketh a wise man mad.' He treated with Sir Edward Bruce, brother to Robert, then king of Scotland, who had conquered Ireland, to bring or send over men to assist him in his design against the English; but Bruce's terms being conceived too unreasonable, the treaty came to nought; however being desperate, he gathered all the forces he could, and, in an instant, like a candle that gives a sudden blaze before it is out, overran all North Wales and the Marches, taking all the castles and holds; but to little purpose, for soon after he was met with, his party discomfited, and himself taken prisoner. This was in the year of our Lord 1322."

I thought so much by way of introduction necessary to commemorate so gallant a person; what became of him afterwards is not mentioned by our historians. However the following poem remains not only as a monument of the hero's bravery, but of the Bard's genius.

BEFORE the beginning of May I lived in pomp and grandeur, but now, alas! I am deprived of daily support, the time is as disastrous as when our Saviour Christ was taken and betrayed. How naked and forlorn is our condition! We are exposed to anxious toils and cares. O how heavy is the Almighty's punishment, that the crimson sword cannot be drawn! I remember how great its size was, and how wide its havoc; numerous are now the oppressed captives who languish in gnashing indignation. Our native Bards are excluded from their accustomed entertainments. How great a stop is put to generosity since a munificent hero, like Nudd,[1] is confined in prison. The valorous hawk of Griffydd,[2] so renowned for ravaging and destroying his enemies, is deplored by the expert Bards, who have lost their festivity and mirth in the place where mead was drunk. I cannot bear to think of his injurious treatment. His hospitality has fed thousands. He is, alas! in a forlorn prison, such is the unjust oppression of the land of the Angles.[3] Years of sorrow have overwhelmed me. I reckon not what becomes of the affairs of this world. The Bards of two hundred regions lament that they have now no protector. This is a certain, but a sad truth. Though the unthinking vulgar do not reflect as I do on the time when my eagle shone in his majesty. I am pierced by the lance of des-

1 Nudd Hael, or the Generous, one of the three liberal heroes of Britain mentioned in the Triads, and celebrated by Taliesin.

2 Griffydd Llwyd, the hero of the poem, was the son of Rhys, son of Griffydd, the son of the famous Ednyfed Fychan, seneschal to Llewelyn the great, and a brave warrior. Edward Philipp Pugh, Esq., of Coetmor, in Carnarvonshire, is a descendant in a direct line from Ednyfed Fychan, and has in his custody a grant from prince Llewelyn the Great of some lands in Creuddyn given to the said Ednyfed, and his posterity, with the prince's seal in green wax affixed to it. To this worthy gentleman, and his lady, I am much obliged for their civility when I lived in those parts.—The royal family of the Tudors are likewise descended from Ednyfed Fychan, as appears by a commission that was sent to the Bards and Heralds of Wales, to enquire into the pedigree of Owain Tudor, king Henry the Seventh's grandfather.

3 The land of the Angles, i. e., England.

pair. Hard is the fate of my protector, Gwynedd[1] is in a heavy melancholy mood, its inhabitants are oppressed because of their transgressions. Long has the bright sword, that shone like a torch, been laid aside, and the brave courage of the dauntless Achilles been stopped. The whole pleasant season of May is spent in dismal sorrow; and June is comfortless and cheerless. It increaseth my tribulation, that Griffydd with the red lance is not at liberty. I am covered with chilly damps. My whole fabric shakes for the loss of my chief. I find no intermission to my pain. May I sink, O Christ! my Saviour, into the grave, where I can have repose; for now, alas! the office of the Bard is but a vain and empty name. I am surprised that my despair has not burst my heart, and that it is not rent through the midst in twain. The heavy stroke of care assails my memory, when I think of his confinement, who was endowed with the valour of Urien[2] in battle. My meditation on past misfortunes is like that of the skilful Cywryd,[3] the Bard of Dunawd.[4] My praise

1 Gwynedd, the name of the country, called by the Romans Venedotia, but by the English North Wales.

2 Urien Reged, a famous king of Cumbria, who fought valiantly with the Saxons, whose brave actions are celebrated by Taliesin and Llywarch Hen. He is mentioned by Nennius, the ancient British historian, who wrote about A.D. 858. This writer is terribly mangled by his editors, both at home and abroad, from their not being versed in the British language. I have collected some manuscripts of his history, but cannot meet a genuine one without the interpolations of Samuel Beulan, otherwise I would publish it. I have in my possession many notes upon this author, collected from ancient British manuscripts, as well as English writers, who have treated of our affairs. This I have been enabled to do, chiefly by having access to the curious library at Llannerch, by the kind permission of the late Robert Davies, Esquire, and since by his worthy son, John Davies, Esquire, which I take this opportunity gratefully to acknowledge.

3 Cywryd. This Bard is not mentioned either by Mr. Davies or Mr. Edward Llwyd, in their catalogues of British writers. It seems he flourished in the sixth century, as did all the ancient British Bards we have now extant. Here let me obviate what may be objected to me as mentioning so many facts, and persons who lived in the sixth century, within the course of this performance. It was the last period our kings fought with any success against the Saxons, and it was natural, therefore, for the Bards of those times, to record such gallant acts of their princes, and for their successors to transmit them to posterity. Every person, though but slightly versed in the British history of that time, knows that Cadwaladr was the last king of Britain. Since his time there are no works of the Bards extant till after the conquest, as I have shewed in my Dissertatio de Bardis.

4 Dunawd, the son of Pabo Post Prydain, one of the heroes of the sixth century, who fought valiantly with the Saxons.

to the worthy hero is without vicious flattery, and my song no less affecting than his. My panegyric is like the fruitful genius of Afan Ferddig[1] in celebrating Cadwallon[2] of royal enterprise. I can no more sing of the lance, in well-laboured verse. Since thou doest not live, what avails it that the world has any further continuance? Every region proclaims thy generosity. The world droops since thou art lost. There are no entertainments or mirth, Bards are no longer honoured: the palaces are no longer open, strangers are neglected, there are no caparizoned steeds, no trusty endearing friendship. No, our country mourns, and wears the aspect of Lent. There is no virtue, goodness, or any thing commendable left among us, but vice, dissoluteness, and cowardice bear the sway. The great and towering strength of Môn[3] is become an empty shadow; and the inhabitants of Arfon[4] are become insignificant below the ford of Rheon.[5] The lofty land of

1 Afan Ferddig, was the Bard of the famous Cadwallon, son of Cadfan king of Britain. I have got a fragment of a poem of his composition on the death of his patron Cadwallon; and as far as I understand it, it is a noble piece, but very obscure on account of its great antiquity; as are the works of all the Bards who wrote about this time. It is as difficult a task, for a modern Welshman to endeavour to understand those venerable remains, as for a young scholar just entered upon the study of the Greek language to attack Lycophron or Pindar, without the help of a dictionary or scholiast. How Mr. Macpherson has been able to translate the Erse used in the time of Ossian, who lived a whole century at least before the earliest British Bard now extant, I cannot comprehend. I wish some of those that are well versed in the Erse or Irish language, would be so kind to the public, as to clear these matters; for I can hardly believe that the Erse language hath been better preserved than the British.

2 Cadwallon, the son of Cadfan, the most victorious king of Britain, fought many battles with the Saxons; and, among the rest, that celebrated one of Meugen, in which he slew Edward king of Mercia, where the men of Powys behaved themselves with distinguished bravery; and had from thence several privileges granted them by that brave prince. These privileges are mentioned by Cynddelw Brydydd Mawr, a Powysian Bard, in a poem entitled "Breintiau Gwyr Powys," or the Privileges of the men of Powys, which is in my custody.

3 Môn, the Mona of the Latins, called by the English Anglesea, in which, at a place called Aberffraw, was the palace of the princes of North Wales. The Bard seems here to hint at the loss of Llewelyn-ap-Griffydd, the last prince of Wales of the British line.

4 Arfon, the country now called Carnarvonshire.

5 Rheon, the name of a river in Carnarvonshire, often mentioned by the Bards; but it must have altered its name since, for I do not recollect any such river which bears that name at present.

Gwynedd is become weak. The heavy blow of care strikes her down. We must now renounce all consolation. We are confined in a close prison by a merciless unrelenting enemy; and what avails a bloody and brave contest for liberty.

HAVING finished the present small collection of the British Bards, I take this opportunity to acquaint the reader, that the time in which they flourished is not accurately set down by Dr. Davies, at the end of his Dictionary, nor by Mr. Llwyd, of the Museum, in his Catalogue of British Writers, in the Archæologia Britannica. Indeed it is impossible to be so exact, as to fix the year when the Bards wrote their several pieces, unless the actions they celebrate are mentioned in our Annals, because some of them lived under several princes. This I thought proper to mention, lest any should blame the translator for his inaccuracy, in settling the Chronology of the Poems.

A SHORT ACCOUNT OF TALIESIN,

The Chief of Bards, and Elphin, the son of Gwyddno Goranhir, his Patron.

GWYDDNO GORANHIR, was a petty king of Cantre'r Gwaelod, whose country was drowned by the sea, in a great inundation that happened about the year 560, through the carelessness of the person into whose care the dams were committed, as appears from a poem of Taliesin upon that sad catastrophe. In his time the famous Taliesin lived, whose birth and education is thus related in our ancient manuscripts. He was found exposed in a wear belonging to Gwyddno, the profit of which he had granted to his son, Prince Elphin, who being an extravagant youth, and not finding the usual success, grew melancholy; and his fishermen attributed his misfortune to his riotous irregular life. When the prodigal Elphin was thus bewailing his misfortune, the fishermen espied a coracle with a child in it, enwrapped in a leathern bag, whom they brought to the young prince, who ordered care to be taken of him, and when he grew up gave him the best education, upon which he became the most celebrated Bard of his time. The accomplished Taliesin was introduced by Elphin to his father Gwyddno's court, where he delivered him a poem, giving an account of himself, entitled, Hanes Taliesin, or Taliesin's History; and at the same time another to his patron and benefactor Elphin, to console him upon his past misfortune, and to exhort him to put his trust in Divine Providence. This is a fine moral piece, and very artfully addressed by the Bard, who introduces himself in the person and character of an exposed infant. As it is probable that the prince's affairs took another turn since that period, this was done with great propriety. Sir John Pryse mentions the poem that Taliesin delivered to king Gwyddno, in his Historiæ Britannicæ defensio. "Taliesinus quidem in odula, quam de suis erroribus composuit, sic inscripta Britannicè (Hanes Taliesin) videlicet errores Taliesini, ait se tandem divertisse ad reliquias Trojæ;

"'Mi a ddaethum yma at Weddillion Troia;'

"neque dubitandum est hoc fuesse opus Taliesini: nam præter innumeros codices vetustissimos, qui inscriptionem hujusmodi attestentur, nullo reclamante, nullus est recentiorum qui vel phrasin illius tam antiquam, carminisve majestatem assequi potuit. Et ideo summus ille vates inter Britannos censetur et nominatur." I never could procure a perfect nor correct copy of this poem of Taliesin, otherwise I would gratify the curious with a translation of it. It is certain from his history, that he was a very learned man for his time, and seems to have been well versed in the doctrine of the Druids, particularly the μετεμψύχωσις, which accounts for the extravagant flights frequent in his poems. I have now in my possession above fifty of them; but they are so difficult to be understood, on account of their great antiquity, and numerous obsolete words, and negligence of transcribers, that it is too great a task for any man at this distance of time to go about a translation of them. However I have selected this ode, as a specimen of his manner of writing, not as it is the best in the collection, but as it is the only one I could thoroughly understand. There are many spurious pieces fathered upon this Bard, in a great many hands in North Wales; but these are all forged either by the monks, to answer the purposes of the church of Rome, or by the British Bards, in the time of the latter princes of Wales, to spirit up their countrymen against the English, which anybody versed in the language may easily find by the style and matter. It has been my luck to meet with a manuscript of all his genuine pieces now extant, which was transcribed by the learned Dr. Davies, of Mallwyd, from an old manuscript on vellum of the great antiquary Mr. R. Vaughan, of Hengwrt. This transcript I have shewn to the best antiquaries and critics in the Welsh language now living. They all confess that they do not understand above one half of any of his poems. The famous Dr. Davies could not, as is plain from the many obsolete words he has left without any interpretation in his dictionary. This should be a caveat to the English reader concerning the great antiquity of the poems that go under the name of Ossian, the son of Fingal, lately published by Mr. Macpherson. It is a great pity Taliesin is so obscure, for there are many particulars in his poems that would throw great light on the history, notions, and manners of the Ancient Britons, especially of the Druids, a great part of whose learning it is certain he had imbibed. This celebrated Bard was in great favour with all the great men of his time, particularly with Maelgwn Gwynedd, the warlike and victorious king of all Britain, with Elphin his patron, whom he redeemed with his songs from the castle of Tyganwy, where he was upon some account confined by his uncle Maelgwn. He likewise celebrated the victories of Urien Reged, king of Cumbria, and a great part of Scotland, as far as the river Clyde. In short, he was held in so great esteem by posterity, that the Bards mentioned him with the greatest honour in their works. In his poem entitled Anrheg Urien, or Urien's Present, he says that his habitation was by Llyn Geirionnydd, in the parish of Llan Rhychwyn, in Carnarvonshire, and mentions therein his cotemporary, the famous Aneurin Gwawdrydd, author of the Gododin, an heroic poem on the battle of Cattraeth, of which some account is given in the Dissertatio de Bardis.

A wn ni enw Aneurin Gwawdrydd Awenydd
A minnau Daliesin o lann Llyn Geirionnydd.

i. e. I know the fame of that celebrated genius Aneurin Gwawdrydd, who am Taliesin, whose habitation is by the pool Geirionnydd.—

Having finished this short account of our author, I shall now proceed to his poem, entitled, Dyhuddiant Elphin, or Elphin's Consolation, which I offer now to the public.

Dr. John David Rhys quotes it at length in his Linguæ Cymraecæ Institutiones Accuratæ; which, to save further trouble, I shall beg leave to transcribe here in his own words. "Cæterum nunc et propter eorum authoritatem, et quod huic loco inter alia maxime quadrant, non pigebit quædem antiquissima Taliesini Cambro-Britannica Carmina subjungere," &c.

I have nothing more to acquaint the reader with, but that I have used two copies in my translation, one in print by the said Dr. John David Rhys, the other in manuscript by Dr. Thomas Williams. I have followed the copy I thought most correct, and have given the different reading of the manuscript in the margin.

TALIESIN'S POEM

To Elphin, the son of Gwyddno Goranhir, king of Cantre'r Gwaelod, to comfort him upon his ill success at the Wear; and to exhort him to trust in Divine providence.

I.

FAIR Elphin, cease to weep, let no man be discontented with his fortune; to despair avails nothing. It is not that which man sees that supports him. Cynllo's prayer will not be ineffectual. God will never break his promise. There never was in Gwyddno's Wear such good luck as to-night.

II.

Fair Elphin, wipe the tears from thy face! Pensive melancholy will never profit thee; though thou thinkest thou hast no gain; certainly too much sorrow will do thee no good; doubt not of the great Creator's wonders; though I am but little, yet am I endowed with great gifts. From the seas and mountains, and from the bottom of rivers, God sends wealth to the good and happy man.

III.

Elphin with the lovely qualities, thy behaviour is unmanly, thou oughtest not to be over pensive. To trust in God is better than to forebode evil. Though I am but small and slender on the beach of the foaming main, I shall do thee more good in the day of distress than three hundred salmons.

IV.

Elphin with the noble qualities, murmur not at thy misfortune: though I am but weak on my leathern couch, there dwelleth a gift on my tongue. While I continue to be thy protection, thou needest not fear any disaster. If thou desirest the assistance of the ever blessed Trinity, nothing can do thee hurt.

DE

BARDIS DISSERTATIO;

IN QUA NONNULLA

QUÆ AD EORUM ANTIQUITATEM ET MUNUS RESPICIUNT,

ET AD PRÆCIPUOS QUI IN CAMBRIA FLORUERUNT,

BREVITER DISCUTIUNTUR.

STUDIO ET OPERA

EVANI EVANS, CERETICENSIS.

Si quid mea carmina possunt,
Aonio statuam sublimeis vertice Bardos;
Bardos Pieridum cultores, atque canentis
Phœbi delicias, quibus est data cura perennis
Dicere nobilium clarissima facta virorum,
Aureaque excelsam famam super astra locare.
JOH. LELANDUS in Assertione ARTURII.

Insigni Viro

GVLIELMO VAVGHAN

De Cors y Gedol Armigero,

et

In Senatu Britannico

Pro Comitatu Meirionnydd *Delegato, Provinciae*

Praefecto, Rotulorum Custodi,

Societatis Cymmrodorion *Londini Praesidi Summo,*

Caeterisque Ejusdem Societatis Membris,

Hanc De Bardis Dissertationem,

Summa, Qua Par Est, Observantia D. D. D.

Evanus Evans.

DE BARDIS DISSERTATIO;

QUUM per multos annos non sine summa voluptate Bardos Britannos horis subsicivis evolverem, et quum hac ætate fere in desuetudinem abiere ejusmodi studia, et quicquid est Britannicae antiquitatis nostrorum pereat incuriâ, non potui quin hanc qualem qualem rudi Minerva dissertatiunculam in vulgus emitterem, quo exteris melius innotescat, quantum in his olim profecêre nostrates.

Bardi apud Celtas originem habuerunt; et Graeci, qui eorum meminerunt, mira omnino de illis produnt, quae eo magis fidem merentur quod non solebant laudes suas in Barbaros effusè impendere. Cum alibi gentium hodie nulla eorum maneant vestigia nisi apud Cambro-Britannos et Hibernos, Celtarum posteros; è re fore duxi, si aliquid de antiquioribus qui apud nos extant, praelibarem, praemissis de iis in genere ex Scriptoribus Graecis et Latinis elogiis, quò augustius in scenam prodeant, et inde venerandae antiquitatis auctoritatem sibi vindicent.

Unde Bardi nomen sunt sortiti, nondum mihi constat; Annii enim Viterbiensis regem Bardum, uti et omnia ejus hujuscemodi commenta, penitus rejicio. Non omnino abludit vox *Bâr* furor, modo sit ille poeticus quo se agitari fingebant Bardi. Si ea fuerit vocis origo, necesse est ut primitùs scriberetur *Barydd*. Uteunque sit, nos a multis retrò Seculis furorem illum poeticum voce Awen designamus, quae dedùci potest a Gwên, *risus* vel *lætitia:* Poetae enim munus est ut homines cantu exhilaret. Non multum ergo contendimus an ea sit vocis origo, cum vocabulorum antiquorum, cujusmodi sunt hominum, officiorum, urbium, montium et fluviorum sit admodum obscura significatio.

His de Bardorum origine praemissis, ad eorum pergamus munus, prout Scriptores Graeci et Latini tradiderunt. Primus sit DIODORUS SICULUS, qui haec scribit. Εἰσὶ καὶ παρ' ἀυτοῖς καὶ ποιηταὶ μελῶν, ὃυς ΒΑΡΔΟΥΣ ὀνομάζουσι, ὄυτοι δὲ μετ' ὀργάνων ταῖς λύραις ὁμοίων ᾄδοντες, ὃυς μὲν ὑμνοῦσι, ὃυς δὲ βλασφημοῦσι.[1] Non multum dissimile est quod de illis prodit AMMIANUS MARCELLINUS. "Bardi (inquit ille) fortia virorum illustrium facta heroicis composita versibus cum dulcibus lyræ modulis cantitarunt." His POSSIDONII apud ATHENAEUM verba addere lubet, qui eorum munus graphicè depingit. Κελτοὶ περιάγονται μεθ' ἑαυτῶν, καὶ πολεμοῦντες συμβιωτὰς ὃυς καλοῦσι παρασίτους. οὗτοι δὲ ἐγκώμια ἀυτῶν, καὶ πρὸς ἀθρόους λέγουσιν ἀνθρώπους συνεστῶτας, καὶ πρὸς ἕκαστον τῶν κατὰ μέρος ἐκείνων ἀκροωμένων. τὰ δὲ ἀκούσματα ἀυτῶν εἰσὶν οἱ καλούμενοι ΒΑΡΔΟΙ. ποιηταὶ δὲ οὗτοι τυγχάνουσι μετ' ᾠδῆς ἐπαίνους λέγοντες.[2] Hinc manifesto liquet eorum præcipuum munus fuisse Heroum laudes in cœlum evehere. Sed quum nulla Celticorum vel Gallicorum extent Bardorum opera, ex quibus quam dignè munus gesserint evincatur, operæ pretium est, alium ex eodem ATHENAEO locum adducere, ex quo patebit haudquaquam iis defuisse sublime dicendi genus, quod Græci ὕψος vocant. Posidonius, Luernii, qui Bittitis pater fuit à Romanis profligati, opes cùm enarrat, tradit eum popularem gratiam aucupantem, per agros curru vehi solitum, aurúmque et argentum in turbas Celtarum innumeras eum prosequentes spargere: quin et septum eundem quadratum stadiorum duodecim aliquando cinxisse, in quo potione sumptuosa et exquisita pleni lacus essent, paratáque cibariorum copia, ut complusculis diebus liceret iis quibus placeret, ingredi, fruíque illo apparatu, cum assiduis ministrorum officiis. Epularum diem aliquando cùm ille constituisset, ac præfiniisset, barbarum quendam Poetam tardius caeteris eo commeantem illi occurrisse, ac canentem laudes ejus, excellentésque virtutes celebrasse, vicem verò suam doluisse, ac deflevisse, quòd serius adventasset: illum cantu delectatum auri sacculum poposcisse, et accur-

1 P. 213. H. Steph. Edit. 1559. 2 P. 246. D.

renti cantori projecisse: quo sublato, poëtam ejus rursum laudes iterantem praedicasse currûs, quo vehebatur, impressa in terram vestigia aurum et beneficia procreare mortalibus. Sed praestat ipsa ATHENAEI verba apponere.

"Ετι ὁ Ποσειδώνιος διηγούμενος ϗ τὸν Λουερνίου τοῦ Βιτύιτος πατρὸς πλοῦτον, τοῦ ὑπὸ Ῥωμαίων καθαιρεθέντος, φησὶ, δημαγωγοῦντα αὐτὸν τὸυς ὄχλους ἐν ἅρμάτι φέρεσθαι διὰ τῶν πεδίων, ϗ σπείρειν χρυσὸν, ϗ ἄργυρον τοῖς ἀκολουθόυσαις τῶν Κελτῶν μυριάσι, φράγμα τε ποιεῖν δωδεκαςάδιον τετράγωνον, ἐν ᾧ πληρȣ̃ν ληνὸυς πολυτελοῦς πόματος, παρασκευάζειν τε τοσοῦτο βρωμάτων πλῆθος, ὥστε ἐφ' ἡμὲρας πλεὶονας ἐξεῖναι τοῖς βουλομένοις τῶν παρασκευασθέντων ἀπολαύειν, ἀδιαλείπτως διακονουμένοις. Ἀφορίσαντος δ' αὐτοῦ προθεσμίαν ποτε τῆς θοινῆς, ἀφυςερήσαντά τινα τῶν Βαρβὰρων ποιητὴν ἀφικέσθαι, καὶ συναντήσαντα μετ' ᾠδῆς ὑμνεῖν ἀυτοῦ τὴν ὑπεροχὴν, ἑαυτὸν δ' ὑποθρήνειν ὅτι ὑςέρηκε τὸν δὲ τερφθέντα θυλάκιον ἀιτῆσαι χρυσίου, καὶ ῥίψαι ἀυτῷ παρατρὲχοντι, ἀνελόμενον δ' ἐκεῖνον πάλιν ὑμνεῖν, λέγοντα, ΔΙΟΤΙ ΤΑ ΙΧΝΗ ΤΗΣ ΓΗΣ (ΕΦ ΗΣ ΑΡΜΑΤΗΛΑΤΕΙ) ΧΡΥΣΟΝ ΚΑΙ ΕΥΕΡΓΕΣΙΑΣ ΑΝΘΡΩΠΟΙΣ ΦΕΡΕΙ.[1]

Haec sunt quae (ut pote cui ad Bibliothecas aditus non patet) de antiquis illis in medium proferre licuit. Ad nostros jam venio in quibus non desunt veri et genuini ὕψους exempla. Nequaquam suo genere Graecis et Latinis poetis cedunt nostri Bardi, quamvis ad eorum normam carmina non texerunt. Quid enim nobis cum exteris? An eorum modulo et pede nostra poemata metenda sunt? Quid, ut taceam de Arabicis et Brachmanicis, et in Europa boreali Scaldis? quid fiet, inquam, de antiquioribus illis Sacrosanctis poetis? quid fiet de JOBO, DAVIDE, et siqui alii θεοδίδακτοι poetae? Sed haec a proposito nostro aliena sunt.

Quum res Britonum, ingruentibus Pictis, Scotis, et Saxonibus, laberentur, dici non potest, quantam libris et veteribus nostrorum monumentis stragem ediderint: adeo ut Bardi et historici verè antiqui, sint admodum rari. E nostris historicis qui Bardorum meminit, primus est GILDAS NENNIUS, qui scripsit, uti ipse narrat, anno 858, et quarto MERVINI regis. Sed is locus in nonnullis exemplaribus deest, et ejus auctor clarissimo VAUGHANO, NENNIO antiquior esse videtur, qui eum "vetustum Saxonicægenealogiae autorem" nominat. Sive verò is fuerit NENNIUS, quod mihi videtur, sive, uti ille mavult, aliquis eo vetustior, omnia quæ ibi narrantur quam verissima sunt, quamvis scribentium oscitantia quam fœdissime sint depravata. Nec mendas castigarunt editores GALE et BERTRAM. Quæ ad Bardos sic se habent. "Item TALHAIARN TATANGEN in poemate claruit, et NUEVIN, et TALIESIN, et BLUCHBAR, et *Cian* qui vocatur *Gweinchgwant*, simul uno tempore in poemate Britannico claruerunt." Qui locus sic restitui debet. "Item *Talhaiarn Tatangwn* claruit, et *Aneurin*, et *Taliesin*, et *Llywarch*, et *Cian* qui vocatur *Gwyngwn* simul uno tempore in poemate Britannico claruerunt." Ex iis quos hic nominat *Nennius* tres tantum extant, nempe *Aneurin*, *Taliesin*, et *Llywarch* cognomento *Hen*. Meminit tamèn *Talhaiarni Taliesinus* in poemate cui titulus *Angar Cyfyndawd*, i. e. Concordia discors.

Trwy iaith TALHAIARN,
Bedydd bi ddydd farn.

"Ex TALHAIARNI sententia
Expiato erit per baptisum in die supremo."

Uti et CIANI in eodem poemate.

CIAN *pan ddarfu*
Lliaws gyfolu.

"Quando CIANUS multos carmine celebratet."

Meminit et ejudem ANEURINUS in suo poemate Heroico, cui nomen *Gododin*.

Un maban y Gian o faen Gwyngwn.

"Unicus CIANI filius ex valido *Gwyngwn* ortus."

SED quum eorum opera aboleverit ætas, nihil ultra de iis dicere possumus. Hoc saltem constat, si NENNIO fides adhibenda sit, eos suo seculo Bardos fuisse eximios. ANEURINUS, TALIESINUS et LLYWARCH HEN habent multa notatu digna, et quæ rei istius seculi historicæ multum lucis adferunt. Sed quum eorum sint rarissima exemplaria, intellectu sunt quam difficillima, quod sit partim ob scribentium oscitantiam, partim ob linguam vetustam et obsoletam, quæ in nullo Lexico vel glossario inveniri potest. Unde fit, ut saepe *non plus dimidio* vel a peritissimo intelligatur. TALIESINUS quem nostrates *Pen Beirdd*; i. e. Bardorum Coryphaeum appellavere, in aulis Britanniae principum vixit, et ibi clara eorum in bello facinora cantavit. Patronos habuit MAELGWYN GWYNEDD, eum scilicet quem GILDAS MAGLOCUNUM vocat, et URIENUM Regedensem Cumbriae principem et ELPHINUM filium GWYDDNO GARANIR Dominum *Cantref Gwaelod*, cujus regio a mari absorpta est circa annum 540. Floruerunt TALIESINUS et ANEURIN GWAWDRYDD *Mychdeyrn Beirdd*, i. e. Bardorum Monarcha, eodem tempore, circa annum 570. ANEURINUS, in suo poemate cui titulus *Gododin*, refert se in bello juxta *Cattraeth* sub auspiciis MYNYDDAWC EIDDIN, bellum adversus Saxones gessisse, et ibi omnes, tribus exceptis, inter quos erat ANEURINUS, bello occubuisse. Fuerunt sub hoc principe in hac expeditione trecenti et sexaginta tres viri nobiles, qui eum ad bellum juxta *Cattraeth* sunt secuti. Fit hujus exercitus mentio libro *Triadum* in hunc modum. Teir gosgordd addwyn Ynys *Prydain*. Gosgordd MYNYDDAWC EIDDIN Yng *Cattraeth*; a gosgordd MELYN a CHYNFELYN; a gosgordd DRYWON mab NUDD yn *Rhodwydd Arderydd*. i. e. Tres fuere nobiles exercitus Insulae Britannicae. Exercitus MYNYDDAWC EIDDIN juxta *Cattraeth*; Exercitus MELYN et CYNFELYN: et Exercitus DRYWON filii NUDD juxta *Rhodwydd Arderydd*.

PLACUIT hic nonnulla ex ANEURINI *Gododinio* excerpere, quae licet ob vetustatem et dialecti varietatem sint admodum obscura (fuit enim si non Pictorum lingua, saltem Britannorum septentrionalium dialectus, et ideo hodiernis Cambro-Britannis minus facilis intellectu) attamen lectori haud injucunda fore judicavi, eo quod salvis Græcis et Latinis sit forsan antiquissimum in Europâ poema. Interpretationem in multis claudicare nullus dubito. Ii quibus plura exemplaria videre contigerit, ea felicius enucleabunt. Ego non nisi unum vidi a THOMA GULIELMO Medico practico scriptum, in quo quae sequuntur sic se habebant.

CAEAWG CYNHORAWG myn ydd elai,
Diphun ym mlaen bun medd a dalai,
Twll tal i rodawr yn i clywai awr,
Ni roddai nawd maint dilynai,
Ni chilia o gamawn, yn i ferai
Waed mal brwyn, gomynei wyr nid elai,
Nis adrawdd Gododin ar llawr MORDAI,
Rhag pebyll MADOG pan atcorei
Namyn un gwr o gant yn y ddelai.

i. e.

"CAEAWG CYNHORAWG ubicunque ivit,
- - - - - hydro meli dedit,
Scutum ejus fuit perforatum, ubicunque audivit
Clamorem, hostibus non pepercit, et eos insecutus est:
Nec prius a bello destitit, quam sanguis effusè fluxerit,
Et eos qui non discedebant securi percussit;
Adeo ut non possit Gododin celebrare facta in aula *Mordai*
Ex *Madoci* castris quum domum profectus est
Unus tantum ex centum rediit."

Caeawg Cynhorawg arfawg yngawr,
Cyno diwygwr gwrdd yngwyawr,

Cynran yn rhagwan rhag byddinawr,
Cwyddai bum pumwnt rhag eu llafnawr,
O wyr *Deifr* a *Bryneich* dychrawr,
Ugeincant eu difant yn unawr,
Cynt i gig i fleidd nog yt i neithiawr,
Cynt e fydd i fran, nog yt i elawr,
Cyn noe argyfrein e waed i lawr,
Gwerth medd ynghyntedd gan *Lliweddawr*,
Hyfeidd Hir ermygir tra fo Cerddawr.

i. e.

"*Caeawg Cynhorawg* vir in bello armatus,
Et *Cyno* qui se strenuum gessit in dimicando,
Ceciderunt numerus ingens eorum hastis transfixi.
Prius lupo parabatur caro, quam nuptiali convivio;
Et corvo prius commodum fuit, quam Libitinæ.
Prius quam humi fluebat ejus sanguis
In aula *Lliweddawr* mulsum bibit,
Et *Hyfeidd Hir* celebrabitur, donec erit Cantor."

Gwyr a aeth *Gattraeth* feddfaeth feddwn,
Ffurf ffrwythlawn, oedd cam nas cymhwyllwn,
I am lafnawr coch, gorfawr, gwrmwn,
Dwys dyngyn ydd ymleddyn aergwn,
Ar deulu *Bryneich* be ich barnaswn,
Diluw, dyn yn fyw nis gadawswn,
Cyfeillt a gollais, diffiais oeddwn,
Rhugl yn ymwrthryn, rhyn rhiadwn.
Ni mynnws gwrawl gwaddawl chwegrwn,
Maban y *Gian* o faen *Gwyngwn*.

i. e.

"Viri festinabant *Cattraeth*, quibus mulsum erat potus,
Formâ eximii, quibus ingratus essem, si non meminerim.
Hastis armati turmatim rubris, magnis et incurvatis,

Pugnabant impetuosi bellatores.
Si mihi liceret[1] sententiam de *Deirorum* populo ferre,
Æque ac diluvium omnes una strage prostrarem;
Amicum enim amisi incautus,
Qui in resistendo firmus erat - - -
Non petiit magnanimus dotem a socero,
Filius *Ciani* ex strenuo *Cwyngwn* ortus."

Yfeis i o win a medd y *Mordai*,
Mawr maint i wewyr,
Ynghyfarfod gwyr,
Bwyd i eryr erysmygai.
Pan gryssiei *Gydywal* cyfddwyreai
Awr, gan wyrdd wawr cyn i dodai,
Aessawr ddellt am bellt a adawai,
Parrau ryn rwygiad, dygymmynai
Ynghat blaen bragat briwai.

i. e.

"Ego bibi ex vino et Mulso MORDAI,
Cujus hasta fuit immanis magnitudinis.
In belli congressu,
Victum aquilis paravit.
Quando CYDYWAL festinavit, exortus est clamor
Ante croceam auroram, cum signum dedit,
Scutum in asseres comminutos fregit,
Et hastis lacerantibus percussit,
Et in bello eos qui primam stationem sunt nacti vulneravit."

Gwyr a aeth *Gattraeth* buant enwawd;
Gwin a medd o aur fu eu gwirawd,
Blwyddyn yn erbyn wrdyn ddefawd,
Trywyr a thriugaint a thrichant eurdorchawd,

1 Fortasse, "Vindictam in Deirorum populum," &c.

O'r sawl yt gryssiassant uch gormant wirawd,
Ni ddiengis namyn tri o wrhydri ffossawd,
Dau gatci *Aeron*, a CHYNON DAEARAWD
A minnau o'm gwaedffreu gwerth fy ngwenwawd.

i. e.

"Viri ibant ad CATTRAETH, et fuere insignes,
Vinum et mulsum ex auries poculis erat eorum potus,
- - - - - - - - - -
Trecenti et sexaginta tres auries torquibus insigniti erant,
Ex iis autem qui nimio potu madidi ad bellum properabant,
Non evasere nisi tres, qui sibi gladiis viam muniebant,
Sc. bellator de *Aeron* et CONANVS DAEARAWD,
Et egomet ipse (sc. Bardus Aneurinus) sanguine rubens,
Aliter ad hoc carmen compingendum non superstes fuissem.'

Pan gryssiei GARADAWG i gad,
Mab baedd coed, trychwn, trychiad,
Tarw byddin yn nhrin gymmyniad,
Ef llithiai wydd gwn oi angad,
Ys fy nhyst EWEIN fab EULAD,
A GWRIEN, a GWYN, a GWRIAD,
O *Gattraeth* o gymmynad,
O *Fryn Hydwn* cyn caffad,
Gwedi medd gloyw ar angad,
Ni weles WRIEN ei dad.

i. e.

"Quando ad bellum properabat CARADOCUS,
Filius apri sylvestris qui truncando mutilavit hostes,
Taurus aciei in pugnæ conflictu,
Is lignum (i. e. hastam) ex manu contorsit,
Cujus rei sunt testes EWEIN filius EULAD.
Et GWRIEN et GWYN et GWRIAD.

Ex *Cattraeth* et congressu ibi,
Ex *Bryn Hydwn* ubi prius habitavit, oriundus,
Postquam mulsum lucidum in manu tenuerat,
Non vidit patrem suum GWRIENUS."

Cyfwyrein cetwyr cyfarfuant,
Ynghyt, yn unfryt yt gyrchassant,
Byrr eu hoedl, hir eu hoed ar eu carant,
Seith gymmaint o Loegrwys a laddassant,
O gyfryssedd gwragedd gwych a wnaethant,
Llawer mam a'i deigr ar ei hamrant.

i. e.

"Laudo bellatores qui congressi sunt omnes,
Et uno animo hostes adorti sunt,
Fuit eorum vita brevis, et longum amicis desiderium reliquerunt,
Occiderunt tamen ex Saxonibus plus scepties
Ex[1] aemulatione mulierum egregiè egerunt.
Et plurima mater lacrymas pofudit."

Arddyledawc canu, cymman o fri,
Twrf tân, a tharan, a rhyferthi,
Gwryd ardderchawg marchawg mysgi,
RHUDD FEDEL rhyfel a eidduni,
Gwr gwnedd, difuddiawg, digymmyni ynghat,
O'r meint gwlad yt glywi.

i. e.

"Debitus est tibi cantus, qui honorem assecutus es maximum,
Qui eras instar ignis, tonitrui et tempestatis,

[1] Quid sibi vult hic Bardus non mihi constat.

Viribus eximie, eques bellicose
RHUDD FEDEL, bellum meditaris.
Licet vir strenuus adoriatur, eum superabis in bello
Ex quacunque regione eum advenisse audieris."

Arddyledawc canu claer orchorddion,
A gwedi dyrraith dyleinw afon,
Dimcones loflen ben eryron llwyd,
Ef gorau bwyd i ysglyfion.
Or a aeth *Gattraeth* o aurdorchogion,
Ar neges MYNYDDAWG mynawg Maon,
Ni ddoeth yn ddiwarth o barth Frython,
Ododin wr bell well no CHYNON.

i. e.

"Carmine debent celebrari nobiles proceres,
Qui post conflictum amnes ripas superare fecerunt.[1]
Ejus manus satiavit aquilarum fuscarum gulas,
Is et optime cibum paravit avibus rapacibus,
Ex omnibus enim eis qui ibant ad *Cattraeth* aureis torquibus insigniti,
Qui partem MYNYDDAWG in bello defendebant clari satellites,
Nullus ex Britonibus melius suum egit munus
In *Gododin*, (ex iis qui ex longinquo venerunt) quam CONANUS."

Truan yw gennyf i gwedi lludded
Goddef gloes angau trwy anghyffred
Ag eil trwm truan gennyf fi, gweled
Dygwyddaw an gwyr ni pen o dräed
Ac uohenaid hir ac eilywed
Yn ol gwyr pybyr tymyr tudwed

1 Sc. cruore fuso.

RHYFAWN a GWGAWN GWIAWN a GWLYGED
Gwyr gorsaf gwriaf gwrdd ynghaled
Ys deupo eu henaid hwy wedi trined
Cynnwys yngwlad nef addef afreued

i. e.

"Me maximè dolet post laborem amicos nostros
Subire mortis angorem more inassueto;
Et iterum me maximè dolet quod ipse vidi
Viros nostros in bello gradatim cadentes.
Gemitus est longus et opprobrium
Post homines alacres patriæ decus,
RHYFAWN et GWGAWN GWIAWN et GWLYGED;
Viri qui erant sustentacula (belli sc.) fortissimi et in angustiis magnanimi
Ascendant eorum animæ post pugnam
In regnum cœlorum ubi habitatio est sine ullo desiderio."

Hæc de ANEURINO sufficiant.

Floruere eodem seculo et multi alii Bardi inter quos eminet MYRDDIN WYLLT, id est, MERLINUS Sylvestris, qui poema composuit cui titulus *Afallennau*, id est, pomarium, in quo patroni sui GWENDDOLAU filii CEIDIO munificentiam prædicat."

Afellen beren bren y sydd fad
Nid bychan dy lwyth sydd ffrwyth arnad
A minnau wyf ofnawg amgelawg am danad
Rhag dyfod y coedwyr coed gymmynad
I gladdu dy wraidd a llygru dy hâd
Fal na thyfo byth afal arnad
A minnau wyf gwyllt gerthrychiad
Im cathrid cythrudd nim cudd dillad
Neum rhoddes GWENDDOLAU tlysau yn rhad
Ac yntau heddyw fal na buad.

i. e.

"O arbos pomifera, dulcis et bona,
Non parvum fers onus fructuum;
Ego tui causa anxius et solicitus sum
Ne lignatores arbores ad cædendas veniant,
Et effodiant tuam radicem, et semen corrumpant,
Ita ut nunquam postea pomum feras:
Ego sum ferus, hominibus spectaculum,
Me occupat horor, et vestes me non amiciunt.
GWENDDOLAU dedit mihi gratis jocularia,
Et ipse est hodie non uti olim fuit."

Fuit MERLINUS MORFRYNII filius et *Albania* oriundus, et alter fuit a MERLINO AMBROSIO qui vixit tempore VORTIGERNI, et eò quod nepotem causu interfecerit in insaniam incidit et in *Calèdoniam* recessit sylvam feri instar, ubi, cum animi compos esset, sortem suam carminibus deploravit.

Floruit hoc seculo et LLYWARCH-HEN, i. e. longævus, URIENI *Cumbriæ* principis consobrinus. Extant ab eo scripta poemata in quibus narrat se a Saxonibus in *Povisiam* pulsum fuisse, et sibi fuisse viginti quatuor filios auries torquibus insignitos, et omnes patriam defendendo bello occubuisse. Qui plura de hoc viro nobili et Bardo desiderat Cl. LLWYDII Archaeologiam Britannicam consulat p. 259.

Vixerunt eodem tempore alii Bardi, sed cum eorum non extent opera, nomina tantum interserere sufficat TRISTFARDD, Bardd URIEN REGED. DYGYNNELW, Bardd OWAIN ap URIEN, AFAN FERDDIG, Bardd CADWALLON ap CADFAN. GOLYDDAN, Bardd CADWALADR FENDIGAID. Sunt in iis qui extant multa quae historico Britannico usui esse possunt: fuere enim Bardi rerum gestarum fidi narratores. Fuit eorum praecipuum munus principum et magnatum laudes, et egregia in bello acta carminibus celebrare, quod et olim de iis observavit LUCANUS.

> Vos quoque, qui fortes animas belloque peremptas
> Laudibus in longum vates dimittis aevum,
> Plurima securi fudistis carmina BARDI. Lib.

"Bardi (inquit Lelandus in Assertione ARTURII) soli musicis numeris, et illustri nobilium memoriæ conservandæ studebant, canebant illi ad lyram heroum inclyta facta, profuit hoc studium mirificè cognitioni, tanquam per manus posteritati traditae. Unde quoque contigit ut ARTURII maximi nomen, fama, gloria utcunque conserventur." Inventus est enim ejus sepulchrum in monasterio *Glastoniensi* juxta id quod Bardus cecinerat coram HENRICO Secundo, quod satis demonstrat illos historicorum fidorum aequè ac poetarum munus egisse.

Habemus praeter hos quos supra citavimus Bardos, nonnulla carmina anonyma pervetusta, quae Druidum esse existimavit EDVARDUS LLUYD, cujusmodi sunt *Englynion yr Eiry, y bidiau, y gorwynnion.* Moris fuisse Druidis carmina almunos docere notavit CAESAR: "Magnum ubi versuum numerum edicere dicuntur. Itaque nonnulli annos vicenos in disciplina permanent, neque fas esse existimant ea litteris mandare, quum in reliquis fere rebus publicis privatisque rationibus, Graecis litteris utuntur. Id mihi duabus de causis instituisse videntur; quod neque in vulgus disciplinam efferri velint, neque eos qui discunt litteris confisos minus memoriae studere, quod feré plerisque accidit ut praesidio litterarum diligentiam in discendo ac memoriam remittant." Genus carminis quo in his usi sunt fuit *Englyn Milwr.*

Haec de antiquissimis quae nunc extant Bardis Britannicis dicere sufficiat, ad illos nunc accedo qui durante Principum Cambriæ gubernaculo floruerunt. A seculo sexto ad decimum nihil quod novi extat scriptum, saltem non vidi, neque quid causæ esse potuit augurari possum, nisi frequens bellorum strages et Britannorum inter dissidia. In HOELI BONI, nostris HYWEL DDA, legibus fit Bardi aulici mentio, et quænam fuerit ejus ibi conditio, quæ,[1] temporis ratione habitâ, fuit perhonesta. Circa annum 1170 GRUFFYDD AP CONAN Cambriæ princeps legem Bardis praescripsit, in qua cautum erat ut nullam praeter suam exercerent artem, in qua et dona et pœnas constituit. Eos autem in tres classes divisit, *Prydydd*, *Teuluwr*, et *Clerwr;* et fixum unicuique secundum ordinem statuit stipendium. Eorum electio fieri solebat in solenni principum et procerum concessu, ubi unicuique secundum meritum assignatus est locus. Ille vero qui praecelliat, sellâ donatus est aureâ vel argenteâ, unde et *Cadeirfardd* dictus, i. e. Bardus qui sellam assecutus est.

Ab eo tempore multi eximii floruerunt Bardi, et a principibus admodum fovebantur. MEILIR qui fuit GRUFFINI filii CONANI Bardus, fuit et ejusdem miles et legatus uti et ipse in ejus epicedio refert.

Yfeis gan deyrn o gyrn eurawg
Arfod faedd feiddiad angad weiniawg

1 "Qui Harpatorem in manum percusserit, componat illum quartà parte majori compositione quàm alteri ejusdem conditionis homini." Inter Legg. Ripuariorum et Wesinorum a Lindenbrochio collectas—Unde patet quanto in honore apud exteros etiam Bardus et Harpator (idem enim plerunque fuit munus) habitus esset. Præter harpam aliud instrumenti genus sibi peculiare Norwallenses vindicant, quod *Crwth* vocant—Hinc verbum Anglicum *Crowdero* apud Hudibrastum pro *Fiddler, or Player upon the Violin*, ad quod *Crwth* principium dedisse videtur. Hoc instrumenti genus ferè in desuetudinem abiit, et *violino* cessit.—Ex sex chordis felinis constat, nec eodem modo quo *violinum* modulatur, quamvis a figurâ haud multùm abludat: in Sudwalliâ penitus ignoratur:

"Romanusque Lyrâ plaudat tibi, Barbarus Harpâ,
Græcus Achilliaca, *Crotta Britanna* canat."

VENANTIUS. Lib. 7. Carm. 8.

Yn llys *Aberffraw* er ffaw ffodiawg
Bum o du Gwledig yn lleithawg
Eilwaith ydd eithum yn negessawg
O leufer lliw camawn iawn dywyssawg
Bu fedd aur gylchwy yn fodrwyawg
Torresid gormes yn llynghessawg
Gwedi tonnau gwyrdd gorewynnawg
Dyphuthynt eu seirch meirch rhygyngawg.

i. e.

"Dedit mihi potum ex cornu deaurato princeps,
Cujus impetus erat instar apri ferocis in bello, cujus
Manus erat liberalis
In aula *Aberffraw,* quod mihi decus et felicitas fuit.
Ex domini mei parte miles fui,
Et iterum legationem obii.
Quum a bello cruento discederet princeps egregius.
Mulsum ex poculo aureo bibebatur in circulo,
Hostium enim invasionem navalem repulimus,
Et post refluxum undarum viridium perspumosarum
Portabant phaleras in littore sicco equi gestientes."

Nec dedignati sunt ipsi principes hanc artem, animi relaxandi causa, colere, ut testantur OWENI CYFEILIOG principis *Povisiæ* et HOELI filii OWENI *Venedotiæ* principis opera, quibus addere licet LLEWELLINUM ultimum Cambriae principem. De eo enim sic MATT. WEST. circa natale domini LLEWELLINUS accessit ad regem misericordiam non justitiam petiturus—et paulo post—Rex EDWARDUS vocalem principem diligenter instructum ad partes Walliae redire permisit.[1] Poematum argumenta erant egregia in bello facinora, libertas, hospitalitas et munifi-

1 Vid. PRYNNE's Coll. of Records, Vol. III. p. 1214.

centia, et si quae alia virtus, quae homines domi ornat, et foris hostibus tremendos reddit. Et fuit eorum in accendendis hominum ad clara incepta animis tanta vis, ut nihil aeque sonaret TYRTAEI musa quum suos ad honestam mortem oppetendam hortaretur. Et quaenam, quaeso, reipublicae tam utilis virtus, quum hostibus utrinque premeretur, et cum sola spes, salus et libertas esset in armis, quam magnanimus periculorum contemptus, et ad ea adeunda ardor egregius? Sed præstat GIRALDUM CAMBRENSEM audire qui iis vixit temporibus, et fuit eorum quæ hic narrantur oculatus testis. "Nec ullo prorsus nisi martio labore vexantur, patriæ tamen tutelæ student et libertatis: pro patria pugnant, pro libertate laborant; pro quibus non solum ferro dimicare, verum etiam vitam dare dulce videtur. Unde et in thoro turpe, in bello mori decus putant. Ac illud poetæ dixerunt—*procul hinc avertite pacem, nobilitas cum pace perit,* nec mirum si non degenerant. Quorum enim hi reliquiae sunt Æneadae in ferrum pro libertate ruebant. De his igitur spectabile, quod nudi multoties cum ferro vestitis, inermes cum armatis, pedites cum equitibus congredi non verentur, in quo plerumque conflictu sola fiunt agilitate, et animositate victrices. Illis quorum poeta sic meminit, sicut situ sic natura non dissimiles."

——— Populus quos despicit arctos
Felices errore suo, quos ille timorum
Maximus haud urget leti metus, inde ruendi
In ferrum mens prona viris, animaeque capaces
Mortis, et ignavum rediturae parcere vitae.

Et nonnullis interjectis—"Illud in hoc loco notandum videtur, quod Anglorum Rex *Henricus* Secundus nostris diebus imperatori Constantinoplitano *Emmanueli* super insulae Britannicae situ ac natura, magisque notabilibus litteris et nunciis inquirenti: inter caetera hoc quasi praecipue notabile rescripsit. In quadam insulae parte sunt gentes quae Wallenses dicuntur, tantae audaciae et ferocitatis ut nudi cum armatis congredi non vereantur, adeo ut sanguinem pro patria fundere promptissime, vitamque velint pro laude pacisci." Hactenus GIRALDUS.

Non immerito Bardis tantus fuit habitus honor; ii enim heroum inclyta canentes acta, et majorum illustria proponentes exempla suos ad ardua incitabant, unde et patriae salutem, principibus et proceribus gloriam conciliabant; nec solum illustria aliorum canebant facta, verum ipsi in bello eodem quo in cantibus ardore incitati, multa praeclara fortitudinis exhibebant documenta. GWALCHMAI filius MEILIR se Cambriae fines adversus Anglos defendisse gloriatur in poemate cui titulus *Gorhoffedd* GWALCHMAI, i. e. *ejus Deliciæ*. Stationem ejus juxta fluvium *Efurnwy* fuisse docet non pocul ab agro *Salopiensi*. Sunt multa in hoc poemate tam heroe quam Bardo digna. Postquam enim excubias per noctem totam egisset GWALCHMAI, ad lucem diei appropinquantis laetus, loci et rerum circumjacentium pulchritudine delectatus, omnem curam et solicitudinem amovit, et philomelae cantui, et aquae juxta labantis murmuri, et arborum herbarumque virori attendit, imminens ab hoste periculum contemnens, Marti aeque ac Mercurio paratus, firmum mehercle et generosum pectus!

Poema in hunc modum incipit.

Mochddwyreawg Huan haf dyffestin
Maws llafar adar, mygr, hyar hin.
Mi ydwyf eurddeddf ddiofn yn nhrin
Mi wyf llew rhag llu, lluch fy ngorddin
Gorwyliais nos yn achadw ffin

Gorloes rydau dwfr *Dygen Freiddin*[1]
Gorlas gwellt didryf, dwfr neud jessin
Gwyrlain yn gware ar wely lliant
Lleithrion eu pluawr, pleidiau eddrin.

i. e.

"O sol æstive, cito oriens propera,
Suavis est cantus avium, et cælum sudum et serenum est.
Ego sum bona indole præditus, et in bello intrepidus,
Sum leo strenuus in fronte exercitus, et meus impetus est violentus,
Totam noctem pervigilavi fines tutando
Ubi sunt vada translucida juxta *Dygen Freiddin*
Ubi herba in loco solitario crescens perviridis est, et aqua limpida
Mergi ludunt in fluctuum lecto,
Quorum plumæ fulgent, et ipsi inter se certant."

Non pigebit hic de alio Bardo, scilicet CYNDDELW Brydydd MAWR, i. e. CONDELAO vate eximio, nonnulla ex OWENI *Venedotiæ* principis epicedio excerpere; fuit enim ille, uti ex historia constat, patriæ propugnator, et in bello fere semper victor. Vixit CYNDDELW in *Povisia*, et fuit MADOCI filii MAREDUDD, illius regionis principis, Bardus aulicus.

Gwersyll torfoedd tew llew lladdai,
Gorsaf tarf, taerfalch fal GWALCHMAI,
Gorfaran GWRFAN gorfyddai,
Gwr yn aer yn aros gwaedd fai,
Bryd EROF gryd, arf greu a ddodai,
Brwydr eurgrwydr, eurgrawn ni guddiai,

1 *Dygen Freiddin*, hodie *Craig Freiddin*, est rupes alta et prærupta in agr. *Salopiensi*, non procul a *Sabrina*.

Bradog waith gwynniaith gwynnygai,
Brys briwgad, brig bragad briwiai,
Brwysc lafneu ynghreu yngrhai celanedd,
Cymminedd cymmynai,

Gwyrdd heli *Teivi* tewychai,
Gwaedlan gwyr, a llyr ai llanwai,
Gwyrach rudd gorfudd goralwai,
Ar donniar gwyar gonofiai,
Gwyddfeirch tonn torrynt yn ertrai,
Gwythur naws fal traws au treifiai,
Gwyddfid *Eingl* ynghladd au trychai,
Gwyddgwn coed colled au porthai,
Gwyddwal dyfneual dyfnasai fy modd,
Fy meddiant a gaffaei.

Colleis Arglwydd call nim collai,
Corf eurdorf, eurdal am rhoddai,
Cof cadflawdd am cawdd, a'm carai,
Car cerddawr, cerddau ai cyrchai,
Gryd wascar, llachar, a'm llochai,
Grym dilludd DILLUS fab ERFAI,
Greddf *Greidwyr*, a *Chywyr a Chai*
Glew ddefawd glyw oesdrawd aesdrai,
Ystre hynt, wastad, westrei gwinfydig
Gwyn ei fyd bieufei.

Gwyth escor tra mor, tra *Menai*,
Gwlydd elfydd elwais o honai,
Tra fu OWAIN mawr ai meddai,
Medd a gwin a gwirawd fyddai,
Gwynedd wen Gwyndyd len ledpai,
Gwedi gwawr, cad fawr ai cadwai,
Pa wladwr, arwr arwyndai,
Pa wledig a wledych arnai?

i. e.

"Densas turmas in conflictu occidit leo

Qui fuit instar GWALCHMAI acris ad fugandum hostes,
Superavit magnas copias GWRVANNI.
Fuit in bello vir qui tubam expectabat,
Similis EROF bellicoso, qui telum cruentum duxit.
Ex bello rediens, in quo aurum nactus est, thesaurum non recondit;
In hostes dolosos certans magnâ excanduit irâ;
Hastæ in bello furiosæ erant in cadaveribus occisorum
Et acies (gladiorum) se invicem contriverunt.
Viridis aqua *Teivii* pinguis facta fuit.
Fluxus virorum sanguinis et maris eum ripas superare fecit,
Et rubra[1] avis aquatilis, pro nagno hebebat emolumento,
Et per fluvios cruoris natabat,
Et alti marini equi (i. e. fluctus) plangebant in littore.
Magnanimus ille princeps eos instar tyranni oppressit,
Et Anglorum cumulos in fossa truncavit.
Sylvestres canes amiserunt opsonatorem,
Quibus in densis vepribus assolebat esse victus, neque meo assensu,
Neque auxilio indigebat.
Perdidi dominum prudentem, qui me non neglexit,
Cujus corpus erat auro amictum, quique mihi aurum dedit
Cujus memoria (mortui) me lædit : qui me dilexit :
Amicus enim erat Bardo, et eum apetebant carmina
Ille qui homines in bello dissipare fecit, et cujus impetus erat violentus me fovit,
Cujus robur erat ineluctabile instar DILLUS filii ERFAI,
Et cujus ingenium erat simile GREIDWYR, CYWYR et CAI
Herois instar hastam gessit comminutam
Domi autem vitæ cursus erat tranquillus, hospes enim erat munificus
Et ad summam felicitatem pervenit.

1 Quaenam sit hæc avis mihi non constat.

Ille victorias reportavit violentus trans aestuarium
Menai
Ubi terra est benigna, ex qua beneficium sum nactus:
Donec extitit OWENUS magnus qui *Monam* possesit,
Mulsum, vinum et *gwirawd*[1] bibimus.
O *Venedotia* olim beata, Venedotorum tutatem asperum,
Post Heroem bellicosum qui te defendet!
Quis ex nostratibus heros in aedibus vivens magnificis,
Quis princeps te gubernare aequo ac ille valebit?"

Sed non semper in bellatorum laudes effusi erant Bardi; saepe etiam principum et magnatum fata indigna lugubriter canebant. Sed infinitum esset haec singulatim recensere. Unum sat est adducere exemplum, ex quo de aliis facile judicari potest. LEOLINO GRUFFINI filio, ultimo Cambriae principe, juxta *Buellt* dolo sublato, dici non potest quanto id Bardos dolore affecit. Inter quos GRUFFYDD AP YR YNAD COCH haec texuit admodum παθητικῶς.

Llawer llef druan, fal pan fu *Gamlan*,
Llawer deigr dros rann gwedi gronniaw,
O leas gwanas gwanar eurllaw,
O laith LLEWELYN cof dyn nim daw,
Oerfelog calon, dan fron o fraw,
Rhewydd, fal crinwydd y sy'n crinaw,
Poni welwch chwi hynt y gwynt ar glaw?
Poni welwch chwi'r deri yn ymdaraw?
Poni welwch chwi'r mor yn merwino'r tir?
Poni welwch chwi'r gwir yn ymg'weiriaw?
Poni welwch chwi'r haul yn hwylio'r awyr?
Poni welwch chwi syr wedi syrthiaw?
Poni chredwch i Dduw ddyniadon ynfyd
Poni welwch chwi'r byd wedi bydiaw?

1 Potûs genus apud veteres Britannos.

Och hyd attat di Dduw na ddaw mor tros dir
Pa beth in gedir i ohiriaw?
Nid oes le i cyrcher rhag carchar braw
Nid oes le i triger och! o'r trigaw,
Nid oes na chyngor, na chlo nag agor,
Na ffordd i esgor brwyn gyngor braw!

i. e.

"Frequens est vox lugubris, veluti olim in *Camlan*,
Multae lacrymae in genis accumulantur,
Eo quod occidit Cambriae sustentaculum, et ejus dominus munificus.
Ex quo occidit LEOLINUS de caeteris non curo;
Cor frigidum est sub pectore ob horrorem,
Et is qui prius hilaris erat, jam marcescit.
Nonne videtis venti et imbris cursum?
Nonne videtis quercus in se invicem ruentes?
Nonne videtis mare terram vastans?
Nonne videtis solem ex cursu aerio deflectentem?
Nonne videtis astra ex orbibus corruisse?
Cur Deo non creditis homines, vesani?
Nonne videtis mundi finem adesse?
Exclamabo usque ad te, o Deus, cur terram non absorbet mare,
Et cur diutius relinquimur in angore languere?
Nullus est locus, quem petamus aegri,
Nullus locus, in quo habitemus miseri,
Nullum restat consilium, nullum effugium,
Nulla via, qua evitemus fatum luctuosum."

Floruere a tempore GRUFFINI CONANI filii ad hunc LEOLINUM et multi alii Bardi insignes, inter quos eminet LLYWARCH cognomine Prydydd y Moch, qui LEOLINI Magni, nostris LLEWELYN AP IORWERTH, victorias multis celebravit odis, uti et fecere DAFYDD BENFRAS, DANIEL AP LLOSGWRN MEW, LLEWELYN FARDD AP CYWRYD.

Floruit eodem tempore in *Ceretia* PHYLYP BRYDYDD, qui Bardus fuit RHYS GRYG et RHYS IEUANC ex familia RHYS AP TEWDWR oriundus.

Longum esset singulos recensere; de praestantioribus pauca praelibasse sufficit. Cum Cambriam in suam potestatem redegerat EDWARDUS primus, in Bardos saeviit tyranni instar, et multos suspendi fecit. Quid mirum, cum ipsum LEOLINUM principem et DAVIDEM fratrem tam inhumaniter tractaverit? Sed EDWARDUS a LEOLINO olim in fugum pulsus, noluit illi nec asseclis ignoscere. Hinc illae lacrymae. Bardis objiciebatur quod cives in seditionem excitarunt, id est revera, quod eos ad vindicandum libertatem pristinam majorum more hortarentur. Bardi enim fuere *Cambris* idem quod olim *Atheniensibus* oratores, quos ut Graeciam in servitutem redigeret, sibi tradi voluit PHILIPPUS Macedo. Regum Angliae justiciarii post *Edwardum* in Cambria ejus exemplum secuti, Bardos legibus iniquis obnoxios ubique sustulerunt; unde fit ut admodum sint rari ab eo tempore usque ad annum 1400, quo, Anglorum excusso servitutis jugo, sub OWENI GLYNDWR auspiciis, se in libertatem priscam vindicarunt Cambri. Hoc aevo multi claruere Bardi, inter quos IOLO GOCH OWENI magnificentiam et victorias ad sydera tulit. Fuit enim OWENUS Bardorum fautor et Maecenas, et eos undiquaque ad aulam liberalitate provocabat. Eo tempore floruit DAFYDD AP GWILYM Bardorum longe venustissimus e *Ceretia* oriundus. Avunculum habuit LLEWELYN AP GWILYM de *Cryngae* et *Dôl Goch,* qui eum liberaliter educabat. Patronus ejus fuit IFOR HAEL de *Bussaleg,* cujus munificentiam et magnanimitatem multis prosequitur laudibus. Cum OWENI retro laberentur res, Cambros more inaudito oppressit HENRICUS IV. et patriae fatum subiere Bardi. Lege enim cautum erat ne annuam peragrationem et conventus, nostris *Clera* et *Cymhortha* celebrarent. Haec fuit causa cur multi hoc saeculo tam obscure scripserint: multis enim cantibus *Cywydd Brut*, i. e. *Carminis fatidici* nomen indidere; quod et fecere postea cum inter *Eboracenses* et *Lancastrenses* grassaretur factio. HENRICUS V. multum a paterna remisit in Cambros saevitia. Ab eo tempore longa floruit Bardorum series, et in magnatum aedibus alebantur, ubi eorum genealogias et signa gentilitia texebant, eorumque virtutes, scilicet magnanimitatem, hospitalitatem et alias animi atque corporis ingenuas et honestas dotes debita prosequebantur laude. Mos enim fuit Britannis olim, uti et nunc Cambris, ut longam majorum seriem producerent, et Bardi qui hoc munere sunt functi *Arwyddfeirdd* sunt appellati, et carmen texuere "parasematicum, quod cum prosapia generisve serie, etiam et παρασήματα, id est insignia nobilium et generosorum describit ea, quae in vestibus et vexillis et hujusmodi aliis insignita conspiciuntur, quaeque fiunt aut feruntur, ita ab iis discreta ut nosci possint quorum sint, sive ad quos pertineant, more antiquorum bene meritis tributa, et tanquam ornamenta laudis et gloriae, vel ob propriam vel suorum majorum virtutem comparata."—Vide JOHANNIS DAVIDIS RHESI Linguae Cymraecae Institutiones accuratas pag. 146. Ex quo et haec de hujuscemodi Bardo transtulimus p. 303. "*Pwy bynnag a ddywetto ei fod yn Arwyddfardd, gwybydded achoedd Brenhinoedd a Thywyssogion, a chyfarwyddyd oddiwrth y tri Phrifardd ynys Prydain, nid amgen,* MYRDDIN AP MORFRYN, *a* MYRDDIN EMRYS *a* THALIESIN BEN BEIRDD." i.e. "Quicunque voluerit esse Bardus parasematicus, necesse est ut sciat regum et principum stemmata, et sit bene versatus in operibus MERLINI MORFRYNII filii, MERLINI AMBROSII et TALIESINI summi Bardi." Et hoc fuisse antiquitus Bardorum munus annotavit GIRALDUS CAMBRENSIS. "Hoc mihi notandum videtur, quod Bardi Cambrenses et cantores seu recitatores genealogias habent prædictorum principum in libris eorum antiquis et autenticis, eandemque memoriter tenent a RODERICO Magno usque ad Belinum Magnum, et inde usque ad Sylvium, Ascanium et Æneam, et ab ea usque ad Adam generationem linealiter producunt."

Non abs re fore judicavi hic monumentum vetus inserere, quod in manuscripto Joh. Dav. Rhesi propria manu exarato inveni. Quod quidem manuscriptum dignum est omnino quod prelo mandetur: nostram enim linguam poesin, et alia vetusta monumenta adversus ignarum quendam calumniatorem, quorum messem innumeram hæc aeque ac superior aetas tulit, strenue vindicat. Hic tractatus in lingua Britannica eleganter scriptus est, et talium nebulonum inscitiam protervam facile retundit. Videtur vir doctissimus hoc monumentum ex vetusto aliquo scriptore nunc deperdito excerpsisse. Utcunque sit, id ego ex ejus autographo hic fideliter exscribere curavi. "Blethinus filius Cynvini patri in principatu *Povisiæ* successit. Hic templa, castra et maneria renovari fecit, leges Howeli observavit. Inter tres principes, videlicet, Gruffinum filium Conani principem *Venedotiæ*, Blethinum filium Cynvini principem Povisiæ, et Rhesum filium Tewdwr principem *Suth-walliæ* inquisitio magna fuit de armis et de regali sanguine antiquorum Britonum. Quibus conquisitis in ditione sapientium Walliæ; repertæ fuerunt tres lineæ regales, et quindecim lineæ de sanguine nobilium senatorum Britanniæ. Hic Blethinus primus omnium principum *Povisiæ*, in armis usus est leone rubeo in sulphure. Hic castrum de *Dol y Forwyn* fundavit, et apud *Mifod* sepultus est."

Sunt in istis genealogiis multa quæ antiquario Britannico usui esse possunt; nihil enim apud nostrates vel antiquius vel magis autenticum extat, et nihil quod magis nostram illustrat et confirmat historiam. Nonnulli enim ex Bardis non solum rei poeticae, verum etiam historicae mentem appulerunt. Erat in monasteriis uber historiarum, genealogiarum et poeseos collectio. Bardi enim ab abbatibus maxime fovebantur, et erant in festis solennibus ab iis laute excepti: uti constat ex operibus GUTTO'R GLYNN, GUTTUN OWAIN, IEUAN DEULWYN et TUDUR ALED. Extant et nunc in nobiliorum ædibus innumera Epicedia, quæ nostrates *Cywyddau Marwnad* nuncupavere: fuit enim Bardi domestici munus, cum aliquis e familia obierit, ejus Epicedium concinnare, quod post exequias ad cognatos fuit delatum et coram iis a Rhapsodis quos nostrates *Datceiniaid* nominavere recitatum. Inter alia quæ in defuncti honorem sunt narrata, ejus genealogiam memorare tenebatur, ex quibus nobilibus ortus fuerit familiis, et quæ præclara fecerint ejus majores facinora. Hujuscemodi poematum multa vidi exemplaria pulchre exarata. Ab ELIZABETHAE Reginæ tempore nullus fuit Bardorum legitimus consessus: unde fit ut nil sit deinceps accurate et secundum prosodiæ regulas scriptum: eousque ut jamdudum Bardorum et historicorum opera (ex quibus solis vera et genuina Britanniæ historia petenda est) in maximo sint periculo ne funditus pereant. Quod multas ob causas in seculo tam docto et sagaci maxime est deplorandum, sunt quidem hoc ævo qui hæc studia velint rediviva, et qui plus ipsi possint in re poetica atque historica quam quos superior tulit aetas. Inter quos societas *Cymmrodorion* Londini, patriae atque maternae linguae amore instigata, inter alia laude digna instituta, nonnulla veterum et recentiorum melioris notae Bardorum poemata typis mandare meditatur. Opus profecto omnibus Cambris ingenuis gratissimum et longe desideratissimum. Optandum est potius quam expectandum, ut ii qui habent aliquid in poesi vel historia notatu dignum in privatis bibliothecis reconditum, id in vulgus emittant, aut saltem ab iis qui hujusmodi rebus operam navant perlegi permittant. Sic enim suae famae et patriae commodo melius consulent quam vermibus et muribus committere.

Ego autem in Cambriae montibus degens a bibliothecis et museis procul, quod potui feci; utinam ii qui plus possint, et materiam uberiorem sunt nacti de Bardis, et caeteris Britannicae antiquitatis reliquiis, meliora cudant.

YCHYDIG

AWDLAU O WAITH YR HEN FEIRDD,

YN AMSER

TYWYSOGION CYMRU;

WEDI EU CYFIEITHU I'R SAESONEG;

Er mwyn dangos ansawdd ein Prydyddiaeth i wyr cywraint, dysgedig, anghyfiaith: â nodau byrrion, i eglurhau enwau Dynion, a Lleoedd, a grybwyllir ynddynt; a hanes byrr o honynt, wedi ei gasglu allan o *Drioedd Ynys Prydain*, a hen Goffadwriaeth eraill; er dywenydd i'r oes hon, ac er adfer ei haeddedigawl barch i'r hen famiaith *Gymraeg*, ac i'n Gwlad; a'u dyledus glod i'w thrigolion dewrwych gynt.

'Αιεὶ τοῦτο Διὸς κόυραις μέλει, ἀιὲν ἀοιδοῖς
'Υμνεῖν ἀθανάτως, ὑμνεῖν ἀγαθῶν κλέα ἄνδρων.

THEOCRITUS Idyll. xvi.

AT

RISIART MORYS, YSWAIN,

LLYWYDD CYMDEITHAS Y CYMMRODORION YN LLUNDAIN;

A'I FRODYR,

LEWIS MORYS, YSWAIN, O BENBRYN,

YNG NGHEREDIGION; A

WILLIAM MORYS, O GAERGYBI, YM MON.

NI bum yn hir yn myfyrio i bwy i cyflwynwn yr ychydig Awdlau sydd yn canlyn, canys ni adwaen i neb heddyw ag sydd yn eu deall cystal â chwi, na neb chwaith sydd yn coledd ac yn mawrhau ein iaith mor anwylgu Frutannaidd. I mae ein gwlad ni yn rhwymedig i bob un o honoch: i chwi y *Llywydd,* yn enwedig, am y gofal a gymmerasoch yn golygu argraffiad diweddaf y *Bibl Cyssegrlan,* er lles tragwyddol eneidiau ein cydwladwyr. Ef a dâl Duw i chwi am y gorchwyl elusengar yma, pan i bo'r byd hwn, a'i holl fawredd a'i wychder, wedi llwyr ddiflannu. Ac i mae'r wlad a'r iaith yn dra rhwymedig i'r *Gwr o Benbryn,* am gasglu cymmaint o *Hanesion ynghylch ein Hynafiaid,* na chlywodd y *Saeson* braidd son erioed am danynt. Ef a ddelwent ddilynwyr *Camden,* pei gwelynt fal i mae yn argyhoeddi ac yn ceryddu eu beiau, a'u tuedd gwyrgam, yn bychanu ac yn distadlu y pethau nad ydynt yn eu deall; ac o wir wenwyn yn taeru mai dychymmygion diweddar ydynt. Gobeithio i cawn ni weled y trysor mawrwerthiog yma ar gyhoedd; i beri gosteg, ac i dorri rhwysg y cyfryw oganwyr ein hen hanesion. Nid bychan o les i mae *y Gwr o Gaergybi* ynteu yn ei wneuthur, trwy gasglu *Gwaith yr hen Feirdd* godidog gynt; ac ir wyf yn cyfaddef mai o'i lyfrau ef i cefais i y rhan fwyaf o'r odlau sydd yn canlyn. Ni fedrwn lai na dywedyd hyn am eich ewyllys da i'ch gwlad a'ch iaith; cynneddfau sydd, ysywaeth, mor brin ac anaml yn yr oes hon. Ef a ddichon hyn beri i'n gwlad agor ei llygaid, a defnyddio yn well rhagllaw yr hen ysgrifenadau sydd heb fyned ar goll. Ac os na wna hi hyny, i mae yn rhaid addef i chwi eich trioedd wneuthur eich rhan yn odiaeth. Hyn a'm hannogodd i roddi blaenffrwyth fy llafur, er nad yw ond bychan, dan eich nodded; a gobeithio nad ydyw lwyr annheilwng i'w gyhoeddi, ag i daw rhywun cywreiniach i ddiwygio yr hyn sydd ammherffaith, ac i osod allan pethau eraill godidoccach. Nid oedd genyfi ond torri'r garw, gobeitho i daw eraill i lyfnhau a gwastattau y balciau. Yn ddiau ni fuaswn i yn cymmeryd yr orchest yma arnaf, ond darfod edliw o'r *Saeson*, nad oes genym ddim mewn Prydyddiaeth a dâl ei ddangos i'r byd: a bod un o drigolion yr *Uch Alban* gwedi cyfieithu swrn o waith hen fardd; neu yn hytrach wedi addurno a thacclu rhyw waith diweddar, a'i osod allan yn ei enw ef. Chwi a wyddoch yn dda, oddiwrth waith ein hen feirdd awduraidd ni, sydd eto i'w gweled, nad ydyw ddim tebygol fod y bardd gogleddig mor henaidd: ond nid af i i ymyrryd ag ef ym mhellach yr awron. Y mae yn ddigon genyfi roddi hyn o brawf o'n hen feirdd ein hunain i'r byd; ac os darfu i mi wneuthur cyfiawnder iddynt, dyna fi wedi cyrraedd fy amcan. Pa fodd bynnag i digwyddo, i mae'n llawen genyf gael odfa i dystiolaethu fy mod yn mawrygu yn ddirfawr eich cariad a'ch traserch chwi at eich gwlad a'ch iaith; yn yr hyn i damunwn, yn ol fy ngallu, eich canlyn; a datcan, yngwydd yr holl fyd, fy mod, frodyr haeddbarch,

Eich Gwasanaethwr rhwymedig, gostyngeiddiaf,

EVAN EVANS.

AT Y CYMRY.

PAN welais fod un o *Ysgodogion Ucheldir Alban*, ac hefyd *Sais* dysgedig, wedi cyfieithu gwaith eu hen Feirdd i'r *Saesoneg*, mi a dybygais mai nid gweddus i ni, y *Cymry*, y rhai sydd genym Gerddi awduraidd, gorhenaidd, o'r einom, fod yn llwyr ddiymdro yn y cyngaws hwnnw: o herwydd, hyd i gwn i, dyna'r unig ragorgamp celfyddyd a adawodd ein hynafiaid ini, sydd heb ei cholli. I mae *gwaith y Derwyddon*, od oedd dim gwiwgof ganddynt wedi ei ysgrifennu, wedi myned ar ddifancoll; ac nid oes dim wedi dyfod i'n hoes ni oddiwrthynt, ond y Brydyddiaeth yn unig. I mae ein hen *Fusic* wedi ei llwyr ebargofio: nid yw'r cyweiriau cwynfanus sydd genym yr awron ond dychymmygion diweddar, pan oedd y *Cymry* yn griddfan tan iau galed y *Sacson*. Am gelfyddydau eraill, od oedd dim mewn perffeithrwydd, i mae gwedi ei lwyr golli. Nid oes genym ddim hanes am ein hynafiaid o'n hawduron ein hunain, ond oddiwrth y Beirdd yn unig, o flaen *Gildas ap Caw*; yr hwn sydd yn ein goganu, ac yn ein llurginio, yn hytrach nag ysgrifennu cywir hanes am danom; ond fo wyr hanesyddion yr achos: heblaw hyn, i mae ei waith ef wedi myned drwy ddwylo'r *Meneich;* gwŷr a fedrai yn dda ddigon dylino pob peth i'w dibenion eu hunain.—Y Beirdd, fal i tystia *Giraldus*, Arch-diacon *Brycheiniog*, oeddynt yn cadw achau y Brenhinoedd, ac yn coffau eu gweithredoedd ardderchog; ac oddiwrthynt hwy yn ddiammau i deryw i *Dysilio* fab *Brochwel Ysgythrog*, tywysog *Powys*, ysgrifennu'r *hanes* sydd yr awron yn myned tan enw BRUT Y BRENHINOEDD, yr hwn a ddarfu i *Galfrid ap Arthur*, o Aber Mynwy, ei gyfieithu o iaith *Llydaw* i'r *Lladin*, ac oddiyno yn

Gymraeg; fel i mae ef ei hunan yn cyfaddef mewn amryw hen gopiau ar femrwn, sydd etto i'w gweled yng Nghymru; ond ysywaith, e ddarfu iddo chwanegu amryw chwedlau at hanes *Tysilio*: *Flamines* ac *Archiflamines*, a phrophwydoliaeth *Myrddin Emrys*, a phethau eraill a fuasai harddach eu gadael heibio. Ped fuasai yn dilyn y Beirdd, e fuasai genym gywirach hanes nag sydd genym yr awron: ond fel ag i mae, ni haeddai yn gwbl mo'r gogan i mae'r *Saeson*, o amser *Camden*, yn ei rhoi iddi; o herwydd i mae *Nennius*, yr hwn a ysgrifennodd drychant o flynyddoedd o'i flaen, yn rhoddi yr un hanes am ein dechreuad. Ir wyf yn amcanu, os Duw a rydd im' hoedl ac iechyd, osod allan yr awdur hwn a nodau helaeth arno, gyd ag amddiffyniad o'r hanes; o herwydd efe yw'r hanesydd hynaf a feddwn yn *Lladin*, oddigerth y *Gildas* uchod, yr hwn nid yw deilwng ei gyfrif yn hanesydd; o herwydd nid dyna ei gyngyd na'i fympwy, yn ei *Epistolæ de excidio Britanniæ*. Ir wyf yn methu a chaffael copi iawn o *Nennius*, ac ir wyf yn meddwl nad oes un yng Nghymru a dâl ddim, ond yn *Hengwrt:* da iawn er lles y wlad a hanesyddion *Prydain*, i gwnai ei berchennog adael i ryw wr dysgedig ei gymharu. I mae genyfi ddau gopi, ond i maent yn dra ammherffaith; felly hefyd i mae'r rhai printiedig, o eiddo'r Dr. *Gale* a *Bertram*. Ni wiw i *Sais*, na neb dieithr, bydded mor ddysgedig ag i mynno, oni ddeall ef Gymraeg yn iawn, ac oni chaiff hefyd weled ein hen ysgrifenadau a'n Beirdd ni, gytcam â'r fath waith. Nid yw *Camden*, er dysgedicced, diwytted, a manyled gwr ydoedd, ond ymleferydd am lawer o bethau yn ei *Britannia;* a hyny yn unig, o achos nad oedd yn medru yr iaith yn well. A gresyn yw, nad oedd y *Saeson*, y rhai oeddynt yn ddiau (rai o naddunt) yn chwilio pethau yn dêg, ac yn ddiduedd dros ben, y cyfryw ag ydoedd *Leland*, *Usher*, a *Selden*, yn deall ein iaith, a medru gwneuthur defnydd o'n hen lyfrau: o herwydd hyn, nid oeddynt, er cymaint eu dysg a'u dawn, ddim i'w cyffelybu ag *Wmffre*

Llwyd o *Ddinbych*, a *Rhobert Fychan* o'r *Hengwrt*, fel i mae eu gwaith yn eglur ddangos. Ac yn ddiau, mae yn ammhosibl i undyn, bydded mor gywreinied ag i myno, wneuthur dim â ffrwyth ynddo, heb gaffael gweled yr hen ysgrifenadau, sydd yn gadwedig yn llyfr-gelloedd y boneddigion yng *Nghymru;* yn enwedig yn *Hengwrt,* a *Llan Fordaf.* Myfi a welais, ac a gefais fenthyg amryw lyfrau o waith llaw, yn llyfrgrawn yr anrhydeddus *Robert Davies,* ysg^r. o *Lannerch* yn Swydd *Dinbych ;* a Sir *Roger Mostyn* yng *Ngloddaith,* seneddwr dros Swydd *Flint ;* a chan yr anrhydeddus *William Fychan,* ysg^r. o *Gors y Gedol,* seneddwr dros Swydd *Feirionydd ;* yr hyn ni fedraf lai nâ'i fynegu yma yngwydd y byd, er coffau eu cymmwynas a'u hewyllys da i'n gwlad a'n iaith, ac i minnau hefyd ; yn ol arfer canmoladwy, a haelioni yr hen *Frython* gynt.

Ond i ddyfod weithion at y Beirdd, yr rhai a adawsom ar ol. Ef a ddarfu imi gyfieithu ychydig odlau o'u gwaith, trwy annogaeth gwyr dysgedig o *Loegr ;* ac mi a ewyllysiwn wneuthur o honof hynny er clod iddynt ; ond i mae yn rhaid im' adael hynny ym marn y darllenyddion : ac nid oes genyfi ddim i'w ddywedyd, os drwg yw'r cyfieithiad, nad arnaf i yn llwyr i mae'r bai yn sefyll; o herwydd i maent y Beirdd yn ddiammau yn orchestol odiaeth; ond i mae'n rhaid addef hefyd eu bod yn anhawdd afrifed eu deongli, o herwydd eu bod yn llawn o eiriau sydd yr awron wedi myned ar gyfrgoll: ac nid ydynt wedi eu heglurhau mewn un Geiriadur argraffedig nac ysgrifenedig a welais i. Ir oedd yr Athraw hynod o *Fallwyd,* yr hwn a astudiodd yr iaith er lles cyffredin y wlad, dros holl ddyddiau ei einioes, yn methu eu deongli. Ac ni wnaeth y dysgedig Mr. *Edward Llwyd* o'r *Musæum,* gamp yn y byd yn y perwyl yma, er ei fod yn gydnabyddus â holl geinciau prifiaith *Prydain.* Ac yn ddiau o'r achos yma, nid oedd genyfi ddim ond ymbalfalu am ystyr a synwyr y

Beirdd, mewn llawer man, oddiwrth flaen ac ol. Ir wyf yn rhyfeddu'n ddirfawr am rai o'r *Cymry* sydd yn haeru fod gwaith *Taliesin*, a'i gydoesiaid *Aneurin Gwawdrydd*, *Llywarch Hen*, a *Merddin Wyllt*, yn hawdd eu deall. Yn ddiau nid wyf i yn deall mo honynt, ac i mae'r rhai dysgediccaf yn yr iaith, y to heddyw, yn addef yr un peth. I mae'r Beirdd, hir oesoedd gwedi hyny, sef ar ol dyfodiad *Gwilym Fasdardd*, hyd farwolaeth, *Llywelyn ap Gruffydd*, yn dywyll iawn; fal i gellwch weled oddiwrth yr odlau sydd yn canlyn. Hyn a barodd i mi beidio â chyfieithu chwaneg o honynt y tro yma, rhag ofn imi, trwy fy anwybodaeth, wneuthur cam â hwynt. Ond gan i'r *Saeson* daeru, na feddwn ddim mewn prydyddiaeth a dâl ei ddangos; mi a wnaethum fy ngorau er cyfieithu y Casgliad bychan yma, i fwrw heibio, os yw bossibl, y gogan hwnnw: ac yn ddiau, os na lwyddodd genyf wneuthur hyny, i mae yn rhaid i'r Beirdd, a'm cydwladwyr, faddeu imi; a gobeithio i derbyniant fy ewyllys da, herwydd na ddichon neb wneuthur ond a allo.—Heblaw hyn oll, i mae hyn o waith yn dyfod i'r byd, mewn amser anghyfaddas i ymddangos mewn dim prydferthwch; o herwydd i mae un o drigolion yr *Uch Alban*, gwedi gosod allan ddau lyfr o waith *Ossian;* hen Fardd, meddai ef, cyn dyfod Cristianogaeth i'w plith. Ac i mae'r llyfrau hyn mewn rhagorbarch gan foneddigion dysgedig y *Saeson*. A rhaid addef eu bod wedi eu cyfieithu yn odidog: ond i mae arnafi ofn, wedi'r cwbl, fod yr *Ysgodog* yn bwrw hug ar lygaid dynion, ac nad ydynt mor hen ag i mae ef yn taeru eu bod. I mae'r *Gwyddelod* yn arddelw *Ossian* megis un o'u cydwladwyr hwynt; ac i mae amryw bethau yn y cerddi a gyhoeddwyd yn ei enw, yn dangos, yn fy nhyb i, oes ddiweddarach nag i mae'r cyfieithydd yn son am dani; yn enwedig dyfodiad Gwyr *Llychlyn* i'r *Iwerddon*, yr hyn ni ddigwyddodd, meddai hanesyddion yr *Iwerddon*, cyn y flwyddyn 700. Ac ni ddaeth yr *Ysgodogion* chwaith i sefydlu yn yr *Alban*, o flaen *Fergus Mac Ein*, ynghylch y flwyddyn 503; fal i mae *William Llwyd*, Esgob *Caerwrangon*, wedi ei brofi yn ddiwrthadl, yn ei lyfr ynghylch llywodraeth eglwysig. Ond pei canniatteid eu bod hwy yno cyn hynny, ni fyddai hynny ronyn nes i brofi *Ossian* mor hyned ag i dywedir ei fod. O herwydd ped fuasai, pa fodd i mae ei gyfieithydd yn medru ei ddeongli mor hyfedr? I mae gwaith ein Beirdd ni, sydd gant o flynyddoedd ar ol hynny, tu hwnt i ddeall y gwir cywreiniaf a medrusaf yn yr hen *Frutaniaith*. Pwy o honom ni a gymerai'r *Gododin*, gwaith *Aneurin Gwawdrydd*, Fychdeyrn Beirdd, a'i. gyfieithu mor llathraidd ag i gwnaeth cyfieithydd *Ffingal* a *Themora?* Ir wyfi yn meddwl nad oes neb a ryfygei gymmeryd y fath orchest arno. Prin iawn i medreis i ddeongli rhai penillion o hono yma a thraw, y rhai a ellwch eu gweled yn y traethawd *Lladin* ynghylch y Beirdd. A gresyn yw ei fod mor dywyll, o herwydd, hyd ir wyf fi yn ei ddeall, gwaith godidog ydyw. Yr un peth a ellir ei ddywedyd am *Daliesin* Ben Beirdd, nid oes neb heddyw, hyd i gwn i, a fedr gyfieithu yn iawn un o'i Awdlau na'i Orchanau. Myfi a wn fod amryw Frudiau ar hyd y wlad, wedi eu tadogi ar *Daliesin* a *Myrddyn;* ond nid ydynt ond dychymygion diweddar, gwedi eu ffurfeiddio ar ol marwolaeth *Llywelyn ap Gruffydd*. Yn enwedig yn amseroedd terfysglyd *Owain Glyndwr*, a'r ymdrech rhwyg pleidiau *Efrog* a *Lancaster*. I mae hefyd eraill, gwedi eu lluniaethu gan y Meneich, i atteb eu dibenion hwythau; ond i mae'r rhain oll yn hawdd eu gwahanu oddiwrth awduraidd waith *Taliesin*, wrth yr iaith.—I mae yn ddiammau genyf, fod y bardd yma yn odidog yn ei amser. Ir oedd yn gydnabyddus ag athrawiaith y *Derwyddon* am y μετεμψύχωσις, a'r Daroganau, y rhai oeddynt yn ddiammau, weddillion o'r Credo paganaidd; canys nid yw daroganu ddim arall ond mynegi pethau i ddyfod, oddiwrth y *Ddar*, yr hon ir oeddynt y *Derwyddon* yn ei pherchi yn fawr iawn. A chan ei fod ef yn wr llys, ac yn byw yn yr oes anwybodus honno, ir oedd yr hyn a ddywedai yn cael ei dderbyn a'i roesawu gan y gwerinos, megis ped fuasai wir broffwyd. A hynny a ellir ei ddywedyd hefyd am Ferddin Emrys, a'i broffwydoliaeth. Mor anhawdd yw tynnu ofergoelion eu hynafiaid, oddiwrth un wlad neu genedl!

E ddichon rhai o honoch ysgatfydd ofyn, Paham na buaswn yn cyfieithu rhai o'r Beirdd godidog diweddar, a ysgrifenasant wedi diwygio yr hen gynghanedd? I'r rhain ir wyf yn ateb, fod y Beirdd yn amser y tywysogion yn fwy ardderchog a mawryddig yn eu gwaith; ac ir oeddynt eu hunain, rai o naddunt, yn dywysogion, ac yn wyr dyledogion; yn enwedig, *Owain Cyfeiliog*, tywysog *Powys*; a *Hywel ap Owain Gwynedd*, Bardd a rhyfelwr godidog: ac felly ir oeddynt yn fwy penigamp na'r Beirdd diweddar, o ran eu testunau. Canys ir oedd y Beirdd diweddar, fel i mae *Sion Dafydd Rhys* yn achwyn arnynt, yn gwenieithio i'r gwyr mawr, ac yn dywedyd celwydd ar eu cân; ac yn haeru iddynt dorri cestyll, lladd a llosgi, pryd ir oeddynt, eb ef, yn cysgu yn eu gwelyau, heb ddim mo'r fath feddwl nac amcan ganddynt. Eithr yn amser y tywysogion, o'r gwrthwyneb, ir oedd y Beirdd yn dystion o ddewredd a mawrfrydigrwydd eu tywysogion; ac ir oeddynt eu hunain yn filwyr glewion. Ir oedd *Meilir Brydydd* yn gennad dros *Ruffydd ap Cynan* at frenin *Lloegr*; ac ir oedd *Gwalchmai*, ei fab, yn flaenor câd ynghyffinydd *Lloegr* a *Chymru*; fel i maent ill dau yn tystiolaethu yn eu cerddi. Heblaw hyn, ir oedd y tywysogion yma yn fuddugawl yn eu rhyfeloedd â'r *Saeson*, ac ir oedd hynny yn peri i'r Beirdd ymorchestu, i dragywyddoli eu gweithredoedd ardderchog; ac i foli eu gwroldeb mewn achos mor glodfawr ag amddiffyn eu gwlad a'u rhyddid, yn erbyn estron genedl, a'u difuddiasei o dreftadaeth eu hynafiaid. Ir oedd y rhain yn ddiau yn destunau gwiw i Feirdd ganu arnynt, ac yn fodd cymmwys i beri i'w deiliaid eu perchi a'u hanrhydeddu; canys ir oedd y cerddi godidog yma yn cael eu datgan gyda'r delyn, mewn cyweiriau cyfaddas, mewn gwleddau yn llys y tywysog, ac yn neuaddau y pendefigion a'r uchelwyr. I mae *Giraldus* yn dywedyd, fod y *Cymry* mor ddrud a milwraidd yn ei amser ef, ag na rusynt ymladd yn noeth ac yn ddiarfog, â'r rhai arfog, llurugog; a'r pedydd yn erbyn y marchogion. Yn ddiau nid oedd un modd a ellid ei ddychymmygu well, i gynnal yr yspryd dihafarch yma yn ein hynafiaid, na chael eu moli gan y Beirdd. Ac e wyddai'r *Saeson* hynny yn dda ddigon; canys ar ol darostwng *Cymru* tan eu llywodraeth, e ddarfu iddynt ddihenyddu'r Beirdd trwy'r holl wlad. I mae llyfrau ystatud Lloegr, yn llawn o gyfreithiau creulon i'w herbyn, ac yn gwarafun yn gaeth iddynt ymarfer o'u hen ddefodau, o glera a chymhortha. Yn amser *Owain Glyndwr*, i cawsant ychydig seibiant a chynhwysiad i ganu; ond gwedi hynny, hyd ddyfodiad *Harri'r Seithfed*, ir oeddynt tan gwmmwl. Gwedi iddo ef ddyfod i lywodraethu, ac yn amser ei fab, *Harri'r Wythfed*, a'r frenhines *Elisabeth*, y rhai a hanoeddynt o waed Cymreig, i cawsant gynhwysiadau i gynnal Eisteddfodau: ond ni pharhaodd hynny ond ennyd fechan, o herwydd bonedd Cymru a ymroisant i fod yn Saeson, fel i maent yn parhau gan mwyaf hyd y dydd heddyw.

Ond i mae rhai yn yr oes yma yn chwenychu eu cadw a'u coledd, er mwyn eu hiaith ddigymmysg, ac er mwyn gwell gwybodaeth o foesau ac ansawdd ein hynafiaid; ac er mwyn eu teilyngdod eu hunain; o herwydd i mae yn rhai o'u Hawdlau a'u Cywyddau, ymadroddion mor gywraint a naturiol ag sydd ym Mhrydyddion Groeg a Rhufain; mal i gwyr y sawl a'u deallant yn dda.—Ymysg eraill i mae Cymdeithas y Cymmrodorion, yn Llundain, yn rhoddi mawrbarch iddynt; ac yn chwenychu cadw cynnifer o'n hen ysgrifenadau ag sydd heb fyned ar goll. A da i gwneynt foneddigion Cymru, ped ymoralwent am argraffu y pethau mwyaf hynod a gwiwgof mewn prydyddiaeth, hanesion, ac eraill hen goffadwriaethau; o herwydd i maent beunydd yn cael eu difrodi, gan y sawl ni wyddant ddim gwell. Hyn, er lles ein gwlad a'n iaith, yw gwir a diffuant ddamuniad

Eich gostyngedig wasanaethwr, a'ch ewyllysiwr da,

EVAN EVANS.

I.

HIRLAS OWAIN.

Owain Cyfeiliog e hun ai cant.

GWAWR pan ddwyre gawr a ddoded,
Galon yn anfon aufudd dynged,
Geleurudd ein gwyr gwedi lludded trwm,
Tremit gofwy mur *Maelawr Drefred.*

Deon a yrrais dygyhyssed,
Diarswyd a'r frwydr arfau goched,
A rygoddwy glew gogeled rhagddaw,
Gnawd yw oi ddygnaw ddefnydd codded!

Dywallaw di fenestr gan foddhäed,
Y corn yn llaw *Rhys* yn llys llyw ced,
Llys *Owain* ar braidd yt ryborthed erioed,
Porth mil a glywi pyrth egored.

Menestr am gorthaw, nam adawed
Estyn y corn er cyd yfed,
Hiraethlawn am llyw lliw ton nawfed,
Hirlas i arwydd aur i dudded:

A dyddwg o fragawd wirawd orgred,
Ar llaw Wgan draws dros i weithred,

Canawon Goronwy, gwrdd gynnired gwyth,
Canawon hydwyth, hydr eu gweithred:
Gwyr a obryn tal ymhob caled,
Gwyr yngawr gwerthfawr gwrdd ymwared,
Bugelydd Hafren balch eu clywed,
Bugunat cyrn medd mawr a wna neued.

Dywallaw di'r corn argynfelyn,
Anrhydeddus, feddw, o fedd gorewyn,
Ac o'r mynni hoedl hyd un blwyddyn,
Na ddidawl i barch, can nid perthyn,
A dyddwc i Ruffydd waewruddelyn,
Gwin a gwydr goleu yn ei gylchyn,
Dragon Arwystli, arwystl terfyn,
Dragon Owain hael o hil Cynfyn,
Dragon iw dechreu, ac niw dychryn cat,
Cyflafan argrat cymwy erlyn.
Cetwyr idd aethant er clod obryn:
Cyfeddon, arfawc, arfau Edwyn,
Talassant i medd mal gwyr Belyn gynt,
Teg i hydrefynt tra bo undyn.

Dywallaw di'r corn, canys amcan cennyf,
Ydd ymgyrryw glyw gloyw ymddiddan,
Ar llaw ddehau ein llyw gyflafan,
Lluch y dan ysgwyd ysgawn lydan,
Ar llaw Ednyfet llawr diogan lew,
Ergyrwayw trylew, trei i darian.
Terfysc ddyffysc ddeu ddiofn anian,
Torrynt torredwynt uch teg adfan,
Teleirw ynghyngrein ynghyfran brwydr,
Tal ysgwyd eurgrwydr torrynt yn fuan:
Tryliw eu pelydr gwedi penwan,
Trylwyn yn amwyn amwiw Garthan.

Cigleu ym Maelawr gawr fawr fuan,
A garw ddisgyrr gwyr, a gwyth erwan,
Ac ymgynnull am drull am dramwyan,
Fal i bu ym Mangor am ongyr dân:
Pan wnaeth dau deyrn uch cyrn cyfrdan,
Pan fu gyfeddach Forach Forfran.

Dywallaw di'r corn, canys myfyr gennyf,
Men ydd amygant medd a'n tymmyr,
Selif diarswyt orsaf *Gwygyr*,
Gogelet ai cawdd calon eryr!
Ac unmab *Madawc*, enwawg *Dudur* hael,
Hawl bleiddiad, lleiddiad, lluch ar ysgyr,
Deu arwreidd, deu lew, yn eu cyngyr,
Deu arial dywal dau fab *Ynyr*,
Dau rydd yn nydd cad eu cyfergyr,
Cyfargor diachor camp diachyr,
Arfod llewod gwrdd, gwrddwan cadwyr,
Aer gunieid, lunieid, coch eu hongyr,
Treis erwyr yn ffwyr ffaw ehegyr,
Trei eu dwy aesawr dan un ystyr,
Gorfu gwynt gwaeddfan uch glan glasfyr,
Gorddwy clau tonnau *Talgarth* ystyr.

Dywallaw di fenestr na fyn angau,
Corn can anrhydedd ynghyfeddau,
Hirlas buelin, breint uchel hen ariant,
Ai gortho nid gorthenau:
A dyddwg i *Dudur*, eryr aerau,
Gwirawd gyssefin o'r gwin gwinau,
Oni ddaw i mewn o'r medd gorau oll,
Gwirawd o ban, dy ben faddau,
Ar llaw *Foreiddig*, llochiad cerddau,
Cerddyn hyn i glod cyn oer adnau,
Dieithr frodyr fryd ucheldau,
Diarchar arial a dan dalau,

16

Cedwyr am gorug gwasanaethau,
Nid ym hyn dihyll nam hen deheu
Cynnifieid, gyrthieid, fleinieid, fleiddiau,
Cynfaran creulawn creulyd ferau,
Glew glyw *Mochnannwys* o *Bowys* beu:
O glew gwnedd arnaddunt deu,
Achubieit pob rheid, rhudd eu harfeu:
Echedwynt rhag terfysc eu terfynau,
Moliant yw eu rhann y rhei gwynnau;
Marwnad fu neud mi newid y ddau!
O chan Grist mor drist wyf o'r anaeleu!
O goll *Moreiddig* mawr ei eissieu.

Dywallaw di'r corn can nim puehant,
Hirlas yn llawen yn llaw *Forgant*,
Gwr a ddyly gwawd gwahan foliant,
Gwenwyn y addwyn, gwan edrywant,
Areglydd defnydd dioddefiant llafn,
Llyfn i deutu llym ei hamgant.

Dywallaw di fenestr o lestr ariant,
Celennyg edmyg, can urdduniant,
Ar llawr *Gwestun* fawr gwelais irdant,
Ardwy *Goronwy* oedd gweith i gant,
Cedwyr cyfarfaeth ydd ymwnaethant,
Cad ymerbynieid, eneid dichwant,
Cyfarfu ysgwn ac ysgarant aer,
Llas aer, llosget maer ger mor lliant:
Mwynfawr o garcharawr a gyrchassant,
Meurig fab Gruffydd grym ddarogant,
Neud oedd gochwys pawb pan atgorsant,
Neud oedd lawn o heul hirfryn a phant.

Dywallaw di'r corn ir cynnifieid,
Canawon *Owain*, cyngrein, cydneid,

Wynt a ddyrllyddant yn lle honneid,
Glud men ydd ant gloyw heyrn ar neid:
Madawc a *Meilir* gwyr gorddyfneid treis,
Tros gyferwyr gyferbynieid:
Tariannogion torf, terfysc ddysgeid,
Trinheion faon, traws ardwyeid.
Ciglau am dal medd myned dreig *Cattraeth*,
Cywir eu harfaeth, arfau lliweid,
Gosgordd Fynyddawc am eu cysgeid,
Cawssant y hadrawdd cas flawdd flaenieid;
Ni wnaeth a wnaeth fynghedwyr ynghalet *Faelor*,
Dillwng carcharor dullest foleid.

Dywallaw di fenestr fedd hidlaid, melus,
Ergyrwayw gwrys gochwys yn rheid,
O gyrn buelin balch oreuraid,
Yr gobryn gobrwyau henaid;
O'r gynnifer anhun a borth cynnieid
Nis gwyr namyn Duw ac ai dywaid.

Gwr ni dal ni dwng, ni bydd wrth wir,
Daniel dreig cannerth, mor ferth hewir,
Menestr mawr a gweith yd ioleithir
Gwyr ni oleith lleith, oni llochir,
Menestr medd ancwyn a'n cydroddir,
Gwrdd-dan gloyw, goleu, gwrddloyw babir
Menestr gwelud dy gwyth yn Llidwm dir
Y gwyr a barchaf wynt a berchir.
Menestr gwelud dy galchdoed Cyngrein,
Ynghylchyn *Owain* gylchwy enwir,
Pan breiddwyd Cawres, taerwres trwy dir,
Preidd ostwng orflwng a orfolir,
Menestr nam didawl, nim didolir,
Boed ym mharadwys in cynhwysir,
Can pen teyrnedd, poed hir eu trwydded,
Yn i mae gweled gwaranred gwir. AMEN.

II.

A W D L

I Fyfanwy Fechan, o Gastell Dinas Bran. Howel ap Einion Lygliw ai cant.

NEUD wyf ddihunwyf, hoen Creirwy hoywdeg,
Am hudodd mal Garwy,
O fan or byd rwymgwyd rwy,
O fynor gaer Fyfanwy.

Trymmaf yw cariad tramwy, hoen eurnef,
Hyn arnaf dy faccwy,
Dy far feinwar Fyfanwy,
Ar ath gar ni fu far fwy.

Gofyn ni allawdd namyn gofwy cur,
Dyn mewn cariad fwy fwy,
Fynawg eirian Fyfanwy,
Fuchudd ael fun hael fyw'n hwy.

Eurais wawd ddidlawd, ddadl rwy adneuboen,
Adnabod Myfanwy,
Poen ath gar afar ofwy,
Poen brwyn ei ryddwyn i ddwy.

Gorwydd, cyrch ebrwydd, ceirch ebran addas,
Dwg dristwas, dig Drystan,
Llwrw buost, farch llary buan,
Lle arlloes fre eurllys Fran.

Gwn beunydd herwydd herw amcan, ddilyd
    Ddelw berw Caswennan:
Golwg, deddf amlwg diddan,
Gwelw, freich fras brenhinblas Bran.

Gyrrais a llidiais farch bronn llydan, hoyw,
    Er hoen blodau sirian:
Gyrrawd ofal yr Alban,
Garrhir braisc ucheldir Bran.

Lluniais wawd, ddefawd ddifan, traul ofer,
    Nid trwy lafur bychan:
Lliw eiry cynnar pen Aran,
Lloer bryd, lwys fryd o lys Fran.

Mireinwawr Drefawr dra fo brad im dwyn,
Gwarando fy nghwyn, frwyn freuddwydiad,
Mau glwyf a mowrnwyf murniad, huno heb
Gwrtheb teg atteb tuac attad
Mi dy fardd digardd, dygn gystuddiad Rhun,
Gyfun laes wannllun ith lys winllad.
Mynnu ddwyf draethu heb druthiad na gwyd
Wrthyd haul gymmryd, gamre wasdad.
Mynnud hoyw fun loyw oleuad gwledydd,
Glodrydd, gain gynnydd, nid gan gennad,
Maint anhun haelfun hwylfad, em cyfoeth
Ddoeth, fain oleugoeth, fy nau lygad,
Medron boen goroen nid digarad was,
Heb ras, mau drachas om edrychiad.
Magwyr murwydr hydr, hydreiddiad lwysle,
Mygrwedd haul fore eurne arnad.
Megis llwyr gludais llawer gwlad, yn ddwys,
Dy glod lwys, cynnwys pob datceiniad,
Mal hy oedd ymmy, am wyl gariad graen,
Myfanwy hoen blaen eiry gaen gawad.

Meddwl serchawl, hawl, lliw ton hwyliad welw,
Arddelw dygynnelw heb dy gynheiliad.
Modd trist im gwnaeth Crist croesdog neirthiad llwyr,
Wanwyr oi synwyr drwy lud senniad.
Murn boen a mi om anynad hawl,
Serchawl eneidiawl un fynediad.
Mul i bwriais, trais tros ddirnad Duw gwyn,
Tremyn ar ddillyn porphor ddillad.
Megis ti ferch rhi, rhoddiad gymmyrredd,
Mwyfwy anrhydedd, wledd wledychiad.
Marw na byw, nwyf glyw gloyw luniad cyngaws,
Hoednaws nid anaws im am danad.
Meddwl ofeiliaint braint braidd im gad llesmair,
I gael yr eilgair wrth offeiriad.
Masw imi brofi, brif draethiad a wnawn,
Lle nim rhoddi iawn, ne gwawn, na gwad.
Mesur cawdd anawdd i ynad eglur,
Adrawdd fy nolur ddwysgur ddysgiad.
Modd nad gwiw, lliw lleuad rhianedd,
Nam gwedd hud garedd, nam hoed girad.
Meinir nith borthir, gwn borthiad poenau,
Yn nenn hoen blodau blawd yspyddad.
Medraist, aur delaist adeilad gwawd,
Im nychdawd ddifrawd ddyfrys golliad.
Meddylia oth ra ath rad, ith brydydd
Talu y carydd Duw dofydd dad.

Prydydd wyf, tros glwyf, trais glud, poen gwaneg,
    Iaith laesdeg ith lwysdud:
Fynawg riain fain funud:
Fun arlludd hun eirllwydd hud.

Im neud glud, dy hud hydr, riain wanlleddf,
    O'r wenllys ger Dinbrain:
Aml yw gwawd gynnefawd gain,
Om araith ith dwf mirain.

III.

A W D L

I Lewelyn fab Iorwerth. *Dafydd Benfras ai cant.*

GWR a wnaeth llewych o'r gorllewin,
Haul a lloer addoer, addef iessin,
Am gwnel, radd uchel, rwyf cyfychwin,
Cyflawn awen, awydd *Fyrddin*,
I ganu moliant mal *Aneurin* gynt,
Dydd i cant *Ododin*.
I foli gwyndawd *Gwyndyd* werin,
Gwynedd bendefig, ffynnedig ffin,
Gwanas deyrnas, deg cywrennin,
Gwreidd, teyrneidd, taer ymrwydrin,
Gwrawl ei fflamdo am fro Freiddin.
Er pan orau Duw dyn gyssefin,
Ni wnaeth ei gystal traws arial trin.
Gorug *Llewelyn*, orllin teyrnedd,
Ar y brenhinedd braw a gorddin
Pan fu yn ymbrofi a brenin *Lloegyr*,
Yn llygru swydd *Erbin*.
Oedd breisc, weisc ei fyddin,
Oedd brwysc rwysc rhag y godorin,
Oedd balch gwalch, golchiad ei laïn,
Oedd beilch gweilch, gweled ei werin,
Oedd clywed cleddyfau finfin,
Oedd clybod clwyf ymhob elin,
Oedd briw rhiw yn nhrabludd odrin,
Oedd braw saw *Saeson* clawdd y *Cnwccin*,

Oedd bwlch llafn yn llaw gynnefin,
Oedd gwaedlyd pennau, gwedi gwaedlin rhwy,
    Yn rhedeg am ddeulin.
Llewelyn, ein llyw cyffredin,
Llywiawdr berth hyd *Borth Ysgewin*,
Ni ryfu gystal *Gwstennin* ag ef,
    I gyfair pob gorllin.
Mi im byw be byddwn ddewin,
Ym marddair, ym mawrddawn gyssefin,
Adrawdd ei ddaed aerdrin ni allwn,
    Ni allai *Daliesin*.
Cyn adaw y byd gyd gyfrin,
Gan hoedyl hir ar dir daierin,
Cyn dyfnfedd escyrnwedd yscrin,
Cyn daear dyfnlas, arlessin,
Gwr a wnaeth o'r dwfr y gwin,
Gan fodd Duw a diwedd gwirin,
Nog a wnaethpwyd trais anwyd trin,
Ymbrefent ymhrysur orllin :
Ni warthäer hael am werthefin nos,
    A nawdd saint boed cyfrin.

IV.

C A N U

I Lewelyn fab Iorwerth. Einiawn fab Gwgawn ai cant.

CYFARCHAF o'm naf, am nefawl Arglwydd,
Crist Celi culwydd, cwl i ddidawl,
Celfydd leferydd o le gweddawl,
Celfyddydau mau ni fo marwawl:
I brofi pob peth o bregeth *Bawl*,
I foli fy rhi, rhwyf angerddawl,
Rhyfel ddiochel, ddiochwyth hawl,
Llewelyn heilyn, hwylfeirdd waddawl,
Llawenydd i ddydd, i ddeddf ai mawl,
Llewychedig llafn yn llaw reddfawl,
Yn lladd, dy wrthladd iwrth lys *Rheidiawl*,
Gweleis a gerais ni gar mantawl,
Gwelygordd *Lleission* llyssoedd gweddawl,
Lluoedd arwoloedd ar weilw didawl,
Llawrwyr am eryr yn ymeiriawl,
Llewelyn lleyn, llyw ardderchawl,
Lluriglas, gwanas, gwanau a hawl,
Gwenwyn yn amwyn am dir breiniawl *Powys*,
Ae diffiwys, ae glwys a glyw ei hawl,
Ef dynniad ynghad, *Eingl* frnd freuawl,
Ef dandde rhuddle *Rhuddlan* is gwawl,
Gweleis *Lewelyn*, eurddyn urddawl,
Yn urddas dreigwas dragywyddawl,
Eil gweleis i dreis dros ganol *Dyfrdwy*,
Yn y trei tramwy llanw rhwy, rhwydd hawl
Gweleis aer am gaer oedd engiriawl,

Talu pwyth dydd gwyth, canyseawl,
Ni ryweleis neb na bo canmawl,
O'r ddau y gorau a fo gwrawl.

Mi ath arwyre, ath arwyrein myfyr,
Eryr yn rhywyr, prifwyr *Prydein.*
Prydfawr *Lewelyn* pryd dyn dadiein,
Prydus, diescus, escar ddilein.
Escynnu ar llu ar lle *Ewein,*
Ysgymmod gorfod, gorfalch am brein,
Ysgymmyn gwerlyn, gwerlid gofiein,
Ysgymydd clodrydd, *Kulwydd* a *Llwyfein*,
Lluddedig edmyg, meirch mawrthig mein;
A lluoedd yngwiscoedd yn ymoscrein,
Ar llinyn ar dynn ar du celein,
A llinon rhag Bron rhag bro *Eurgein,*
Tyrfa *Clawdd Offa* clod yn hoffiein,
A thorfoedd *Gwynedd* a gwyr *Llundein,*
Cyfran tonn a glan, glafdir gwylein,
Golud mowr ystrud, ysgryd *Norddmein,*
Llewelyn terwyn, torf anghyngein,
Biau'r gwyr gorau, bachau bycheiu,
Priodawr mwynglawr *Mon* glod yscein,
Areul golud pentud, *Pentir Gwychein.*
Gwawr *Dehau* gorau, gwyr yn dyrein,
Gwenwyn a gwanar y ddau gar gein,
Ae lyw cyferyw, cyfwyrein a thrin,
A thrychieid gwerin *Caer Fyrddin* fein,
Ni sefis na thwr, na bwr, bu crein,
Nag argoed, na choed, na chadlys drein,
A rhag pyrth bu syrth *Saeson* ynghreiu.
Oedd trist maer, oedd claer cleddyf heb wein,
A chan llu pannu, pen ar ddigrein,
A chan llaw lludwaw *Llan Huadein,*
Cil Geran achlan, a chlod goelfein,
A chlwyr ar dyhedd, mawredd mirein,

Yn *Aber Teifi* tew oedd frein uch benn,
Yn yd oedd perchen parchus gyfrein.
Oedd tew peleidr creu, creuynt gigfrein,
Calanedd gorwedd gorddyfnassein,
Llewelyn boed hyn boed hwy ddichwein,
No *Llywarch* hybarch, hybar gigwein.
Nid celadwy dreig, dragon gyngein,
Nid calan cyman gwr y gymein,
Hydwf yngnif ai lif ọ lein,
Hyd ydd el yn rhyfel hyd yn *Rhufein*,
Ai raglod ai rod o riw Feddgein,
Hyd i dwyre haul hyd y dwyrein.

Ys imi rwydd Arglwydd, argleidrad,
Argledr tir, a gwir a gwenwlad,
Ys imi or cyngor cyngwasdad,
Cywesti peri peleidrad,
Ys imi ri ryfel ddiffreiddiad,
Diffryd gwyr, eryr ardwyad,
Ys imi rwydd Arglwydd, erglywiad
A glywir o'r tir gar *Tanad*,
Ys imi glew, a llew a lleiddiad
Yn rhyfel a rhon orddyfniad,
Ys imi wr a wared i rad,
I reidus, galarus, geilwad.
Ys imi ner yn arwyn ddillad,
Yn arwein ysgin ysgarlad,
Ys imi *Nudd*, hael fudd, Hueil feiddiad,
Ar Lloegr ryllygrwys heb wad.
Ys imi *Rydderch*, roddiad aur melyn,
Molitor ymhob gwlad.
A mawrdud olud olygad,
A *Mordaf* am alaf eiliad,
Ys imi *Run* gatcun gytcam rad,
Cydgaffael, a hael, a hwyliad

Ef imi y meddwl difrad,
Mi iddaw yn llaw yn llygad,
Ni henyw o afryw afrad,
Mi hanwyf o henwyr ei dad,
Llachar far, aerfar, erfynniad,
Llachar fron o frydau *Gwriad.*
Lluchieint gweilch am walch gynnifiad,
Fal lluchynt estrawn wynt *Ystrad.*
Hunydd nen perchen parchus fad,
Parch arfawr, *Arfon* angoriad.
Llewelyn dreis, erlyn drwssiad,
Dros dehau angau oth angad,
Angor mor y mawr gymynad,
Angawr llawr llurig Duw am danad.

Rhy chyngein *Prydein* yn ddibryder,
I Briodawr llawr yn llawn nifer.
Llewelyn gelyn yn i galwer
I gelwir am dir am dud tymer.
Llawenydd lluoedd llew ymhryder,
Llywiawdr ymmerawdr mor a lleufer,
I ddylif cynnif cynhebyccer
I ddylann am lann, am leissiaid ffer.
Terfysc tonn ddilysc ddyleinw aber:
Dylad anwasdad ni osteccer.
Terwynt twrf rhywynt yn rhyw amser,
A rhialluoedd lluoedd llawer.
Torfoedd ynghyoedd ynghyflawnder
Tariannau golau mal i gweler:
Ry folant anant, anaw cymer,
Ry molir i wir i orober,
I wryd yn rhyd yn rheid nifer,
I orofn gwraf yn ydd eler,
I orfod gorfod glod a glywer,
I wyr am eryr ni amharer,
I warae orau pan waräer,

I wayw a orau yn ddau hanner,
Dinidir yn nydd brwydr yn yd brofer,
Dinoding perging, pargoch hydrfer,
Dinas, dreig urddas, eurddawn haelder
Dinag o fynag pan ofynner,
Dyn yw *Llewelyn* llywiawdr tyner,
Doeth coeth cywrennin, gwin a gwener,
A'r gwr ai rhoddes ni ran o'r pader,
Ai rhoddo ef gwenfro gwynfryn uch ser.

V.

ARWYRAIN

Owain Gwynedd. Gwalchmai ai cant.

ARDDWYREAF hael o hil *Rodri*,
Ardwyad gorwlad, gwerlin teithi,
Teithiawg *Prydain*, twyth arfdwyth *Owain*,
Teyrnain ni grain, ni grawn rëi.
Teir lleng i daethant, liant lestri,
Teir praff prif lynges wy bres brofi,
Un o'r *Iwerddon*, arall arfogion
Or *Llychlynigion*, llwrw hirion lli.
Ar drydedd dros for o *Norddmandi*,
Ar drafferth anferth, anfad iddi.
A dreig *Mon* mor ddrud i eissillyd yn aer,
A bu terfysc taer i haer holi,
A rhagddaw rhewys dwys dyfysci,
A rhewin a thrin a thranc Cymri,
A'r gad gad greudde, a'r gryd gryd graendde,
Ac am dal *Moelfre* mil fannieri,
A'r ladd ladd lachar, ar bar beri,
A ffwyr ffwyr ffyrfgawdd ar fawdd foddi,
A *Menai* heb drai o drallanw gwaedryar,
A lliw gwyar gwyr yn heli:
A llurygawr glas, a gloes trychni,
A thrychion yn nhud rhag rheiddrudd ri,
A dygyfor *Lloegr*, a dygyfranc a hi,
Ag ei dygyfwrw yn astrusi,
A dygyfod clod cleddyf difri,
Yn saith ugain iaith wy faith foli.

A W D L

I Nest ferch Hywel. Einiawn fab Gwalchmai ai cant.

AMSER Mai maith ddydd, neud rhydd rhoddi,
Neud coed nad ceithiw, ceinlliw celli,
Neud llafar adar, neu gwar gweilgi,
Neud gwaeddgreg gwaneg, gwynt yn edwi,
Neud arfeu douiau, goddau gwedi,
Neud argel dawel nid meu dewi,
Endeweis i wenyg o Wynnofi dir,
I am derfyn mawr meibion *Beli*,
Oedd hydreidd wychr llyr yn llenwi,
Oedd hydr am ddylan gwynfan genddi,
Hyll nid oedd ei deddf hi hwyreddf holi,
Hallt oedd i dagrau, digrawn heli,
Ar helw bun araf uch bannieri ton,
Tynhegl a gerddais i gorddwfr *Teifi*,
Ceintum gerdd i *Nest* cyn noi threngi,
Cânt cant i moliant mal *Elifri*,
Canaf gan feddwl awrddwl erddi,
Caniad i marwnad, mawr drueni!
Canwyll *Cadfan* lan o lenn bali.
Canneid i synnieid gar *Dysynni*,
Gwan, wargan, wyrygall, ddeall ddogni,
Gwreig nid oedd un frad gariad genthi,
Gweryd rhudd ai cudd gwedi tewi,
Gwael neuedd maenwedd mynwent iddi,
Golo *Nest* goleu ddireidi.
Golwg gwalch dwythfalch o brif deithi,

Gwenned gwawn ai dawn oi daioni,
Gwynedd anrhydedd, oedd rhaid wrthi,
Nid oedd ffawd rhy gnawd rhin y genthi,
Gnawd oedd dâl eur mal er i moli,
Ni ryfu dognach er i dogni poen,
    Penyd a fo mwy no'r meu hebddi,
Neum gorau angau anghyfnerthi,
Nid ymglyw dyn byw o'r byd fal mi,
Ni chyfeirch angen iawlwen ioli,
Er neb rhy barther i rhyborthi,
Nest yn ei haddawd, wenwawd weini,
Ydd wyf pryderus fal pryderi.
Pryderwawd ceudawd, cyfnerthi ni wnn,
    Nid parabl yw hwn ni fô peri.
Llen argel issel y sy'm poeni,
Lludd *Gwen* lliw arien ar *Eryri.*
Archaf im Arglwydd culwydd celi,
Nid ef a archaf arch egregi,
Arch, ydd wyf un arch yn i erchi,
Am archfein riein, reid y meini,
Trwy ddiwyd eiriawl deddfawl *Dewi.*
A deg cymmeint seint senedd *Frefi,*
Am fun a undydd i hammodi,
A'r gystlwn pryffwn y prophwydi,
Ar gyfoeth Duw doeth i detholi,
Ar anghyweir *Meir* a'r merthyri,
Ag yn i goddau gweddi a ddodaf,
    Am dodeis nwyf im addoedi.
Ni bu ddyn mor gu gennyf a hi
Ni bo poen oddef, *Pedr* wy noddi,
Ni bydd da gan Dduw i diddoli,
Ni bo diddawl *Nest,* nef boed eiddi.

VII.

A W D L

I Lewelyn fab Iorwerth. Llywarch Brydydd y Moch ai cant.

CRIST Greawdr, llywiawdr llu daear a nef
Am noddwy rhag afar,
Crist celi, bwyf celfydd a gwar,
Cyn diwedd gyfyngwedd gyfar.
Crist fab Duw am rhydd arllafar,
I foli fy rhwyf rhwysg o ddyar,
Crist fab Mair am pair o'r pedwar defnydd,
Dofn awen ddiarchar.
Llewelyn llyw *Prydain* ai phâr,
Llew a glew a glyw gyfarwar,
Fab Iorwerth ein cannerth an car,
Fab Owain ffrawddiein, ffrwyth cynnar,
Ef dyfu dreig llu yn llasar dillat,
Yn ddillyn cyfarpar,
Yn erfid, yn arfod abar,
Yn arfau bu cenau cynnar,
Yn ddengmlwydd hylwydd hylafar,
Yn ddidranc ei gyfranc ai gar,
Yn *Aber Conwy*, cyn daffar fy llyw,
Llewelyn athrugar,
A *Dafydd*, defawd *Ul Caissar*,
Difai ddraig, ddragon adwyar,
Difwlch udd difalch i esgar,
Difwng blwng blaen ufel trwy far,
Dybryd in feirdd byd bod daear arnaw,
Ac arnam i alar.

Ef yn llyw cyn llid gyfysgar,
Ysglyfion ysglyfiynt llwrw bar,
Oedd rynn rudd ebyr or gwyr gwar,
Oedd ran feirw fwyaf o'r drydar,
Oedd amliw tonnau, twnn ambar eu neid,
Neud oeddynt dilafar.
Ton heli ehelaeth i bar,
Ton arall guall, goch gwyar.
Porth Aethwy pan aetham ni ar feirch mordwy,
Uch mowrdwrf tonniar,
Oedd ongyr, oedd engir ei bar,
Oedd angudd godrudd gwaedryar,
Oedd enghyrth ein hynt, oedd angar,
Oedd ing, oedd angau anghymar,
Oedd ammau ir byd bod abar o honam,
O henaint lleithiar.
Mawr gadau, anghau anghlaear,
Meirw sengi, mal seri sathar,
Cyn plygu *Rodri*, rwydd esgar, ym *Mon*
Mynwennoedd bu braenar,
Pan orfu pen llu llachar,
Llewelyn llyw *Alun* athafar,
Myrdd bu lladd, llith brein gorddyar,
O'r milwyr, a mil yngharchar.
Llewelyn cyd laddwy trwy far,
Cyd llosgwy, nid llesg ufeliar,
Llary deyrn, uch cyrn cyfarwar
Llwrw cydfod ir clod is claiar,
Ry llofies rwyf treis tros fanniar i feirdd,
Oedd fawrllwyth ir ddaear,
Gwisci aur ag ariant nis car.
Gwascwynfeirch gosseirch, gosathar,
Ysginfawr gorfawr, gorwymp par,
Yscarlad lliw ffleimiad, fflamiar,
Meirch Mawrthig, ffrwythig, ffraeth, anwar,
Ffrawddus, a phreiddiau ewiar.

Mwth i rhydd, arwydd yngwascar,
Mal *Arthur* cein fodur cibddar,
Cann a chann, a chein wyllt a gwar,
Cant a chant a chynt nog adar

Adar weinidawg, caeawg Cynran drud,
Dreig *Prydein* pedryddan,
Addod Lloegr, lluossawg am bann,
Addaf hir in herwydd calan,
Adwedd teyrnedd tir nis rhan,
A dan ser ys sef i amcan,
Adnes i franhes i frein bann,
Dychre dychrein gwyr yngrheulan,
Gwrdd i gwnaeth uch Deudraeth *Dryfan*,
Gwr hydwf, gwrhydri *Ogyrfan*
Dygwydd gwyr heb lafar heb lan,
Dygoch llawr dwygad fawr faran,
Un am fro *Alun*, elfydd can,
A *Ffrainc* yn ffrawddus mal *Camlan*;
Ar eil yn *Arfon* ar forfan,
Yn undydd an un Duw in a ran,
A dwy dreig ffeleig, ffaw gymman
Mal deulew ein dylochassan,
Ag un traws gatcun, treis faran,
Fal gwr yn gorfod ymhobman,
Llewelyn llafn-eur anghyfan,
Lloegr ddiwreidd, llu rhuddfleidd *Rhuddlan*,
Llu rhagddaw a llaw ar llumman,
Llwybr yn wybr yn ebrwydd allan,
Llwrw ddawn *Cadwallawn fab Cadfan*.
I mae am *Brydain* yn gyfan,
Llary ni ddel ei law ettaw attan,
Llyried tra myned tramor dylan,
Rhag llaith anolaith anolo llan,
A llafnawr lledrudd uch grudd a gran,
Ninnau Feirdd *Prydein*, prydus eirian berth,

Gwyr a byrth fy rhwyf ymhob calan,
Er digabl barabl gan bawb oi fan,
Digrifwch elwch elyf egwan,
Oi ariant gormant gorym ni drudran,
O'i alaf ai aur ai ariant can.

Gan i ddwyn dychryn a ddechreuo bleid,
Uch blaenwel yn oed llo,
Gnaws achaws yn ych cyn adfo,
Gnawd i ladd ni lwydd i abo.
Caer Lleon llyw *Mon* mwyn *Pabo* ath dug,
Ef ath dwg ynghodo,
Llewelyn ef llosges dy fro,
Llas dy wyr dra llyn, dra llwyfo,
Llwyr dug y *Wyddgrug*, nid ffug ffo,
Lloegrwys i llugfryd i synnio,
Llewdir teyrn lluddiwyd yn agro,
Llas i glas, i glwystei neud glo,
Llys *Elsmer*, bu ffêr, bu ffwyrngno,
Llwyr llosged i thudwed ai tho,
Llwrw gwelwch neud heddwch heno
Gan fy rhwyf, nid rhyfedd cyd bo,
Hyd i del i dorf ar dyno a bryn,
Udd breiniawg bieufo,
Llew ai dug, ai dwg pan fynno,
Ir *Trallwng* trillu anwosgo,
Llys efnys, afneued tra fo.
Lles i fyrdd o feirdd ai cyrcho.
Addug y *Wyddgrug* ai dycco,
Gwyliwch gwylyddwr, pwy ai lluddio,
Llwrw *Fochnant* edrywant ar dro,
Llwytcwn llwyth llithiwyd am honno,
Lletcynt *Argoedwys*, gwys grendo,
Llys a dwy neud einym ni heno.
Edryched *Powys* pwy fo,
Brenin breisg werin, brwysg agdo,

Ai gwellygio pwyll rhydwyllo:
Ai gwell *Ffranc* no ffrawddus *Gymro*.
Llyw y sy ym, synniwch cyd tawo,
Lloegr gychwyn, a fynn a fynno,
Llwyr i dyd i fryd ar fro *Gadwallawn*
Fab Cadfan, fab Iago,
Llary yspar ys penyd iblo,
Llwrw espyd yspeid anolo,
Llew prydfawr llyw *Prydain* ai chlo,
Llewelyn lliaws ei fran fro,
Llary deyrn cedyrn, cad wosgo; ynghur
Ys fy nghar a orffo.

Gorfydd Udd dremrudd, dramor lliant,
Ym *Môn Mam Gymru* bedryddant,
Gorllwybr llu llenwis ewyngant,
Gwarthaf bryn a phenrhyn a phant,
Gorllanw gwaed am draed a ymdrychant,
Amdrychion pan ymdrechassant,
Cad y *Coed Anau*, Cadr anant borthi,
Burthiaist wyr yn nifant.
Ail gad trom i tremynasant,
Udd addien uch *Dygen Ddyfnant*,
Eil miloedd mal gwyr dybuant,
Eil yrth gyrth in gwrthfynnassant,
Eil agwrdd ymwrdd am hardd amgant bre
Bron yr Erw i galwant,
Cynwan llu fal llew yth welsant,
Cadr eryr ith wyr yn warant,
Can hynny cynhennu ni wnant,
Can wyllon *Celyddon* cerddant,
Dugost y *Wyddgrug*, a dygant i dreis
Adryssedd cyfnofant,
A *Rhuddlan* yn rhuddliw amgant,
Rhun can clawdd adrawdd edrywant
A *Dinbych* wrthrych gorthorrant ar fil,

Ar *Foelas* a *Gronant*
A *chaer yn Arfon*, a charant yngnif,
Yngnaws coll am peiriant,
A *Dinas Emreis* a ymrygant,
Amrygyr ni wneir na wnant
Neur orfydd dy orofyn nad ant
Ith erbyn ith erbarch feddiant
Neu'r orfuwyd yn orenw Morgant
Ar filwyr *Prydain* pedryddant
Dy gynnygn ni gennyw cwddant,
Ni gaiff hoen na hun ar amrant,
Mad ymddugost waed, mad yth want,
Arall yn arfoll ysgarant,
A chleddyf, a chlodfawr yth wnant,
Ag ysgwyd ar ysgwydd anchwant,
Mad tywyssaisd dy lu, Lloegr irdant,
Ar derfyn *Mechain* a *Mochnant*,
Mad yth ymddug dy fam, wyd doeth,
Wyd dinam, wyd didawl o bob chwant,
O borffor o bryffwn fliant,
O bali ag aur ag ariant,
O emys gochwys gochanant dy feirdd,
Yn fyrddoedd i caffant.
Minnau om rhadau rhymfuant,
Yn rhuddaur yn rhwydd ardduniant,
O bob rhif im Rhwyf im doniant,
O bob rhyw im rhodded yn gant
Cyd archwyf im llyw y lloergant yn rhodd,
Ef am rhydd yn geugant.
Lliwelydd lledawdd dy foliant,
Llewelyn, a *Llywarch* rwy cant.
Munerawd ym marw fy mwyniant fal yn byw
Lleissiawn ryw *Run* blant.
Nyd gormod fy ngair it gormant !
Teyrn wyd tebyg *Eliphant*,
Can orfod pob rhod yn rhamant,

Can folawd a thafawd a thant.
Cein deyrn, cyn bych yngreifiant,
Can difwyn o ysgwn esgarant,
Can Dduw ren yn ran westifiant
Can ddiwedd pob buchedd, bych sant.

VIII.

PUM AWDL

I Lewelyn fab Gruffydd. *Llygad Gwr ai cant.*

I.

CYFARCHAF i Dduw, ddawn orfoledd,
Cynnechreu doniau, dinam fawredd,
Cynnyddu canu, can nid rhyfedd dreth,
O draethawd gyfannedd,
I foli fy Rhi rhwyf *Arllechwedd,*
Rhuddfäawg freiniawg o frenhinedd,
Rhyfyg udd *Caissar,* treis far trossedd,
Rhuthrlym, grym *Gruffydd* etifedd,
Rhwysg frwysg, freisg, o freint a dewredd,
Rhudd barau o beri cochwedd,
Rhyw iddaw diriaw eraill diredd,
Rhwydd galon, golofn teyrnedd.
Nid wyf wr gwaglaw wrth y gogledd,
O Arglwydd gwladlwydd, glod edryssedd,
Nid newidiaf naf un awrwedd a neb,
Anebrwydd dangnefedd.
Llyw y sy ym ys aml anrhydedd,
Lloegr ddifa o ddifefl fonedd,
Llewelyn gelyn, galon dachwedd,
Llary wledig gwynfydig *Gwynedd,*
Llofrudd brwydr, *Brydein* gywryssedd,
Llawhir falch, gwreiddfalch gorsedd,
Llary, hylwydd, hael Arglwydd eurgledd,
Llew *Cemmais,* llym dreis drachywedd,

Lle bo cad fragad, friwgoch ryssedd,
Llwyr orborth hyborth heb gymwedd,
Gnaws mawrdraws am ardal dyhedd,
Gnawd iddaw dreiddiaw drwyddi berfedd,
Am i wir bydd dir or diwedd,
Amgylch *Dyganwy* mwyfwy i medd,
A chiliaw rhagddaw a chalanedd creu,
Ag odduch gwadneu gwaed ar ddarwedd.
Dreig *Arfon* arfod wythlonedd
Dragon diheufeirch heirddfeirch harddedd,
Ni chaiff *Sais* i drais y droedfedd oi fro,
Nid oes o *Gymro* i Gymrodedd.

II.

Cymmrodedd fy llyw lluoedd beri,
Nid oes rwyf eirioes, aer dyfysgu,
Cymro yw haelryw o hil *Beli* hir,
    Yn herwydd i brofi.
Eurfudd ni oludd, olud roddi,
Aerfleidd arwreidd o *Eryri*,
Eryr ar geinwyr gamwri dinam,
    Neud einym i foli.
Eurgorf torf tyroedd olosci,
Argae gryd, Greidiawl wrhydri,
Arwr bar, taerfar, yn torri cadau,
    Cadarnfrwydr ystofi.
Aer dalmithyr, hylithr haelioni,
Arf lluoedd eurwisgoedd wisgi
Arwymp Ner, hyder, hyd *Teifi* feddiant,
    Ni faidd neb i gospi.
Llewelyn Lloegrwys teistroli,
Llyw breiniawl, brenhinedd teithi,
Llary deyrn cedyrn, yn cadw gwesti cyrdd
    Cerddorion gyflochi.
Coelfein brein *Bryneich* gyfogi,

Celennig branes, berthles borthi,
Ciliaw ni orug er caledi gawr,
Gwr eofn ynghyni.
Parawd fydd meddiant medd Beirdd im Rhi,
Pob cymman darogan derfi,
O *Bwlffordd* osgordd ysgwyd gochi hydr,
Hyd eithaf *Cydweli*.
Can gaffael yn dda dra heb drengi,
Gan fab Duw didwyll gymmodi,
Ys bo i ddiwedd ddawn berchi ar nef,
Ar neilliaw Crist Geli.

III.

Llyw y sy'n synhwyrfawr riydd,
Lliwgoch i lafnawr, aesawr uswydd,
Lliw deifniawg, llidiawg, lledled fydd ei blas,
Llwyr waeth yw ei gas noi garennydd.
Llewelyn gelyn, galofydd,
Llwyrgyrch darogan cymman celfydd,
Ni thyccia rhybudd hael rebydd rhagddaw,
Llaw drallaw drin wychydd.
Y gwr ai rhoddes yn rhwyf dedwydd,
Ar *Wynedd* arwynawl drefydd,
Ai cadarnhao, ced hylwydd yn hir,
I amddeffyn tir rhag torf oswydd.
Nid aniw, nid anhoff gynnydd,
Neud enwawg farchawg, feirch gorewydd,
I fod yn hynod hynefydd *Gymro*,
A'r *Gymry* a'u helfydd.
Ef difeiaf Naf rhy wnaeth Dofydd,
Yn y byd o bedwar defnydd,
Ef goreu riau reg ofydd a wnn,
Eryr *Snawtwn* aer gyfludwydd.
Cad a wnaeth, cadarn ymgerydd,
Am gyfoeth, am Gefn Gelorwydd,

Ni bu gad, hwyliad hefelydd gyfred,
Er pan fu weithred waith *Arderydd.*
    Breisclew *Mon*, mwynfawr *Wyndodydd*,
Bryn *Dernwyn* clo byddin clodrydd,
Ni bu edifar y dydd i cyrchawdd,
    Cyrch ehofn essillydd.
Gwelais wawr ar wyr lluosydd,
Fal gwr yn gwrthladd cywilydd,
A welei *Lewelyn*, lawenydd dragon,
    Ynghymysc *Arfon* ac *Eiddionydd*,
Nid oedd hawdd llew aerflawdd llüydd,
I dreissiaw gar Drws Daufynydd,
Nis plygodd Mab Dyn bu doniawg ffydd,
    Nis plycco Mab Duw yn dragywydd.

IV.

Terfysc taerllew glew, glod ganhymdaith,
Twrf torredwynt mawr uch mor diffaith,
Taleithiawg deifniawg dyfniaith *Aberffraw*,
    Terwyn anrheithiaw, rhuthar onolaith.
Tylwyth, ffrwyth, ffraethlym eu mawrwaith,
Teilwng blwng, blaengar fal goddaith,
Taleithawg arfawg aerbeir *Dinefwr*,
Teilu hysgwr, ysgwfl anrhaith.
Telediw gad gywiw gyfiaith,
Toledo balch a bylchlafn eurwaith,
Taleithawg *Mathrafal*, maith yw dy derfyn,
Arglwydd *Lewelyn*, lyw pedeiriaith,
Sefis yn rhyfel, dymgel daith,
Rhag estrawn genedl, gwyn anghyfiaith,
Sefid Brenin nef, breiniawl gyfraith,
Gan eurwawr aerbeir y teir taleith.

V.

Cyfarchaf i Dduw o ddechrau moliant,
    Mal i gallwyf orau,

Clodfori o'r gwyr a geiriau
I'm pen, y penaf a giglau,
Cynnwrf tân, lluch faran llechau,
Cyfnewid newydd las ferau,
Cyfarf wyf a rhwyf, rhudd lafnau yngnif,
Cyfoethawg gynnif cynflaen cadau.
Llewelyn nid llesg ddefodau,
Llwybr ehang, ehofn fydd mau,
Llyw yw hyd *Gernyw* aed garnedd i feirch,
Lliaws ai cyfeirch, cyfaill nid gau,
Llew *Gwynedd* gwynfeith ardalau,
Llywiawdr pobl, *Powys* ar *Dehau*,
Llwyrwys caer, yn aer, yn arfau,
Lloegr breiddiaw am brudd anrheithiau,
Yn rhyfel, ffrwythlawn, dawn diammau,
Yn lladd yn llosci yn torri tyrau,
Yn *Rhos* a *Phenfro*, yn rhysfäau *Ffrainc*,
Llwyddedig i ainc yn llüyddau.
Hil *Gruffydd*, grymmus gynneddfau,
Hael gyngor, gyngyd wrth gerddau,
Hylathr i ysgwyd, escud barau gwrdd,
Hylym yn cyhwrdd cyhoedd waedffrau.
Hylwrw fwrw far, gymmell trethau,
Hawlwr gwlad arall gwledig riau,
Harddedd o fonedd, faen gaerau dreisddwyn,
Hirbell fal *Fflamddwyn* i fflamgyrchau.
Hwylfawr ddreig, ddragon cyfeddau,
Heirdd i feirdd ynghylch ei fyrddau,
Hylithr i gweleis ddydd golau i fudd,
Ai feddgyrn wirodau.
Iddaw i gynnal cleddyfal clau,
Mal *Arthur* wayw dur i derfynau,
Gwir frenin *Cymru* cymmreisc ddoniau,
Gwrawl hawl boed hwyl o ddehau.

IX.

ODLAU'R MISOEDD,

I Sir Gruffydd Llwyd o Dref-garnedd a Dinorweg yn Arfon; allan or Llyfr Coch o Hergest, yngholeg yr Iesu yn Rhyd Ychen. Gwilym Ddu o Arfon ai cant. 1322.

NEUD cyn nechrau Mai mau anrhydedd,
Neud aeth ysgwaeth a maeth a medd,
Neud cynhebyg, ddig, ddygn adrossedd drist,
Er pan ddelid Crist, weddw athrist wedd!
Neud cur a lafur im wylofedd,
Neud cerydd Dofydd, nad rhydd rhuddgledd.
Neud cof sy ynnof, ys anwedd ei faint,
Neud cywala haint, hynt diryfedd.
Neud caeth im dilyd llid llaweredd,
Neud caith Beirdd cyfiaith am eu cyfedd.
Neud caethiwed ced, nad rhydd cydwedd *Nudd*,
Cadrwalch *Ruffydd*, brudd, breiddin tachwedd,
Neud cwyn Beirdd trylwyn, meddw ancwyn medd,
Neud cawdd im anawdd, menestr canwledd,
Neud carchar anwar enwiredd Eingl-dud,
Aerddraig *Llan Rhystud* funud fonedd.
Neud nim dyhudd budd, bum arygledd,
Neud nam dilyd llid, lliaws blynedd.
Neud nam dawr, Duw mawr, maranedd, Nef glyw,
Neud nad rhydd fy llyw, llew *Trefgarnedd*,
Neud trwm oi eisiau dau digyfedd.
Neu'r wyr Beirdd canwlad, nad rhad rheufedd,
Neud ef arwydd gwir, neud oferedd gwyr,
Wrth weled f' eryr yn ei fowredd;
Neud truan i'm gwân gwayw lledfrydedd,
Neud trwydded galed im amgeledd.

Neud trymfryd *Gwynedd*, gwander dyedd braw:
Neud hwy eu treisiaw am eu trossedd.
Neud trahir gohir gloyw babir gledd,
Oedd trablwng echwng *Achel* ddewredd.
Neud trai cwbl or Mai, mawredd allwynin,
Neud mis Mehefin weddw orllin wedd.
    Neud mis Mehefin, mau hefyd gystudd,
Neud nam rhydd *Gruffydd* wayw rhudd yn rhyd.
Neum rhywan im gwân gwayw cryd engiriawl,
Neud am Ddraig urddawl didawl im dyd.
Neum erwyr om gwyr im gweryd Crist Ner,
Neud arfer ofer, Beirdd nifer byd.
Neud arwydd nam llwydd lledfryd im calon,
Neud eres nad tonn honn ar ei hyd.
Mau ynnof mowrgof am ergyd gofal,
Am attal arial *Urien* yngryd.
Mal cofain cywrain *Cynwryd*, fardd *Dunawd*,
Meu im Dreig priawd gwawd ni bo gwyd.
Mau gwawdgan *Afan*, ufuddfryd ffrwythlawn,
O gof *Gadwallawn*, brenhinddawn bryd.
Ni wn waith gwaywdwn, gwawd ddihewyd clod,
A thi heb ddyfod pa dda bod byd?
Neud wyr pawb yn llwyr, lleyrfryd gynnat,
Nad hylithr aur mâl mal oddiwrthyd.
Nid oes nerth madferth ym myd, oth eisiau,
Gwleddau na byrddau na Beirdd ynghlyd.
Nid oes lys ysbys, esbyd neud dibeirch,
Nad oes meirch na seirch na serch hyfryd.
Nad oes wedd na moes, masw ynyd yw'n gwlad,
Nad oes mad eithr gwad a gwyd.
Neud gwagedd trossedd, traws gaderuid *Môn*,
Neud gweigion *Arfon* is *Reon* ryd.
Neud gwann *Wynedd* fann, fen ydd ergyd cur,
Neud gwael am fodur eglur oglyd.
Neud blwyddyn i ddyn ddiofryd a gar,
Neud blaengar carchar, grym aerbar gryd.

X.

DYHUDDIANT ELPHIN.

Taliesin ai dywawd.

I.

ELPHIN deg taw ath wylo
Na chabled neb yr eiddo
Ni wna les drwg-obeithio
Ni wyl dyn ddim ai portho
Ni fydd goeg gweddi *Cynllo*
Ni thyrr Duw ar addawo:
Ni chad yngored *Wyddno,*
Erioed cystal a heno.

II.

Elphin deg sych dy ddeurudd
Ni weryd bod yn rhy brudd
Cyt tybiaist na chefaist fudd
Nith wna da gormod cystudd
Nag ammau wrthiau Dofydd
Cyt bwyf bychan wyf gelfydd,
O foroedd ac o fynydd
Ag o eigion afonydd
I daw Duw a da i ddedwydd.

III.

Elphin gynneddfau diddan
Anfilwraidd yw d' amcan
Nid rhaid yt ddirfawr gwynfan
Gwell Duw na drwg ddarogan

Cyd bwyf eiddil a bychan
Ar fin gorferw mor dylan
Mi a wnaf yn nydd cyfrdan
Yt well no thrychan maran.

IV.

Elphin gynneddfau hynod
Na sorr ar dy gyffaelod
Cyt bwyf gwan ar lawr fy nghod
Mae rhinwedd ar fy nhafod
Tra fwyf fi yth gyfragod
Nid rhaid yt ddirfawr ofnod
Drwy goffau enwau'r Drindod
Ni ddichon neb dy orfod.

It may not be improper to inform the Reader that the ORTHOGRAPHY *used in these Poems is the* ORTHOGRAPHY *of the* MSS. *and not that of the* WELSH BIBLE.

APPENDIX.

1. A method how to retrieve the ancient British language, in order that the Bards of the sixth century may be understood, and that the genuineness of Tyssilio's British History, which was translated from the Armoric language into Latin by Galfridus Arturius of Monmouth may be decided; and concerning a new edition of Gildas Nennius's Eulogium Brittanniæ, with notes, from ancient British MSS. This old British writer has been shamefully mangled by Dr. Gale, his editor, in the Scriptores Brittannici; and not much mended by Mr. Bertram in his late edition of it at Copenhagen.

Whether the ancient British language can be so far recovered as to understand the most ancient British writings now extant, is, I think, a consideration by no means beneath the notice of a society of Antiquarians, and of all learned men in general. There has been, it is true, an attempt of this nature made by the very learned Mr. Edward Llwyd, of the Museum, and in part laudably executed in his Archæologia Britannica, which reflects honour on those worthy persons who supported him in his five years travels into Ireland, Scotland, Cornwal, Basse Bretagne, and Wales. But as his plan was too extensive to bring every branch of what he undertook to perfection, I think a continuation of the same, restrained within certain limits, might still be useful.—Natural history is itself a province sufficient to engross a man's whole attention; but it was only a part of this great man's undertaking: and the learned world is abundantly convinced of the uncommon proficiency he made in natural philosophy; and how industrious he was in tracing the dialects of the ancient Celtic language. But still it must be acknowledged that he did very little towards the thorough understanding the ancient British Bards and historians. And indeed he owns himself that he was not encouraged in this part of his intended work, as appears by his proposals. Far be it from me to censure those very learned men who generously contributed to support the ingenious author in his travels, and dictated the method he was to persue. But, after all, I cannot help lamenting that he did not pay more attention to the old MSS. and compile a glossary to understand them. What he has done of this nature is very imperfect, few words being added to what there are in Dr. Davies's Dictionary, and those chiefly from writings of the fourteenth and fifteenth century. Indeed it appears he had not seen the works but of one of the Bards of the sixth century, and that in the red book of Hergest, in the Archives of Jesus's College, Oxon. He complains he could not procure access to the collections at Hengwrt and Llan Fordaf, and without perusing those venerable remains, and leisure to collate them with other copies, it was impossible for him to do anything effectual.—Now the method I would propose to a person that would carry this project into execution, is, that as soon as he is become master of the ancient British language, as far as it can be learned, by the assistance of Dr. Davies's dictionary, and Moses Williams's glossary at the end of Dr. Wotton's translation of Howel Dda's laws, he should endeavour to procure access to the great collections of ancient British MSS. in the libraries of the Earl of Macclesfield, Lady Wynne of Wynstay, the Duke of Ancaster, Sir Roger Mostyn at Gloddaith, John Davies, Esquire, at Llannerch, Miss Wynne of Bod Yscallen, William Vaughan, Esquire, at Cors y Gedol, and in other places both in South and North Wales in private hands. By this means he would be enabled in time to ascertain the true reading in many MSS. that have been altered and mangled by the ignorance of transcribers. I am satisfied there are not many copies of the Bards of the sixth century extant, nor indeed of those from the conquest to the death of Llewelyn. But two or three ancient copies on vellom, if such can be met with, will be sufficient; for in some transcripts by good hands that I have seen, they are imperfect in some copies. This would in a great measure enable our traveller to fill up the blanks, and help him to understand what, for want of this, must remain obscure, if not altogether unintelligible. We should by the means of such a person have a great many monuments of genius brought to light, that are now mouldering away with age, and a great many passages in history illustrated and confirmed that are now dark and dubious. Whole poems of great length and merit might be retrieved, not inferior, perhaps, to Ossian's productions, if indeed those extraordinary poems are of so ancient date, as his translator avers them to be. The Gododin of Aneurin Gwawdrydd is a noble heroic poem. So are likewise the works of Llywarch Hen about his battles with the Saxons, in which he lost twenty-four sons, who all were distinguished for their bravery with golden torques's. *Aurdorchogion.*

Taliesin's poems to Maelgwn Gwynedd, to Elphin ap Gwyddno, to Gwynn ap Nudd, and Urien Reged, and other great personages of his time, are great curiosities. We have, besides these, some remains of the works of Merddin ap Morfryn, to his patron Gwenddolau ap Ceidis, and of Afan Ferddig to Cadwallon ap Cadfan; and, perhaps, there may be in those collections some besides that we have not heard of. All these treasures might be brought to light, by a person well qualified for the undertaking, properly recommended by men of character and learning: and I think, in an age wherein all parts of literature are cultivated, it would be a pity to lose the few remaining monuments now left of the ancient British Bards, some of which are by their very antiquity become venerable. Aneurin Gwawdrydd above-mentioned is said, by Mr. Robert Vaughan of Hengwrt, to be brother to Gildas ap Caw, author of the *Epistle de excidio Britanniæ*, which is the most ancient account of Great Britain extant in Latin by a native.—No manner of estimate can be made of the works of our Bards and Historians that have been destroyed from time to time; nay some very curious ones have been lost within this century and a half. I think, therefore, it would be an act becoming the Antiquarian Society, and all patrons of learning in general, to encourage and support such an undertaking, which would redound much to their honour, and be a fund of a rational and instructive amusement.—Nor would those benefits alone accrue from a thorough knowledge of our Bards, but still more solid and substantial ones. For who would be better qualified than such a person to decide the controversy about the genuineness of the British History, by Tyssilio, from the oldest copies of it now extant, which differ in a great many particulars from the Latin translation of Galfrid, who owns that he received his copy from a person who brought it from Armorica; and why may there not be some copies of it still behind in some monasteries of that country, and of other works still more valuable? Mr. Llwyd, of the Museum, intended to visit them all, in order to get a catalogue of them to be printed in his Archæologia Britannica; but he was prevented by the war which then broke out, of which he gives an account in a letter to Mr. Rowlands, author of Mona Antiqua restaurata, and which is published at the end of that treatise. Who can be better qualified to succeed in such an undertaking than a person that is thoroughly well versed in all the old MSS. now extant in Wales. I find that the Armoric historians, particularly Father Lobineau, quote some of their ancient Bards to confirm historical facts. This is demonstration that some of their oldest Bards are still extant; and who knows but that some of the books they took with them when they first went to settle in Gaul, under Maximus and Conau Meiriadoc, may be still extant, at least transcripts of some of them; for that some were carried over is plain, by what Gildas himself says, "quæ vel si qua fuerint, aut ignibus hostium exusta, aut civium exulum classe longius deportata non compareant." So that I would have our traveller pass two years at least in Basse Bretagne, in order to make enquiry after such ancient monuments, and I make no doubt but he would make great discoveries.—Thus furnished, he might proceed to the British Museum, the Bodleian library, and the library of the two Universities, and elsewhere, where any ancient British MSS. are preserved. We might then have better editions of British authors than we have had from the English antiquaries, though in other respects very learned men; but, being unacquainted with our language, Bards, and antiquities, they have nothing but bare conjectures, and some scraps from the Roman writers to produce. No one likewise would be better qualified to fix the ancient Roman stations in Britain, as they are set down in Antoninus's intinerary, and their ancient British names.—I wish learned men would think of this ere it be too late; for one century makes a great havoc of old MSS. especially such as are in the hands of private persons, who understand not their true value, or are suffered to rot in such libraries, where nobody is permitted to have access to them.

2. *The following curious Commission published and inserted in some of the copies of Dr. Brown's Dissertation on the Union, &c., of Poetry and Music, and communicated from a Manuscript Copy in my possession, having so near a Relation to the Family of the noble Patron of these Poems, I thought it right to reprint it on this occasion.*

"By the QUEEN,

"ELIZABETH, by the Grace of GOD, of England, France, and Ireland, Queen, Defender of the Faith, &c. To our trusty and right well beloved Sir Richard Bulkely, Knight, Sir Rees Griffith, Knight, Ellis Price, Esq. Dr. in Civil Law, and one of our Council in the Marchesse of Wales, William Mostyn, Ieuan Lloyd of Yale, John Salisbury of Rhug, Rice Thomas, Maurice Wynne, William Lewis, Pierce Mostyn, Owen John ap Howel Fychan, John William ap John, John Lewis Owen, Morris Griffith, Symwd Thelwal, John Griffith, Ellis ap William Lloyd, Robert Puleston, Harri ap Harri, William Glynn, and Rees Hughes, Esqrs. and to every of them Greeting.

"Whereas it is come to the Knowledg of the Lord President, and other our Council in our Marchesse of Wales, that vagrant and idle Persons naming themselves *Minstrels*, *Rythmers*, and *Burds*, are lately grown into such *intolerable Multitude* within the Principality of North Wales, that not only Gentlemen and others by their *shameless Disorders* are oftentimes disquieted in their Habitations, but also the expert *Minstrels* and *Musicians* in *Tonge* and *Cunynge* thereby much discouraged to travaile in the Exercise and Practice of their Knowledg, and also not a little hindred *(of)* Livings and Preferment; the Reformation whereof, and the putting these People in Order, the said Lord President and

Council have thought very necessary: And knowing you to be Men of both Wisdom and upright Dealing, and also of Experience and good Knowledg in the Scyence, have appointed and authorised You to be Commissioners for that Purpose: And forasmuch as our said Council, of late travailing in some Part of the said Principality, had perfect Understanding by credible Report, that the accustomed Place for the Execution of the like Commission hath been heretofore at Cayroes in our County of Flynt, and that William Mostyn, Esq. and his Ancestors have had the Gift and bestowing of the *Sylver Harp* appertaining to the *Chief of that Faculty*, and that a *Year's Warning* (at least) hath been accustomed to be given of the *Assembly* and Execution of the like Commission; Our said Council have therefore appointed the Execution of this Commission to be at the said Town of Cayroes, the Monday next after the Feast of the Blessed Trinity which shall be in the Year of our Lord 1568. And therefore we require and command You by the Authority of these Presents, not only to cause *open Proclamation* to be made in all *Fairs, Market-Towns,* and other *Places of Assembly* within our Counties of Aglere, Carnarvon, Meryonydd, Denbigh and Flynt, that all and every Person and Persons that intend to *maintain* their *Living* by name or Colour of *Minstrels, Rythmers,* or *Bards,* within the Talaith of Aberffraw, comprehending the said five Shires, shall be and appear before You the said Day and Place to *shew* their *Learnings* accordingly: But also, that You, twenty, nineteen, eighteen, seventeen, sixteen, fifteen, fourteen, thirteen, twelve, eleven, ten, nine, eight, seven, or six of you, whereof You the said Sir Richard Bulkely, Sir Rees Griffith, Ellis Price, and William Mostyn, Esqs. or three or two of you, to be of the number; to repair to the said Place the Days aforesaid, and calling to you such *expert men* in the said *Faculty* of the *Welsh Music* as to You shall be thought convenient, to proceed to the Execution of the Premises, and to admit such and so many, as by your Wisdoms and Knowledges you shall find *worthy*, into and under the *Degrees* heretofore *(in Use)* in semblable Sort to *use, exercise,* and *follow* the *Sciences* and *Faculties* of their *Professions,* in such decent Order as shall appertain to each of their Degrees, and as your Discretions and Wisdoms shall prescribe unto them: Giving streight Monition and Commandment in our Name and on our Behalf to the rest not worthy, that they return to some honest Labour, and due Exercise, such as they be most apt unto for Maintenance of their Living, upon Pain to be taken as sturdy and idle Vagabonds, and to be used according to the Laws and Statutes provided in that Behalf; letting You with our said Council look for Advertisement, by Certificate at your Hands, of your Doings in the Execution of the said Premises; foreseeing in any wise, that upon the said Assembly the Peace and good Order be observed and kept accordingly; ascertaining you that the said William Mostyn hath promised to see Furniture and Things necessary provided for that Assembly, at the Place aforesaid.

"Given under our Signet at our City of Chester, the twenty third of October in the ninth Year of our Reign, 1567.

"Signed
Her Highness's Counsail
in the Marchesse of Wales."

"*N.B.* This Commission was copied exactly from the original now at Mostyn, A.D. 1693: where the *Silver Harp* also is."

3. *Since this Commission has been in the Press, the Author has had an opportunity to see the following Account of what has been done in consequence of such a Commission in the tenth Year of the Reign of Queen* Elizabeth. *This is translated from the Original in* Welsh.

KNOW all Men, by these Presents, that there is a Congress of Bards, and Musicians, to be held in the Town of Caerwys, in the County of Flint, on the twenty-sixth day of May, in the tenth Year of the Reign of her Majesty Queen Elizabeth, before Ellis Price, Esquire, Doctor of the Civil Law, and one of her Majesty's Council in the Marches of Wales, and before William Mostyn, Peres Mostyn, Owen John ap Hywel Vaughan, John William ap John, John Lewis Owen, Morris Griffith, Simon Thelwat, John Griffith Serjeant, Robert Pulesdon, Evan Lloyd of Iâl, and William Glyn, Esquires.

And that we the said Commissioners, by virtue of the said Commission, being her Majesty's Council, do give and grant to Simwnt Vychan, Bard, the degree of Pencerdd; and do order that Persons receive and hospitably entertain him in all Places fit for him to go and come to receive his Perquisites according to the Princely Statutes in that Case made and provided. Given under our Hands, in the Year 1568.

A

BIOGRAPHICAL SKETCH OF THE AUTHOR

Of the preceding Work.

"In the church-yard of Llanfihangel Lledrod, situated at some distance from Crosswood, on the other side of Ystwyth, are deposited, without stone or epitaph, the remains of the Rev. Evan Evans, the author of 'Specimens of the Poetry of the Ancient Welsh Bards,' &c., and equally distinguished for his genius as a poet, and his knowledge of the British language and antiquities. He was born at Cynhawdref in this parish, about the year 1730, and received the first part of his education at the Grammar School at Ystrad Meirig, then under the care of the celebrated Mr. Richards. Hence he removed to Jesus College, Oxford, towards the beginning of 1751. He afterwards took orders, and served successively several churches in the capacity of curate, but was never fortunate enough to hold a living of his own. His disappointment in his profession preyed considerably on his mind, and led him to seek an oblivion to his vexation in excesses which impaired his health and greatly limited his usefulness. He devoted considerable attention in early life to the study of his native language, in which he composed several poetical pieces. Some of these, as appears from a correspondence inserted in the 'Cambrian Register,' were submitted to the criticism, and received the corrections of Mr. Lewis Morris, who speaks highly of Mr. Evans's talents and promise of future excellence. His chief literary productions are the 'Specimens,' above mentioned, which were published in 4to. in 1764. In these he has given a literal prose version of the writings of some of the earlier Welsh bards. For the copy-right he received thirty pounds. He wrote also several English poems, and a great number of short poems in Welsh, (some of which are inserted in the following pages,) and a translation into Welsh of two volumes of sermons, selected out of Tillotson and other eminent divines. A great part of his life was spent in collecting and transcribing ancient Welsh manuscripts. He was admitted to the collection of Sir Roger Mostyn, which preserves a very great number of ancient manuscripts, of great value: he likewise copied the works of the oldest bards, from a very large vellum manuscript, called 'Y Llyfr Coch,' in the library of Jesus College, Oxford. He thence also copied several valuable historical tracts of the 12th century. He, besides what has been mentioned, explored every corner of Wales, in quest of manuscripts, and met with considerable success; but the neccessary encouragement, which was solicited towards putting a part of what he had thus collected to press was withheld from him."—*Partly extracted from Rees's Historical description of South Wales.*

We are told that the ancient Welsh MSS. which our industrious author collected and transcribed, occupy upwards of eighty volumes. They were purchased by the late Paul Panton Esq., of Plasgwyn, Anglesea.

Mr. Evans had a lengthy correspondence with Bishop Percy and other eminent antiquaries; the most interesting portions of which will be found in the following pages, together with selections from his poetical works. He was of tall stature,—hence his Bardic name of Prydydd Hir, (the tall poet.) He was very benevolently disposed, and highly national and patriotic, and as might be expected, was most averse to the appointment of English prelates to Welsh dioceses. That will partly account for his stationary position in the Establishment. His excessive love of the 'wine cup' may also have had something to do in preventing his appointment to a more lucrative position in the Church. Mr. Evans died suddenly in the month of May 1789; *some* say that he perished on a mountain; *others* say that he died at, or near his native home; but *none* deny that poverty and sorrow hastened the death of our talented but unfortunate author.

21

AN ELEGY

On the Death of the Rev. E. Evans, (Ieuan Prydydd Hir,) by the Rev. R. Williams, (Companion to Mr. Pennant in his Welsh tours.)

ON Snowdon's haughty brow I stood,
And view'd afar old Menai's flood;
Carnarvon Castle, eagle crowned
And all the beauteous prospect round;
But soon each gay idea fled,
For Snowdon's favourite bard was dead.
Poor bard accept one genuine tear,
And read thy true eulogium here;
Here in my heart, that rues the day,
Which stole Eryri's pride away.
But, lo, where seen by Fancy's eye
His visionary form glides by,
Pale, ghastly pale, that hollow cheek,
That frantic look does more than speak,
And tells a tale so full of woe,
My bosom swells, my eyes o'erflow.
On Snowdon's rocks, unhomed, unfed,
The tempest howling round his head;
Far from the haunts of men, alone,
Unheard, unpitied, and unknown,
To want and to despair a prey,
He pined and sighed his soul away.
Ungrateful countrymen, your pride,
Your glory, wanted bread, and died!
Whilst ignorance and vice are fed,
Shall wit and genius droop their head?
Shall fawning sycophants be paid,
For flattering fools? while thou art laid

On thy sick bed, the mountain heath,
Waiting the slow approach of death,
Beneath inhospitable skies,
Without a friend to close thine eyes.
Thus shall the chief of bards expire,
The master of the British lyre;
And shall thy hapless reliques rot,
Unwept, unhallowed, and forgot?
No! while one grateful muse remains,
And Pity dwells on Cambria's plains,
Thy mournful story shall be told,
And wept, till time itself grows old.

SELECTIONS

FROM THE

POETICAL WORKS & CORRESPONDENCE

OF THE

REV. EVAN EVANS, (IEUAN PRYDYDD HIR.)

A PARAPHRASE OF THE 137TH PSALM.

Alluding to the captivity and treatment of the Welsh Bards by King Edward I.

SAD near the willowy Thames we stood,
And curs'd the inhospitable flood;
Tears such as patients weep, 'gan flow,
The silent eloquence of woe,
When Cambria rushed into our mind,
And pity with just vengeance joined;
Vengeance to injured Cambria due,
And pity, O ye Bards, to you.

Silent, neglected, and unstrung,
Our harps upon the willows hung,
That, softly sweet in Cambrian measures,
Used to sooth our souls to pleasures,
When, lo, the insulting foe appears,
And bid us dry our useless tears.

"Resume your harps," the Saxons cry,
"And change your grief to songs of joy;
Such strains as old Taliesin sang,
What time your native mountains rang
With his wild notes, and all around
Seas, rivers, woods return'd the sound."

What!—shall the Saxons hear us sing,
Or their dull vales with Cambrian music ring?
No—let old Conway cease to flow,
Back to her source Sabrina go:
Let huge Plinlimmon hide his head,
Or let the tyrant strike me dead,
If I attempt to raise a song
Unmindful of my country's wrong.
What!—shall a haughty king command
Cambrians' free strain on Saxon land?
May this right arm first wither'd be,
Ere I may touch one string to thee,
Proud monarch; nay, may instant death
Arrest my tongue and stop my breath,
If I attempt to weave a song,
Regardless of my country's wrong!

Thou God of vengeance, dost thou sleep,
When thy insulted Druids weep,
The Victor's jest the Saxon's scorn,
Unheard, unpitied, and forlorn?
Bare thy right arm, thou God of ire,
And set their vaunted towers on fire.

Remember our inhuman foes,
When the first Edward furious rose,
And, like a whirlwind's rapid sway,
Swept armies, cities, Bards away.

"High on a rock o'er Conway's flood"
The last surviving poet stood,
And curs'd the tyrant, as he pass'd
With cruel pomp and murderous haste.
What now avail our tuneful strains,
Midst savage taunts and galling chains?
Say, will the lark imprison'd sing
So sweet, as when, on towering wing,
He wakes the songsters of the sky,
And tunes his notes to liberty?
Ah no, the Cambrian lyre no more
Shall sweetly sound on Arvon's shore,
No more the silver harp be won,
Ye Muses, by your favourite son;
Or I, even I, by glory fir'd,
Had to the honour'd prize aspir'd.
No more shall Mona's oaks be spar'd
Or Druid circle be rever'd.
On Conway's banks, and Menai's streams
The solitary bittern screams;
And, where was erst Llewelyn's court,
Ill-omened birds and wolves resort.
There oft at midnight's silent hour,
Near yon ivy-mantled tower,
By the glow-worm's twinkling fire,
Tuning his romantic lyre,
Gray's pale spectre seems to sing,
"Ruin seize thee, ruthless King."

THE PENITENT SHEPHERD.

A PENSIVE Shepherd, on a summer's day,
Unto a neighb'ring mountain bent his way,
And solitary mus'd, with thoughts profound,
Whilst ev'ry thing was silent all around;
The firmament was clear, the sky serene,
And not a cloud eclips'd the rural scene.
Not so the Shepherd, all was storm within,
He mourn'd his frailty, and bewail'd his sin;
His soul alone engross'd his utmost care,
Decoy'd by cursed Satan to his snare;
(Alas! with what success he tempts mankind,
And leads them to their ruin with the blind!)
Awhile he stood, as one in woeful pain;
At last, he broke in melancholy strain,
And cried,—

"O great Creator, ever good and wise,
I dare not lift to thee mine eyes—
Thy violated laws for vengeance call,
And on offenders heavy judgment fall;
Which hurl them flaming to eternal pains,
To suffer ever on infernal plains.
The terrors of thy justice make me fear,
For who can everlasting torment bear?
My soul with grief is rent, Oh! stop thy hand,
Shivering before thy Majesty I stand;
Long have I trod the 'luring path of vice,
And tire thy patience, and thy grace despise.
Before thy throne I bow with suppliant knee,
Grant gracious God, thy pardon unto me:
In solitude my follies I repent,
The life so long, so viciously, I spent,

O God! I wish undone my wicked deeds,
My contrite heart with inward sorrows bleeds.
Thou, O my God! art witness of my grief,
And thou alone canst grant me a relief.
I promise faithfully to sin no more,
(I sue for mercy, and thy grace implore,)
And spend my life, for ever, in thy fear,
Thy laws to keep, thy holy name revere."
Thus plain'd the pensive Shepherd, and his moan,
Christ, his Mediator, brought before the throne!
Him graciously answer'd God to Sire,
His face resplendent with a globe of fire:—
"My Son hath paid thy ransom, go in peace,
Eternal justice bids thee be at ease!"
He said, and all the choir of angels sung,
Harmonious melody, their harps they strung,
And heaven's Empyreum to their music rung,
Such is the joy when a poor sinner turns,
That with uncommon glow each seraph burns.
Thus I may compare small things with great,
The Prodigal his tender father met;
Such as the Gospel paints in tatter'd weed,
Willing with husks to satisfy his need:
And none would give them, though the hungry roam,
Till he returned unto his Father's home;
Who kill'd the fatted calf, and spread the feast,
Where wine and minstrelsy his joy exprest.
The Shepherd thus refresh'd with heavenly grace,
Return'd with joy eternal in his face;
The Saviour's wond'rous love to man he prais'd,
And thus his voice with gratitude he rais'd:—

"All glory to the gracious Son of God,
Who hast alone the grevious wine-press trod,
To satisfy his justice, and for me
Hast wrought endless salvation on the tree;

Who hast redeem'd us, and destroyed our foes,
That neither death nor grave can work our woes:
Hast overthrown the dragon, and no more
Hell, nor its gates have terrors left in store!"

Thus did the Shepherd testify his joy,
A theme that might an angel's tongue employ;
He praised Christ, who for mankind did die;
His praise let all resound, to all eternity.

VERSES

On seeing the Ruins of Ivor Hael's Palace.

AMIDST its alders IVOR's palace lies,
In heaps of ruins to my wondering eyes;
Where greatness dwelt in pomp, now thistles reign,
And prickly thorns assert their wide domain.

No longer Bards inspired, thy tables grace.
Nor hospitable deeds adorn the place;
No more the generous owner gives his gold
To modest merit, as to Bards of old.

In plaintive verse his IVOR—GWILYM moans,
His Patron lost the pensive Poet groans;
What mighty loss, that IVOR's lofty hall,
Should now with schreeching owls rehearse its fall!

Attend, ye great, and hear the solemn sound,
How short your greatness this proclaims around,
Strange that such pride should fill the human breast,
Yon mouldering walls the vanity attest.

A Letter from Mr. Thomas Carte to the Rev. Evan Evans.

Dear Sir,

I cannot sufficiently acknowledge Sir Thomas Mostyn's kindness, in the trouble he has taken, of sending up the catalogue of his historical MSS. and in his obliging offer of communicating them to me. Those which I am desirous to see more than the rest, are these, viz.—

"The Annals of the Abbey of Chester, to A.D. 1297.

"Beda de Gestis Anglorum, if it be a different work from his Chronicon and Ecclesiastical History. It is the same.

"History of England, from William the Conqueror to the 6th of Edward the 6th.

"Annales Cambriæ ignoti autoris, et Chronica Cambriæ; both which seem to be in the same volume, which begins with a Welsh history of the Kings of the Britons and Saxons, and Princes of Wales, to the time of Edward 4th.

"A chronology from Vortigern downwards, supposed to be collected by Robert Vaughan, of Hengwrt, Esquire, which seems to be in the volume beginning with Sir John Wynne's pedigree of the family of Gwydir.

"Treatises concerning the courts of wards and chancery."

As Sir Thomas proposes to come to town soon, I hope he will be so good as to bring those MSS. with him (as Sir W. W. Wynne will several others, that he has found at Llanvorda) because they will be very useful to me as I conceive, for my first volume.

There are some others I should be glad to look over, but shall have more time for it. Were I on the spot, I should be very curious to consult the MS. of Froissart, though that author's history, so favourable to the English, is printed. My edition of it is that of Paris, 1520, which I take to be the last of any: but there is a MS. finely wrote and illuminated of this author, in the monastery called Elizabeth, at Breslaw, in Silesia, which contains a third part more than any printed edition. Count Bicklar, a Silesian nobleman, who was at Paris, A. D. 1727, promised me to get a printed edition of Froissart collated with that MS. but he could find no monk in the monastery, or any about the place, capable of doing it. I desired him to buy a MS. that seemeth useless to the convent, at the price of 200 ducats, but my offer made them fancy it the more valuable, and they would not sell it. I have seen a MS. in the king's library at Paris, and that of the capuchins at Rouen, but they contained no more than my edition: I should be glad to know if Sir Thomas's does. I gave the Benedictine, who has the care of the new collections of French historians, notice of the MS. at Breslaw, that he might make use of it in his new edition of Froissart; but I have not heard whether he has got the MS. collated, and the supplement copied.

Adredus Rievallensis, Robert of Gloucester, Caradoc of Llancarvan, and Geoffry of Monmouth, are printed; and I have examined several MSS. of the case in the Cotton, Oxford, and Cambridge libraries; so are the MSS. of Giraldus Cambrensis; but if Sir Thomas's MSS. contain more than the printed editions, I shall be extremely glad to see them, as also Trussel's original of cities, and antiquities of Westminster, as also the digression left out of Milton's history. The tracts of state in the times of Elizabeth, James I., and Charles I. I shall be very glad to see: but they, as well as some others, I can the better stay for, because they relate to more modern times.

Pray make my humble service and acknowledgments acceptable to Sir Thomas; which will oblige me to be more, if possible, than I am,

Dear Sir,

Your affectionate, and obedient servant,

Gray's Inn, Nov. 14, 1744. Thos. Carte.

Mr. Lewis Morris to the Rev. Evan Evans.

Dear Bard,

I received your's last post, without date, with a *Cowydd Merch*, for which I am very much obliged to you. I cannot see why you should be afraid of that subject being the favourite of your *Awen*. It is the most copious subject under heaven, and takes in all others; and, for a fruitful fancy, is certainly the best field to play in, during the poet's tender years. Descriptions of wars, strife, and the blustering part of man's life, require the greatest ripeness of understanding, and knowledge of the world; and is not to be undertaken but by strong and solid heads, after all the experience they can come at.

Is it not odd, that you will find no mention made of *Venus* and *Cupid* amongst our Britons, though they were very well acquainted with the Roman and Greek writers? That god and his mother are implements that modern poets can hardly write a love-poem without them: but the Britons scorned such poor machines. They have their *Essyllt*, *Nyf*, *Enid*, *Bronwen*, *Dwynwen*, of their own nation, which excelled all the Roman and Greek goddesses.—I am now, at my leisure hours, collecting the names of these famous men and women, mentioned by our poets, (as Mr. Edward Llwyd once intended,) with a short history of them; as we have in our common Latin dictionaries, of those of the Romans and Grecians. And I find great pleasure in comparing the *Triades*, *Beddau*, *Milwyr Ynys Prydain*, and other old records, with the poets of the fourteenth and fifteenth centuries; which is the time when our Britons wrote most and best.

Let me have a short *Cowydd* from you now and then; and I will send you my observations upon them, which may be of no disservice to you. That sent in your last letter, I here return to you; with a few corrections. It doth not want many: use them, or throw them in the fire, which you please. Do not swallow them without examination. The authority of good poets must determine all.

Y forwyn gynt, fawr iawn gais,
Deg aruthr erioed a gerais.

The word *Aruthr*, though much used, in the sense you take it, seems not proper here; yet Dr. Davies translates it *Mirus*. I cannot think but the original import of the word is *terrible*; and they cannot say in English of a woman, she is *terribly fair*. *Rhuthr*, from whence *Aruthr* is compounded, I dare say had that sense, at least:—

"Y cythraul accw ruthrwas."
W. Llbyn.

Deg wawr erioed a gerais,

may do as well, and sounds better.

A roist ofal i'm calon,
A brâth o hiraeth i'm bron:
Ni wyr un ar a anwyd
A roist o gur, os teg wyd;
Enwa anhunedd yn henaint
A yr wyn fyth yr un faint.

The first line of the last couplet is too long, and I should write both thus:

Enwa'n hunedd yn henaint
E yr wyn fyth yr un faint.

Again:

Cyrchaf, ac ni fynnaf au,
I dir angov drwy angau.

The last couplet is a beautiful expression; but it hath too much sweet in it; what our poets call *Eisiau Cyfnewid Bogail*. *Ang*, *ang*, is a fault, which our musicians term *too many concords;* and therefore they mix discords in music, to make it more agreeable to the ear. So the rhetoricians call the same fault in their science, *Caniad y gôg*. Therefore, suppose you would turn it thus:

O dir ing af drwy angeu.

Again:

Lle bo dyfnaf yr afon,
Ar fy hynt yr af i hon,
Oni roi, Gwen eurog wedd,
Drwy gariad ryw drugaredd.

Eurog wedd is no great compliment to a fair woman; for *Gwen*, a Flavia, loves to be called white; and the last line hath *gar—gar*, therefore I would write thus, or the like:

Oni roi, Gwen ir ei gwedd,
Yn gywrain, ryw drugaredd.

But I do not like *ir ei gwedd.*

Af i graig fwyaf o grêd
Y môr, i gael ymwared,
Ag o'r graig fawr i'r eigion
Dygaf gyrch i dyrch y dòn—

An excellent expression—

Ag o'r dòn egr hyd annwfn
Af ar y dafi i fôr dwfn.

Here is a charming opening for you, to describe the country you go to, and the wonders of the deep; and something like the following lines might be insérted:

Lle mae'r morfil friwfil fron,
A'r enwog *fôrforwynion*,

To proceed:

A fynno Gwen ysplennydd
Yn ddiau o'm rhwymau 'n rhydd,
Ni chaf gur, ni chaf garu
Na phoen gwn, na hoffi 'n gu;
Ni roddaf gam i dramwy,
I gred i'th ymweled mwy:
Dyna'r modd dan wir i mi,
A dyr unwaith drueni.

The expression *Dan wir*, is too local, and is not understood all over Wales. Local expressions must be avoided as much as possible. Suppose you said then,

Oni chaf heb warafun
Dy fodd fyth difeiwedd fun.

After all these corrections, which are not very material, you have this comfort, (and I mention it that you may not be discouraged,) that I do not know a man in our country who can write a poem which shall want as few corrections. So make poetry and antiquity (when you can come at materials) branches of your study; and, depend upon it, you will make a figure in the world. There are flights and turns in this poem, which even David ab Gwilym would not have been ashamed of.

I would have you write to my brother, and let him know the reason of your not going to London, and that you are alive. If you send him this poem, he will be pleased with it.

Is there any hopes of your seeing the Llyfr Coch n Hergest? Who is keeper, or underkeeper, of Jesus-College Library? And who is principal; and who are the fellows? Perhaps I may know some of them; or can make interest some way or other for you to get the use of those MSS.

But it ought to be considered, that you are to mind the main chance of reading the classics, in order to come to a tolerable being, before you launch too far into any other studies; and you must only take a snatch by the bye, which will serve to whet your genius; *oblegid mae newid gwaith cystal a gorphwyso.*

When you can come at Llyfr Coch o Hergest, or any other ancient MSS., I will send you directions to read it, and understand it: the chief difficulty being in the orthography: the language of all Britain (even Scotland) was the same as it is now in Wales, 1200 years ago.

I wrote to you lately, which I suppose you had not received when you sent your dateless letter. I desire your answer when convenient.

Yours sincerely,

Galltvadog, July 14, 1751. LEWIS MORRIS.

The same to the same.

DEAR EVAN,

Your letter of the second instant, I received this day; and I was very glad to hear that you had procured leave to go to the private library in Jesus College. It is charming to get into conversation with *Llywarch Hen*, *Aneurin*, *Merddin*, &c. They are most pleasing old companions.

I understand that my copy of *Brut y Brenhinoedd* is not the same with that in *Llyfr Coch o Hergest.* Mine was copied out of five MSS. three of them upon vellum, very ancient; but the transcriber, not understanding the occasion of the difference between the copies, stuffed all into this, that he could find in all the MSS. Had he known that some of those MSS. were from Walter the Archdeacon's original translation of the history, out of the Armoric; and some again from his second translation from Galfrid's Latin, he would have kept the copies separate. The transcriber of my copy mentions sometimes—"thus in uch a MS. and thus in such a MS.," but it is impossible to find which is which.

Brut y Tywysogion is only the history of Caradoc of Llancarvan, which was Englished by Humphrey Lloyd, and published by Dr. Powell; and afterwards a very bad edition by Mr. W. Wynne. I would not have you take the trouble upon you to transcribe that; for there are many copies of it. What is most worth your care is the works of the poets; especially that part of them that is historical, as some of Taliesin, Merddin, Llywarch Hen's are. Merddin mentions the war in Scotland, between Rhydderch Hael, Aeddan ab Gafran, Gwenddolau ab Ceidio, &c., and Taliesin mentions several battles, that none of our historians ever so much as heard of. These are matters of great curiosity—Llywarch Hen in one of his Elegies, mentions *Eglwysau Bassa*, that was destroyed by the Saxons. Nennius says, that one of the twelve battles fought by Arthur against the Saxons, was upon the river *Bassas.* Who is that great Apollo among our historians who knows anything of these affairs?—Is there ever a MS. of Nennius, which you can come at? I wish that book was translated into English: it is but small. However, since you are now about the Llyfr Coch, I would have you first to write an index of the contents of it, and send it me, sheet by sheet, and I will give you my opinion what is best to transcribe, and is most uncommon or curious. I do not remember whether the book is paged; let it be as it will, you cannot be long in making such an index, with the first line of each piece. There are some other curious MSS. there; some *Bucheddau* (Lives) as far as I recollect. But the silly copy of *Brut y Brenhinoedd*, in a modern hand, there, is not worth talking of.—How do you know it is the same with the Bodleian? I presume, that the *Brut y Brenhinoedd*, in *Llyfr Coch*, is not the original translation from the Bretonic copy; for I think it mentions Galfrid's translation in the conclusion of it.—But it is many years since I saw it. I shall ask some questions about certain passages in it, when I have leisure to look into my own copy. I have written abundance of notes, in defence of mine, since you saw it; and the more I examine into it, the better I like it. I had at first but a poor opinion of it; being prepossessed with the character given it by English writers; but when I find the poets, and our genealogies, and ancient inscriptions, and coins agree with it; and some foreign writers, I do not wonder that the inveteracy of the old Saxons should still remain against it, as long as Bede is in being. I shall only ask you now,—whether the son of Ascanius is called *Silius* or *Silvius*, in Llyfr Coch? It is in the beginning of my copy, which begins—Eneas gwedi ymladd Troya, &c. Mine is not divided into chapters or books. I have time to write no more, but that

I am,

Yours sincerely,

Galltvadog, Oct. 13, 1751, LEWIS MORRIS.

The same to the same.

SIR,

I happened to come upon business to this place; and being so near you, and having an hour's leisure, I could not help sending this to remind you that there is such a one alive, who wishes you well, and who is really glad you have got into such a worthy family. I hope that you will make the best use of your time; you will not be able to see how precious it is till most part of it is gone. This world (or this age) is so full of people that take no time to think at all, that a young fellow is in the greatest danger as can be to launch out among them. The terrestrial part of men being predominant, is as apt as a monkey to imitate everything that is bad. So that the little good which is to be done, must be done in spite of nature.

I expected a line from you upon your being settled, and that you had time to look about you; and when you have leisure, I shall be glad to hear of your doing well. I make no doubt but you will follow your British studies, as well as other languages: for I suppose it will hardly leave you, whether you will or no. Therefore to whet your parts, and in order to improve yourself that way, I propose to you a correspondent, a friend of mine, an Anglesea man; who will be glad of your acquaintance, and I daresay *you* of *his*; especially when you have seen some of his performances. His name is Gronw Owen; and you may direct to him at Donnington, near Salop; he keeps a school there, and is curate of a place hard by. He is but lately commenced a Welsh poet; and the first ode he ever wrote, was an imitation of your ode on melancholy. His *Cowydd y Farn* is the best thing I ever read in Welsh. You will be more surprised with his language and poetry than with anything you ever saw. His ode is styled *The Wish*, or Gofuned Gronw Ddu o Fon; and is certainly equal, if not superior, to anything I ever read of the ancients.

I have shared the dominion of poetry in Wales among you. He shall have the north, and you the south. But he has more subjects, a hundred to one, than you have, unless Glamorgan affords some.

Mr. Gronw Owen has been for some years laying a foundation for a Welsh rational Grammar, not upon the Latin and Greek plan, but upon the plan that the language will bear. It would be unreasonable to expect an old archbishop to dance a jig and rigadoon with boys and girls; it is certain that the Greek and Latin are such when compared with the Celtic. He has desired of me to bring you acquainted together; and here I do it, unless it is your own faults. He does not know how to write to you, nor I neither; but direct this at a venture.

I am,

Your assured friend,

And servant,

Llandeilo Vawr, April 23, 1752. LEWIS MORRIS.

The same to the same.

Dear Sir,

My brother gave me yours of the third, with an excellent ode to the King of Prussia. The faults in it I take to be owing to your careless writing of it; for they are such as cannot be from want of knowledge, as the ode itself shows. However, as you desire my corrections (which seems to be a sort of menial office, like a plaisterer, who daubs mortar on a grand piece of building, designed by a great architect) I give you my labour for nothing, and choose whether you follow my opinion or no; for I am no oracle.

In my last alterations, in Cowydd Teifi, your line—

Dy llf y loywaf afon—

is certainly best. I only wrote something that came uppermost, to egg you on to do better. Your notion of *Maelienydd* is wrong. You have been imposed upon by Camden, Selden, or perhaps, by Girald. Cambrensis; or by some of those strangers that knew nothing of the matter. *Maelienydd* was the country to the south and east of those mountains. But this is besides my purpose. Well, as you think the unity of design, scene, and action of your poem was about *Llyn Teifi*, I shall not urge the description of *Teifi* as low as the sea (for there it goes.) And I could have wished you had done it; for nobody else in Cardiganshire is able to do poor *Teifi* that kindness. As for your sheltering under Horace's adage, I mind it as nothing. He was a stranger to our methods, handed down to us by his masters, the druidical bards; who knew how to sing before Rome had a name. So never, hereafter, mention such moderns as Horace and Virgil, when you talk of British poetry. Llywarch Hen, Aneurin, and followers of the Druids, are our men; and nature our rule.

With respect to your borrowing Gronw's manuscript, you may make yourself easy about it. I dare say he would sooner part with his wife, and, for aught I know, children too; but his wife I am sure. Your sentiments of Gronw's capacity as a poet, are I believe just; for he has had greater opportunities than any poet since the Norman Conquest. But, if you take my word, you will not be behind him, if you stick to it. And, that you may not complain for want of the necessary requisites, as soon as ever I have any leisure, I will send you an ode or two of the ancients, which are not in Gronw's book, to whet your Awen with. I have a fine collection of the eleventh and twelfth centuries, which I value more than their weight in fine gold.

Your most humble Servant,

London, *Nov.* 13, 1756. Lewis Morris.

The same to the same.

Dear Sir,

It is now almost an age since I heard from you. From an annual animal it would be a proper expression; and I am but little better, as I change for the worse every year, till I shall be no more.

I was glad to hear you had got to Llanrhychwyn; a place scarcely ever heard of by the inhabitants of the level countries; where you roll I suppose, in ancient MSS. and curiosities; and where the arms of the invaders hardly ever reached.

Mr. W. Wynne was with me one night lately; and it seems he hath as many ancient MSS. as other people have printed books: *Gwyn ei fyd!* I was very much out of order when he was here, which deprived me of the pleasure I should otherwise have had.

I had a visit paid me lately by John Bradford, of Glamorganshire (darn o brydydd, &c.) It seems that country is entirely drained of its valuable antiquities; or else, their MSS. are buried among the rubbish of old libraries unheeded.

The more I look into Nennius the difficulties encrease: for he has been so mangled by ignorant or unskilful readers and transcribers, and by Gale the editor, that, without a body had a sight of all the manuscript copies of it in the public libraries, or elsewhere, there is no attempting to interpret it. Mr. R. Vaughan's MS. at Hengwrt would be a vast help; but I see no likelihood to come at a sight of that. Any ancient copy of it on vellum, which has not been dabbled with, or compared with the Cambridge, the Oxford MSS. &c.; that is, one which we might call a virgin manuscript, which hath not been ravished by Camden, Markham, Sir S. D'Ewes, or Usher, would give great satisfaction; but where is that to be found? That which Sir. J. Pryse had may possibly exist somewhere; and that which Humphrey Lloyd had, may likely be in the neighbourhood of Denbigh still.

I have not had a week's health since I saw you, and therefore have been in no good humour to read or write.

Have you, among Taliesin's works, Ymddyddan rhwng Ugnach ab Mydno o Gaerleon a Thaliesin o Gaerdyganwy? If you have it not, I will send it you. It is from the Llyfr Du o Gaerfyrddin.

My chief business of late has been to put the names of men and places in an alphabetical order, and to prepare them for my Celtic remains, from Taliesin's works, Sir J. Pryse's Cambria, the Triades, the Gododin, Beddau Milwyr, Aera Cambr. Brit. L. G. Cothi, and extent of Anglesea.

Remember that you promised me the remainder of the Gododin, and never performed it. The last lines of the fragment which I have, are

Tymor tymhestyl
Tymhestyl dymor
Y beri rhestr rhac rhiallu.

I am now out of the way of all curious antiquities; and you who have an opportunity of seeing every body's treasures, keep them all to yourself. I long to see the Legends of our Welsh Saints (Buchedd y seintiau). I forgot to tell you, that I am at this very time putting the names of all the parishes in Wales into alphabetical order, for the above purpose. But I find my catalogue of the parishes is not very correct; therefore I must desire the assistance of some that live near the places that are doubtful, and have their correction, or opinion of them. One of them is Llangynsarn. I never heard but of three Plwy'r Creuddyn. Is there a Llangedol near Bangor? Are there parishes called Llangedyrn, Bodfrenin, Llandydwen, Betwnog in Lleyn, or how otherwise called? Is there a parish called Llansilien, near Corwen in Edeyrnion? Or is it Llansilian, or Tyssilio? Are there parishes called Llanelidan, and Y Fynechdid, in Cantref Dyffryn Clwyd: and what is the etymology of them; and also of Llanhychen; and whence is Llanferrys yn Ial derived; and who is Trillo, and Trillo Caenog; and what is the common opinion of the derivation of the name of Gyffylliog?

I shall stop here at present; and leave Flintshire, Montgomeryshire, &c. to another time; and shall hint only what is come just now into my head.

I think you have a vote for a knight of the shire, in this county; if you have not made a positive promise to Mr. Vaughan, or that party, I would advise you to do yourself greater service than you expect at their hands; and I believe you know, that I would not advise to any thing but what would be of advantage to you. Let me hear from you about this point.

I am surprised Dewi Fardd does not come with his books, to deliver to the subscribers. I do not hear that they are come to Aberystwith. He has murdered a good book, by inserting in it the works of the greatest blockheads of the creation, and the most illiterate creatures that bear human shapes; such as Robert Humphrey, &c., &c.—Ffei ffei o honynt! Or were they put as beauty spots, to set you and others off? If it is otherwise, you are alive, and may defend yourself, for standing in such company; but I am heartily sorry for poor Hugh Morris. If he knows of this, that he must stand in spite of his teeth, in company with people that were not worthy to carry the feathers of his quill; and the room which his poem should have filled up, taken by persons as far below him as a *Crythor Crwth Trithiant* is below Corelli or Vivaldi.

Let me have your opinion upon the names of the parishes as soon as you can.

I am,

Yours sincerely,

Penbryn, Dec. 20, 1759. LEWIS MORRIS.

The same to the same.

DEAR SIR,

I received your kind favour by Dewi, with the remainder of the Gododin, and some of the Gorchanau. Be so good as to let me know from whence these have been copied, and whether I can depend upon their being correct. I suppose it is your mistake in writing Breint mab *Bleidgi*, for *Bleidig*. It seems the Gododin was not one entire piece, but was written in distinct odes; or else what means the preface to the Gorchanau? But where are the distinctions in the copy? I wish we had a correct one: I can make little or nothing of this.

David Jones tells me of a Llanerch copy of *Brut y Brenhinoedd*, in folio on paper, written by Edward Kyffin, for John Trefor, of Trevalun. I wish I had the beginning and ending of it, as I took off the vellum book, that you brought here; and if you would do the same by the other copies there, I should be glad to see it. By this management we shall be able to distinguish between Galfrid's, Walter's translation, and Tyssilio's original.

I thank you for the inscription at Llanfor, and that at Foel-las. I dare determine nothing about them as yet; only that Mr. Edward Llwyd's reading is only the froth of a fertile brain. When you copy inscriptions, cut a bit of chalk into a pencil, and trace the letters. In old inscriptions there are often natural lines in the stone; and sometimes lines worn out, which must be supplied with chalk. I suspect you had no chalk at Llanfor; and that your ENIARCH may be Llywarch, or LYVARCH. I wish I could see it. Are you sure, there is not part of it covered still with lime?

I thank you also for John Owen's Elegy—a good one—I had got it from the navy office; and also Mr. W. Wynne's.

Mr. Pegge, in a letter lately to Dr. Phillips, says that he has borrowed a MS. of Mr. Davies of Llanerch, which Mr. Pegge has now in his study; and which he says will be of good use to him. Pray what can it be? I have converted Mr. Pegge from the Camdenian faction; and we shall by and by see whether he is an ally of consequence. He is perfectly satisfied with my defence of Tyssilio; and wishes to see a translation of his book. Mr. Davies knows something of him I suppose.

I am glad your spitting of blood is over; take care, your life is precious, whether you have a fat living or no. Dont despair; some men of sense may take notice of you; though, even among the ancient Britons, canonization went seldom out of great families, as appears by *Bonedd y Saint*, which I have at last completed, as far as my materials reached. I now plainly see that the Llanerch MS. of Bonedd is but a fragment; for there is not a syllable of the Brychan family in it; and but very little of the Caw family. I have reduced the whole into genealogical order; and they take but a very narrow compass. I shall have some difficulty in fixing the times of these saints; for there is some confusion among them, occasioned by the blunders of transcribers.

They have been all hunting after the Llanerch MS. of *Bonedd*, even Dr. Thomas Williams, and the Anglesea Man, as well as Thomas Wynne, and Thomas ab Llewelyn, &c., and have stumbled in the reading of it, as now plainly appears to me; and what, if I tell you, that you and I also have slipped in one place: I am sure we have.

I am tired now, and have no more to say, but I cough a little less than I did a week ago; and am likely to live till winter at least, unless some unforeseen accident happens. It will be a hard battle, if I hold out all the winter. You are now in your bloom of body and spirit; do not lose a moment; you will be sorry if you do. God be with you, and keep you.

I am yours sincerely,

Penbryn, July 4, 1760. LEWIS MORRIS.

The same to the same.

DEAR SIR,

It is a long while since I heard from you, and really I don't know when; for my long and dangerous illness has eradicated all former transactions out of my memory, so that I have but a very faint idea of my former letters sent or received. From the beginning of November to this time, I have been struggling with death at his door; and in the very height of my fever, an accident by fire had likely to have destroyed me and mine. Such shocks are terrible, and enough to deface all correspondence. I am now beginning to be able to sit down to write a little, and but very little; for I am severely troubled with an asthma, which I suppose will finish me one day or other. *Chwilio, chwilio a ffaelio cael eich llythyr diwaethaf mewn modd yn y byd.* At the time when a pleuretic fever knocked me down, I was fitting up a new closet for my books and papers, and ever since everything has been in confusion, so that I am as long finding out a book or paper, as if I was in Mostyn Library.

Now I think on it, my brother of the navy office tells me, that you have lately met with two or three copies of Brut y Brenhinoedd at Mostyn. I shall be very much obliged to you for an extract of the beginning of each, and of the conclusion, to see if we can come at a genuine copy, which hath not been mixed with Galfrid or Walter; and should be glad to know if you have met with any British books written in the old letter (called now the Saxon), besides a line or two, in the beginning of the Welsh Charter, in Liber Landavensis, which you sent me; and whether all that charter be not written in the same character, or any thing else in that book. This seems to me to be the case with respect to that character, that it was the one which the Druids used, and all Britain and its islands, before the Roman conquest. That the provincial Britains, immediately under the Roman power took the Roman letters; therefore we are not to look for the old character among the Loegrian Britains, nor the Armoricans, nor the Cornish. That the Druids taking their shelter in Wales, Ireland, and the highlands of the North, the British party *there* retained the old character; but the Roman party took to their new letter; and in process of time, both the Roman and British characters were mixed; as we find them upon some tombstones in Wales, (but not in England) soon after the Saxon conquest. The Irish still retain their old letter; but it seems the Britains laid it quite aside, about the time of the Norman conquest, or before. The North Britains retained it for some time, as appears by those ancient verses, which Mr. Edward Llwyd mentions, and which he takes to be the Pictish. The inscriptions on Pabo's and Iestin's tombs, are proofs of what I say; and that of Catamanus, in Llangadwaladyr, of the mixed letter. Mr. Thomas Carte, who had the loan of the Liber Landav. sent me word, that it was written in the Saxon character. It seems he only dipt into the beginning of it, and took all the rest to be the same, or perhaps there may be passages in it here and there, which are in that character. You told me that all the old grants were written in a good strong hand, like my *Cnute's grant*, but better rather; and yet in the donation of Iudhail, which you sent me, I find some of the old characters. I also observe that if all the book is written in the same strong good hand, it is not an original; for it is impossible to find persons to write the same hand for hundreds of years successively; and if I remember well, Sir John Pryse, in his defence of British History, mentions some grants, which were scarcely legible in the Liber Landav. in his time; and yet you say, that there are donations therein down to bishop Herwaldus, about 1104. Doth not that shew that the book is only a copy, taken after the Norman conquest, with some notes of later date?

Set me right in these things; for I am at an entire loss about them. This is all I have leisure to write at present, and should be glad to hear from you—who am,

Yours sincerely,

LEWIS MORRIS.

Penbryn, February 4, 1761.

The same to the same.

DEAR SIR,

A person told me lately, that he had seen you at Hengwrt, in your way home from me; and that you were permitted to look over what MSS. you pleased; and that you translated them off hand into English, as if they had been the common text of the Welsh Bible.

I was very glad of this, and I hope you have met there with the so much desired copy of Nennius, which has had the benefit of Mr. Robert Vaughan's hand, and which must be the test to all others; and then we shall see a genuine Nennius come out in English, as far as the nature of the thing will bear.

If I can be of any service to you in this arduous task, nothing of my endeavours shall be wanting; and for God's sake begin to translate into English, as fast as you can, and let me see it as you go on, perhaps I may help you to some notes, or some illustrations or other. I have Nennius and Tyssilio much at heart, and I cannot be long on this side the grave.

Inclosed I send you the old papers, you talked of when here. I never looked into them till now; and cannot guess at the authors quoted therein, except G. for Galfrid; T. W. Thomas Williams, and H. Lh. Humphry Llwyd. What is Scr. Sc., and H. C.?

Be sure to keep up your correspondence with that very curious and valuable man, Mr. Percy. I am afraid that there are not many such learned critics in the kingdom.

I was heartily sorry to see you in those foolish difficulties, when you were here last. For heaven's sake, for your own sake, and for the sake of us all, do not run yourself into those excesses; but shew the world that you have not only learning and knowledge, far above the common herd; but that you have also discretion and prudence, without which no man will ever arrive at greatness. Nennius will set you up out of the reach of little folks, if you stick to him.

I am yours sincerely,

LEWIS MORRIS.

Penbryn, June 26, 1763.

Rev. W. Wynn to the Rev. Evan Evans.

Iolo Goch, o Goed Puntwn, yn Mhlwy Llan Nefydd yn Sir Ddinbych; y mae yno glwt o dir a elwir, y dydd heddyw, Gardd Iolo.—The tradition is fresh in the neighbourhood. I have read in the little book many good C. of D. ap Gwilym since I saw you, tho' there are some very poor ones amongst them. What I had then read were looked over in haste, and it is impossible to form a right judgment of such things, without a careful perusal, especially when there are uncommon words or various readings to disturb the attention, as there are many in this book. I desire you'll dash out of my Cywydd y Farn—*Tawdd y mellt greigiau gelltydd*, and insert these two in their stead—*Rhed fflfil rhawd ufelfellt, Rhua drwy'r main rheieider mellt*—See Edm. Pr. and Wm. Cynwal, Cyw. 29. I have had access to Llannerch library for three days successively, where there are a great many MSS., though few to your taste or mine.—English history, exploded philosophy, monkish theology, and such trash in abundance, written on fine vellum, in a most curious manner. Three good pedigree books, six or seven volumes of Welsh poetry, but for the most part very incorrect. Some of them are most shamefully mangled by the transcribers. I have borrowed one large quarto, transcribed about the conclusion of Queen Elizabeth's reign, by an ignorant, slovenly fellow, who has murdered the orthography in a most barbarous manner. Yet I think it valuable, because, upon collating some parts of it with other copies, I found it in the general more genuine than the common run, notwithstanding the barbarity of the orthography. Where *tarw garw* occur, this scribbler always robs the line of a syllable, which is the greatest injury he commits. I have transcribed *Duchan Gwyddelyn*, o waith Iolo. Marwnad Mad. ap Gr. Mailor, 1236, by Ein. Wan, Mar. Tywysog Llew. ap Gr. by Gwgon, Mar. Ow. Goch; a gânt Bleddyn Fardd; Cyw. merch da, o waith G. O.; Cyw. da i ofyn Cledd, o waith G. O.; Mar. Lleucu Llwyd, o waith I. Ll. G. M. H. Mar. Ll. G. M. H., o waith Iolo.

There is at Llannerch a little old rag, consisting of about 20 pages accurately written, out of which I have transcribed a curious ode if not two. It begins thus: *Nid wyf ddihynwyf hoen. Kreirwy hoywdec am hudawdd mal Garwy.* After eight Englyns, there is a blank, without the author's name, and below that begins either another ode of the same person's, or a remainder of the foregoing, beginning thus: *Mireinwawr drefawr dra vo brad ymddwyn*, and subscribed Howel ap Eignion ai cant i Vevanwy vechan o Gastell Dinas Bran. After the last stanza is written *Mireinwawr drefawr*, with a dash, which makes me suppose they are two poems, though on the same subject; because it is common to conclude an ode with a repetition of the first stanza.—Quare, Whether the first of these is not the same with your Awdl Myfanwy? I cannot recollect, but I think it is longer than yours; it ends thus:

Lliw eiry cynnar pen Aran—
Lloer bryd lwys fryd o lys Vran.

I lately borrowed a quarto, fairly written by a man of learning and great knowledge in antiquities, but ignorant of the Welsh prosody, for which reason it is not very correct. There are many of D. G. in it, Owdl Fair, by I. R. I. Ll. of Gogerddan; one quarter of which is Latin. I have seen the same in another book given to D. N—, Mawl Edw. 3 ryw bryd gwedi Aarfa Cressi, o waith Iolo.—That battle was fought in the year 1346.—Edw. IIId. died 1377.—This is demonstration that Iolo ought to have been placed much higher in chronology than the year 1400; and by his own testimony we find he was a mere *Cleiriach* before the commencement of the 15th century, though he lived about ten years after. This, though in Iolo's usual style, I think the most ancient Cywydd I ever saw, excepting one of D. Ddu, *Digam gwnaeth Duw oi gymwyd;* and even this is, by some, fathered upon Iolo. *Mar. Tywysog Llewelyn*—Gwaith Bleddyn Fardd—Iolo Goch was of the family of the Pantons, of Coed Panton, and Plas Panton, in the parish of Llan Nefydd, Denbighshire. The Latin version in Saphics of Taliesin's ode *Ef a wnaeth Panton,* and some good *Cywydds* of Iolo's, that I never saw before, M. D. ap Gr. ap Llew—a lâs yn y Mwythig, a gant

Bleddyn Fardd, Dadolwch Rhys, ap Gr. ap Rhys ap Tewdwr, Gwelygorddiau Powys, Breiniau Powys: those three by Cynddelw Br. Mawr.

A small volume was lately given me collected by Mr. Ellis Wynne, of Lasynys, it contains a great many fragments of British prophecies; by Rys Fardd eight; by Ithel Bardd y Bendro one; by Merddin (wyllt I presume) nineteen; by Robin Ddu two; by Ieu. Drwch y Daran one; by Bercam one; by Adda Fras; by Gronwy Ddu; by Jonas Mynyw one; Proffwydoliaeth Dewi St. Bardd Cwsc nine; by Taliesin, on various subjects, fifteen. The matter of those that bear the name of Merddin, may be his, but I judge they are not his compositions by the style, though it is not modern. Some called Taliesin's, I believe were forged by the Monks, others I think genuine. The prophecies are worth reading, on account of the style and names of places.

I have the constitutions of the Cymmrodorion, and am highly pleased with their scheme. I will contribute something in money, tho I have children, towards promoting it, and with pleasure do all in my power as a corresponding member. Gronwy's ode is an excellent thing; but what he calls *Cadwyn fyr* is erroneous, because it is in reality *Cadwyn gyflawn*. I do not blame him for this, because Dr. IDR's imperfect rule and false examples led him into this error. Some, perhaps, may be offended because the ode part is not *unirythm*, which it is supposed to be by the very name; but I do not like the poem the worse for that. I shewed you the true *Cadwyn fyr* in W. Ll's grammar, and likewise in S. F's.—I have since had the same in a book of Gr. Hira, who was the chief professor of the age, and a perfect master of the faculty, though, in my opinion he had no extraordinary genius. His tutor was Tudur Aled, who was nephew and pupil to D. Edm., yr hwn a ddychymygawdd y mesur Cadwyn fyr.

It were false concord to call it *Cadwyn fyr*. D. ap Edmund's tutor was Mered. ap Rhys, of Rhiwabon, witness G. Gl.—Y mae genyf bedwar pedwar ar hugain cerdd Dant Crwth. —Ar 24 cerdd dant telyn, a hanes yr eisteddfod gyntaf yn Nghaerwys.—To-day I saw an account of Merddin a' Mhorfryn's being buried in Ynys Enlli. Here patience and paper end together. Remember me to my old neighbours.

Yours affectionately,

WM. WYNN.

Ll. Gynhafal, Dec. 13, 1755.

Dr. Percy, late Bishop Dromore, to the Rev. Evan Evans.

SIR,

By my friend Mr. Williams, rector of Weston, Staffordshire, I have been informed of the great attention you have bestowed on British Literature, and the pains you have taken to rescue the productions of your ancient Bards from oblivion. Though I have not the happiness to understand, yet I have a great veneration for, the ancient language of this Island, and have always had a great desire to see some of the most early and most original productions in it. I could never yet obtain a proper gratification of this desire; for, to their shame be it spoken, most of your countrymen, instead of vindicating their ancient and truly venerable mother tongue from that contempt, which is only the result of ignorance, rather encourage it by endeavouring to forget it themselves. Besides my friend Mr. Williams, whose constant residence in England has deprived him of the means of cultivating his native language so much as he would have done, I never met with one native of Wales, who could give me any satisfactory account of the literary productions of his own country, or seemed to have bestowed any attention on its language and antiquities. Not so the Scots:—they are everywhere recommending the antiquity of their own country to public notice, vindicating its history, and setting off its poetry, and, by dint of constant attention to their grand national concern, have prevailed so far, as to have the broken jargon they speak to be considered as the most proper language for our pastoral poetry. Our most polite ladies affect to lisp out Scottish airs; and in the Senate itself whatever relates to the Scottish Nation is always mentioned with peculiar respect. Far from blaming this attention in the Scotch, I think it much to their credit, and am sorry, that a large class of our fellow-subjects, with whom we were united in the most intimate union for many ages, before Scotland ceased to be our *most* inveterate enemy, have not shewn the same respect to the peculiarities of their own country. But, by their supineness and neglect, have suffered a foolish and inveterate prejudice to root itself in the minds of their compatriots, the English,—a prejudice which might have been in a good measure prevented, had the Welsh gentlemen occasionally given them specimens of the treasures contained in their native language, which may even yet be in part removed by the same means.

You have translated, I am informed, some of the Odes of your ancient Bards. I wish you would proceed and make a select collection of the best of them, and so give them to the world. You have probably heard what a favourable reception the public has given to an English version of some Erse Fragments imported from the Highlands of Scotland, and, if you have never seen them, I will send them to you. I am verily persuaded, an elegant translation of some curious pieces of ancient British Poetry would be as well received, if executed in the same manner. I may modestly pretend to have some credit with the booksellers, and with Mr. Dodsley in particular, who is my intimate friend. I shall be very happy to do you any good office with him, and shall be glad to make such an attempt as profitable to you as, I am persuaded, it will be reputable both to you and your country.

I have prevailed on a friend to attempt a Translation of some ancient Runic Odes, composed among the snows of Norway, which will make their appearance at Mr. Dodsley's shop next winter. My very learned friend and neighbour, the Rev. Mr. Lye, editor of Junius's Etymologicon, and of Ulphila's Gothic Gospels, (whose skill in the northern languages has rendered him famous all over Europe,) is now rescuing some valuable remains of Saxon Poetry from oblivion, and I can perhaps obtain leave of him to let you see one of these odes by way of specimen, accompanied with his version. I have not been altogether idle myself; but my attention has been chiefly bestowed on the languages spoken in the southern parts of Europe. I have collected some curious pieces of ancient Spanish Poetry, and when I have translated a select collection of them, may perhaps, give them to the public. Amidst the general attention of ancient and foreign poetry it would be a pity to leave that of the Ancient Britons forgotten and neglected, and therefore, when I heard that a person so capable was employed in collecting and translating those valuable remains, it gave me a very sensible pleasure, and I could not help expressing in a *volunteer* letter to you, the sense I entertain of the obligation, which you will undoubtedly confer on all real lovers of literature and the productions of antiquity.

If you will favour me with a line containing a more particular account of what has been the object of your labours, I shall be able to form a more exact idea of the success, that may be expected from them than I can at present. I will also communicate them to several eminent Literati of my acquaintance, and to mention one in particular, Mr. Johnson, the author of the Dictionary, Rambler, &c., who will, I am sure, be glad to recommend your work, and to give you any advice for the most advantageous disposal of it. If you take these voluntary offers of service in good part, you will please to favour me with a line, and I would wish also a specimen of your labours, together with a full direction where to write to you. I am a Clergyman, and shall receive any favour of this kind, that is enclosed under a cover to the Right Honourable Henry Earl of Sussex, at Easton Maudit Castle, by the Ashby Bag, Northamptonshire.

I am Sir, though unknown,

Your very faithful obedient servant,

Easton Maudit, July 21, 1761. THOMAS PERCY.

P. S. I am told you are acquainted with Mr. Gray, the poet. Pray has he any foundation for what he has asserted in his Ode on the British Bards, viz. that there is a tradition among the inhabitants of Wales, that our Edward the First destroyed all the British Bards that fell into his hands? The existence of such a tradition has been doubted.

The same to the same.

DEAR SIR,

That I have so long defer'd answering your very obliging letter has been altogether owing to the following cause. I proposed sending you a Saxon ode, accompanied with a Latin literal and an English free version; the former done by my very learned friend Mr. Lye, from out of whose curious collections I transcribed both it and the original. But, having left it with him to give it a revise, he has unfortunately mislaid both the original and copy, so that, although he has for this month past occasionally endeavour'd to recover them, he has not been able to succeed. As soon as they emerge from the immense ocean of his papers, you may depend upon receiving this curious specimen of Saxon poetry. In the mean time I would not defer any longer returning you thanks for the curious and valuable contents of your letter. I admire your Welsh ode very much; it contains a large portion of the sublime. The images are very bold and animated, and poured forth with such rapidity, as argues an uncommon warmth of imagination in the bard, whose mind seems to have been so filled with his subject, and the several scenes of the war appear to have so crowded in upon him, that he has not leisure to mark the transitions with that cool accuracy, which a feebler genius would have been careful to have done. It is one continued fiery torrent of poetic flame, which, like the eruptions of Etna, bears down all opposition.

You must pardon me if I think your critical friend quite mistaken in his remarks on this ode. He confounds two species of poetry as distinct and different as black and white. Epic poetry delights in circumstance, and it is only in proportion as it is circumstantial that it has merit; the very essence of it (as its name implies) is narration. So a narrative, deveid of all circumstances, must be very jejune, confused, and unsatisfactory. But here lies the great art of the epic poet,—that he can be minute and circumstantial without descending from the sublime, or exciting other than grand and noble ideas. Thus, when Homer describes the stone, which Diomede threw at Æneas, had he only told us in general terms, that it was a large one,

——— Ο δε χερμαδιον λαβε χειρι
Τυδειδης, μεγα εργον, ———

had he stopped here, as many an inferior poet would have done, should we have had so great an idea of the hero's strength or vigour, as when he adds the following particular and striking circumstances?

——— Ο ου δυω γ' ανδρε φεροιεν,
Οιοι νυν βροτοι εισ', ο δε μιν ρεα παλλε και οιος.
Iliad E. l. 304.

On the other hand, it is the essence of ode to neglect circumstance, being more confin'd in its plan, and having the sublime equally for its object. In order to attain this, it is obliged to deal in general terms, to give only such hints as will forcibly strike the imagination, from which we may infer the particulars ourselves. It is no demerit or disparagement in your bard to have neglected the minute circumstances of the battle, because it would have been impossible for him to have described them within the narrow limits of his ode. Here lies his great merit, that he hints, he drops, and the images he throws out, supply the absence of a more minute detail, and excite as grand ideas as the best description could have done. And so far I agree with your critical friend, that no poet ever hit upon a grander image than that of "*A Menai heb drai o drallanw*," &c., nor could take a nobler method to excite our admiration at the prodigious cause of so amazing an effect. So much for criticism.

Soon after I received your letter I was down at Cambridge, where I had the good fortune to meet with Mr. Gray, the poet, and spent an afternoon with him at his chambers. Our discourse turned on you and the Welsh poetry: I shewed him your letter, and he desired leave to transcribe the passage relating to King Edward's massacre of the Welsh bards. All the authority he had before, it seems, was only a short hint in Carte's history: he seemed very glad of this authentic extract. We both join'd in wishing a speedy conclusion to your historical labours, that you might be at leisure to enter upon this far more noble field of ancient British poetry. Excuse me if I think the recovery of particular facts from oblivion, any further than as they contribute to throw light upon compositions, not half of so much consequence to the world, as to recover the compositions themselves.

Your nation and ours are now happily consolidated in one firm indissoluble mass, and it is of very little importance, whether Llewelyn or Edward had the advantage in such a particular encounter. At least very few (even learned and inquisitive readers) will interest themselves in such an enquiry,—whereas the productions of genius, let them come from what quarter they will, are sure to attract the attention of all. Every reader of taste, of whatever country or faction, listens with pleasure, and forms a higher or meaner opinion of any people, in proportion as they are affected by this exertion of their intellectual powers. To give an instance, that is parallel to your own case, the Danes and Swedes have, for this century past, been rescuing their ancient writings from oblivion; they have printed off their Icelandic Histories, and collected what they could of their ancient Runic Poems. The latter have attracted the attention of all Europe; while the former are no otherwise regarded, than as they contribute to throw light on the latter. A very celebrated Frenchman has lately translated some curious specimens of them into his own language; and Mr. Dodsley will soon print a curious Spicilegium of the same kind in English, of which I will procure a copy and send you when printed off. But who will be at the pains (except a few northern antiquaries) to give a careful perusal to the other? I have this moment a voluminous *corpus* of them (lately borrowed) before me. Even curious and inquisitive, as you are yourself, into historical facts, let me ask you if you would be willing to read 800 pages folio, in a barbarous literal Latin version, concerning the exploits of King Haquin Sarli; the mighty achievements of Ghorfinna Harlecefni, and of twenty other valiant barbarians? Yet, when you come to read the native undenied poetic descriptions of the ancient Runic Bards, their forcible images, their strong paintings, their curious display of ancient manners, I defy the most torpid reader not to be animated and affected; and then we are content to make some enquiry after the history of these savage heroes, that we may understand the songs, of which they are the subjects. In like manner, with regard to your own Owain Gwynedd, without intending the least disrespect to so valiant a prince, I believe few readers will desire to know any further of his history, than as it will serve for a comment to Gwalchmai's very sublime and animated Ode. After all, I would not have any historical monuments perish, or be totally neglected. They may come into use upon a thousand occasions, that we cannot at present foresee, and therefore I am glad, that the northern nations have been careful to secure even the above (to us uninteresting) narratives from destruction. And I should be very glad to have the same care taken of those of the ancient Britons. But I think the first care is due to these noble remains of ancient genius, which are in so much greater danger of perishing, because so much harder to be understood.

How strongly is our curiosity excited by the mention you make (in your letter to Mr. Williams), of the Epic Poem, written in A.D. 578, and the other works of Aneurin Gwawdrydd. What a noble field for literary application to rescue such a fine monument of antiquity from oblivion : to which every revolving year of delay will most certainly consign it, till it is lost for ever! *His Labor, hoc opus.* I hope, dear Sir, you will take in good part the freedom, with which I have ventured to advise you on a subject, of which you are so much a better judge than myself; but my zeal, though it may be blind, is well meant. I would fain excite you to direct that application, which you so laudably bestow on your ancient language, in such a manner as may be most profitable to yourself, and most reputable to your country.

Macpherson goes on furiously in picking up subscriptions for his proposed Translation of the ancient Epic Poem in the Erse Language ; though hardly one reader in ten believes the specimens produced to be genuine. Much greater attention would be due to an editor, who rescues the original itself from oblivion, and fixes its meaning by an accurate version. I entirely agree with you, that a Latin version, as literal as possible, should accompany such ancient pieces, but then I would also have you subjoin at the same time a liberal English translation. By this means your book will take in all readers, both the learned and the superficial. This method of publication has been attended with great success among the northern nations, where all their Runic Pieces have been confronted both with a literal version in Latin, aud a more spirited one in the modern languages either of Sweden or Denmark. Were you to endeavour to collect into a *corpus* all the remains of your ancient poetry, and print it by subscription begun among your own countrymen, and warmly recommended by them to us, it would certainly pay well, and be a very valuable present to the public ; but then you ought to send forth a few select pieces into the world, previous to such an undertaking, to bespeak the good opinion of mankind, and this, whenever you please to execute it, shall be attended with my warmest services. In the mean time I hope you will continue to favour me with specimens of your ancient poetry as often as your leisure will permit; and, if any thing else that is curious should occur in the course of your studies, you will confer a great pleasure by imparting it to,

Dear Sir, your very faithful and obedient servant,

Easton Maudit, Oct. 15, 1761. THOMAS PERCY.

N.B. I shall defer sending a specimen of Runic Poetry till I send you the whole collection printed, which you may depend on. May I hope to see your Latin Essay on British Poetry?

The same to the same.

DEAR SIR,

I know not whether the favour you have done me, in having wrote to me once or twice, entitles me to address you with the familiarity of a near acquaintance; but I have ventured to trouble you with a voluntary letter. I presume you have received a very long one from me through the medium of Mr. Williams. In that I requested to know if you had any good old popular ballads in the Welsh language on historical and romantic subjects. This was not a random question. I have in my possession a very ancient MS. collection of such pieces in our own language, some of which will throw great light on our old poets. I have selected two for your inspection, which, when perused, do me the favour to return, and inform me whether you can remember any on the same subjects in the

Cambrian tongue. I have reason to believe both the inclosed pieces are of great antiquity. The fragment is certainly more ancient than the time of Chaucer, who took his Old Wife of Bath's tale from it, as any one upon perusal will be convinced, and consequently that the song was not taken from Chaucer. I cannot help thinking many of these pieces, about King Arthur, translations from the ancient British tongue; and it is in order to receive information on this subject, that I now apply to you. I am going to print a select collection of these old pieces, not only on account of the merit of the poetry which they contain, (and even these display proofs of great invention,) but also as conducing to illustrate our best old poets, who frequently allude to these compositions. As the press waits, I would intreat the favour of a speedy answer. I shall soon be able to send you a specimen of some Runic poetry; which, you will find, bears a surprising similitude to your own Welsh songs, more specimens of which, at your leisure, will oblige,

Dear Sir, your most faithful servant,

Easton Maudit, Nov. 22, 1761. THOMAS PERCY.

The same to the same.

DEAR SIR,

I received the favour of your obliging letter and the valuable present of the two British Odes translated into English. They have afforded me great pleasure, and they display a rich vein of poetry. I think a select collection of such pieces, thrown into a shilling pamphlet, would not fail to prove as acceptable to the public as the Erse Fragments, and would be far more satisfactory, because you could remove all suspicions of their genuineness, which, I am afraid, Mr. Macpherson is not able to do. I observe with you a remarkable similarity between our Runic and your British pieces. As our Runic Poetry will be fit for publication towards Michaelmas, I wish you could get ready such another Collection of British Poetry to follow it in due time, while the curiosity of the public is fixed on these subjects. And, when all these pamphlets have had their day, then throw them into a volume under some such title as this, "Specimens of the Ancient Poetry of different Nations." I have for some time had a project of this kind, and, with a view to it, I am exciting several of my friends to contribute their share. Such a work might fill up two neat pocket volumes. Besides the Erse Poetry, the Runic Poetry, and some Chinese Poetry, that was published last winter, at the end of a book called "Han Kirn Choaan," or the Pleasing History, 4 vols.,—besides these, I have procured a MS. translation of the "Tagrai Carmen," from the Arabic; and have set a friend to translate Solomon's Song afresh from the Hebrew, with a view to the Poetry. This also is printing off, and will soon be published in a shilling pamphlet. Then I have myself gleaned up specimens of East Indian Poetry, Peruvian Poetry, Lapland Poetry, Greenland Poetry; and inclosed I send you a specimen of Saxon Poetry. The subject is a victory gained by the Anglo-Saxon, Athelstan, over the Dane Anlafe and his confederate Constantine King of Scotland. If you compare it with the Runic Ode of *Regner Lodbrog*, you will see a remarkable affinity between them, some of the phrases and imagery being common to both, as the play of arms, &c., &c. The Latin version falls from the pen of my very learned friend Mr. Lye, who has made many important emendations in the original. The English was a slight attempt of my own, to see if one could not throw a little spirit into a literal interlineary version, but I have no reason to boast of my success. I believe the best way would be to publish the English by itself, like the Runic Odes, and throw the two columns of Latin and Saxon to the end. Give me your opinion of my proposal, with regard to the various specimens mentioned above, and the share I would recommend to yourself in particular. Be pleased also to return my Saxon Ode, when perused, for I have kept no copy.

I suppose you have no British Poetry extant, that was written before the conversion to Christianity, as we have of the Runic, and as they affect to have of the Erse; if not, then the most ancient you have is to be chosen. Could not you give some of the Poetry of Taliesin and Merddin? I must observe one thing, that your Odes will require a few explanatory Notes, chiefly with regard to the proper names; and, if you would not think it too great an innovation, I could wish you would accommodate some of your ancient British names somewhat more to our English pronunciation. This is what the Erse translator has done, and, I think, with great judgment. The word might be a little smoothed and liquidated in the text, and the original spelling retained in the margin. Thus Macpherson has converted Lambhdearg into Lamderg, Geolchopack (a woman's name) into the soft word Gealcossa, &c. This is a liberty assumed in all languages; and indeed, without it, it would not be possible for the inhabitants of one nation to pronounce the proper names of another.

You tell me you have read Bartholinus's book of Danish Antiquities; it is a most excellent performance. There is a celebrated Frenchman, the Chevalier Mallet, historiographer to the present King of Denmark, who has lately published a work in French on the same subject, at the end of which he has given a French translation of the famous Edda or Alcoran (if you suffer me to use the word) of the ancient Teutonic nations. If I have health and leisure, I intend to translate this book into English, though it is a formidable undertaking, being a quarto of no small size. I have got the book, which is a capital performance.

I should have one advantage over most others for such an attempt, which is, that my learned neighbour, Mr. Lye, has got the Islandic original of the Edda, and would compare my version with it. I have one thing still to mention, and then I have done. I have lately been employed in a small literary controversy with a learned friend, about the original and antiquity of the popular notion concerning Fairies and Goblins. My friend is for fetching that whimsical opinion from the East, so late as the time of the Crusades, and derives the words Elf and Goblin from the Guelfs and Gibbeline factions in Italy. But I think it would be impossible for notions so arbitrary to have obtained so universally, so uniformly, and so early (see Chaucer's Wife of Bath's Tale), if they had not got possession of the minds of men many ages before. Nay, I make no doubt but Fairies are derived from the *Daergar* or Dwarfs, whose existence was so generally believed among all the northern nations. Can you, from any of your ancient British writers, enable me to ascertain any of these disputed points, or any resemblance to the name of Fairy, Elf, Goblin, in your language? I should think, that these popular superstitions are aboriginal in the island, and are remains of the ancient Pagan creed. Favour me with your opinion on this subject when you write next, which, as your letters are so extremely curious and fraught with entertainment, I beg may be soon.

I remain, Sir, your very faithful servant,

Thomas Percy.

The same to the same.

Dear Sir,

I received your obliging letter, which is so curious, that I cannot but request the repetition of such valuable favours. I am going to draw up a short Essay on the origin and progress of our English poetry, in which I shall have occasion to be very particular in my account of our metrical Romances; and, as I believe many of these are drawn from old British fables, if not downright translations from the ancient British language, I should be extremely obliged to you, if you would give the titles, and, if possible, a short account of the subjects, of all such Romances, as are contained in the vellum manuscript, which you mention, or any other, which you may remember to have seen. I have a notion, that we have many of them translated into English and thence into French and other southern languages.

Inclosed I send you a little Essay on the origin &c. of the English drama. Bishop Warburton has handled the subject before me in the 5th vol. of his Shakespeare; but, as he derives all his information from the French critics, and his instances from the French stage, you will conclude, that he is often wide of the mark and generally superficial. Yet he has one extract from Carew's Survey of Cornwall, relating to the old Cornish plays, which I recommend to your notice; because I could wish to know, (not now, but at any future leisure,) whether you have any thing similar in Wales. The passage from Carew is this. "The Guary Miracle, in English, Miracle-Play, is a kind of interlude compiled, in Cornish, out of some scripture history. For representing this they raise an earthen amphitheatre, in some open field, having the diameter of this inclosed plain some 40 or 50 feet. The country people flock from all sides to see and hear it: for they have therein devils and devices to delight as well the eye as the ear. The players conne not their parts without books, but are more prompted by one called the Ordinary, who followeth at their heels, with the book in his hand." In an act of Parliament, 4th Hen. IV., mention is made of certain *Wastours*, Master Rimours (Rimers) and Minstrels, who infested the land of Wales, to make commorths or gatherings upon the people there. Query the meaning of this? I am afraid, lest I should be too troublesome with my queries, and, therefore, reserve what you please to answer at any future hour; only send me an account of your romances now, which will oblige, dear Sir, your affectionate and faithful servant,

THOMAS PERCY.

Easton Maudit, *March*, 20, 1763.

The same to the same.

DEAR SIR,

I have been many months indebted to you for a very obliging letter. I delayed to answer it, in expectation of seeing your curious Specimens of the Ancient British Poetry, advertised, from the press before this time. Permit me to enquire, what forwardness that intended publication (which you gave me hopes in your last of seeing speedily printed) is in? From the translations, you have already favoured me with a sight of, I conceive a very favourable idea of the merits of your ancient bards, and should be sorry to have their precious relics swallowed up and lost, in the gulph of time; a danger which they will incur, if you, that are so well acquainted with their beauties, and so capable of making them understood by others, neglect this opportunity of preserving them. I can readily conceive, that many of their most beautiful peculiarities cannot possibly be translated into another language, but even through the medium of a prose translation one can discern a rich vein of poetry, and even classical correctness, infinitely superior to any other compositions of that age, that we are acquainted with. Certain I am, that our own nation, at that time, produced nothing that wears the most distant resemblance to their merit.

I have lately been collecting specimens of English poetry, through every age, from the time of the Saxons, down to that of Elizabeth, and am ashamed to show you what wretched stuff our rhimers produced at the same time that your bards were celebrating the praise of Llewelyn, with a spirit scarce inferior to Pindar. Inclosed I send you a specimen of an Elegy on the death of Edward I.—that cruel Edward, who made such havoc among the Cambrian poets. I know not whether you will be able to decipher these foul scrawls, or distinguish them from the marginal explications, with which I have accompanied them.

But you will see enough to be convinced of the infinite superiority of your own bards; nor do I know, that any of the nations of the continent (unless perchance Italy, which now about began to be honoured by Dante) were able at that time to write better than the English. The French, I am well assured, were not. One thing is observable in the Elegy on Edward the First, which is, that the poet, in order to do the more honour to his hero, puts his eulogium in the mouth of the Pope, with the same kind of fiction as a modern bard would have raised up Britannia or the genius of Europe, sounding forth his praises. Considering the destruction which our merciless monarch made among the last sons of ancient genius, it may be looked upon as a just judgment upon him, that he had no better than these miserable rhimes to disgrace his memory.

With regard to your Specimens, should they not yet be put to the press, I should take it for a great favour if you would indulge me with a sight of them in MS., or at least the Dissertation to be prefixed to them; an indulgence that would not be abused, and which, under whatever restrictions you please, would oblige, dear Sir,

Your very affectionate and faithful servant,

Thomas Percy.

Easton Maudit, Dec. 31, 1763.

The same to the same.

Dear Sir,

It is with pleasure I perform all your requests: inclosed you have the transcript from Wormius which you desired. As his book relates only to the Runic letters and ancient manner of writing, it did not fall within his subject professedly to treat of the Islandic prosody; he has, therefore, only described one species of verse out of innumerable others, and this, as it were, by the bye and by way of specimen. He refers to the *Edda*, or old Islandic book of prosody, for the rest; this book I have not seen.—There is another *Edda*, which I have, that explains the Islandic mythology, and of this I shall publish, ere long, a translation, with some curious notes and dissertations of *M. Mallet*, the present historiographer to the King of Denmark, as you may remember I have hinted in the preface to my specimens of Runic Poetry.

When may one hope to see your *Dissertatio de Bardis*? I am fond of the subject, and have great expectations of your manner of handling it. I thank you for your friend's preface; though he is not much master of English style, the particulars he produces are curious. I have turned to my learned friend Mr. Lye's edition of *Junii Etymologicon Anglicanum* for the etymology of such words as your friend mentions, and I find nothing, that does not confirm his derivations; I have not time now to descend to particulars, but shall be glad to hear from you as soon as agreeable. One so much master, as you are, of British antiquities, whether historic or poetical, can never want means of entertaining,

Dear Sir, your very affectionate servant,

Easton Maudit, April 10, 1764. Thomas Percy.

P. S. Pray, are the Welsh romances, you have described, in prose or verse? If they are in prose, then let me ask if you have ever seen any in verse? I take it, these subjects were treated in verse before they came to plain prose in most nations. This, at least, I find to be the case in the old Erse and Islandic languages, as well as in the more modern Italian, French, Spanish, and English tongues. I have got curious specimens in the last I mentioned. Pray is the word St. *Great*, or St. *Greal*, in the first article of your curious letter?

WELSH PROVERBS.

It appears that the Rev. E. Evans *(Ieuan Prydydd Hir)*, had prepared for publication a Collection of our Ancient Welsh Proverbs; for a writer in the second volume of the "Cambro Briton," gives the following translation of the Latin Preface preffixed to the MSS., which we here reprint.

Having discovered Dr. Davies of Mallwyd's Latin Translation of our Welsh Proverbs among many other ancient MSS. in the library at Llanvorda, and soon after having found, also, the original, from which his was transcribed, among the same valuable collection, I thought I could not undertake a more useful work to my country, than to publish the same, and dedicate it, as the first fruits of my labours, to my munificent patron, Sir W. W. Wynn. The exact time when that ancient bard and philosopher, called by the Welsh *Hen Gyrys o Iâl*, flourished, cannot be accurately ascertained. Two collections of Proverbs, made by him, and written on parchment, are now extant in the above library, and, at the end of the said book, a fair copy of Hywel Dda's laws; and from the best judgment, which can be formed from the appearance of the said MSS. and the mode of writing, or form of the hand, it may with safety be pronounced to be about five hundred years old. To the former of these two collections is annexed the following note respecting the author: "Mabieith Hen Gyrys o Iâl, yr hwn a elwit Bach Buddugre a Gado Gyfarwydd, a Gwynfarch Gyfarwydd, a'r hen wyrda a ddyvawt y Diarhebion o Ddoethineb, hyd pan veint gadwedig, gwedy hwynt, i roddi dysg i'r neb a synio arnynt; canys crynodeb parablan llawer a synwyren y cynghoren doethbrud a ddangosir ar vyrder, i'r neb a'u dyallo yn y diarhebion." Iâl, where this celebrated old Cyrys resided, is a mountainous district, containing five parishes, situated towards the north-east corner of the county of Denbigh; and Buddigre, where he lived, is near, if not within, the limits of the parish of Bryn Eglwys. It is evident, that this collection of Proverbs was made from various works of a great number of old bards, living in different ages; for many of them are taken from the compositions of Llywarch Hen (Llywarch the Aged), and from the poems of Aneurin and Taliesin, and several from those of other bards much more ancient, whose effusions have unfortunately perished.

It is more than probable, that many of these pithy sentences and proverbial sayings, these aphorisms of wisdom and axioms of prudence, were the productions of the venerable Druids; and they exhibit, in the present imperfect form, in which they have been delivered to us, no despicable specimens of those verses mentioned by Cæsar, in the seemingly enigmatical mysteries of which their pupils were initiated, and spent many years in acquiring and committing them to memory. And he farther informs us, that, notwithstanding these learned sages made use of Greek characters in transacting both their public and private affairs, yet their disciples were not permitted to *write* these verses, principally, (as it appeared to him,) for two reasons; in the first place, because, if they were allowed to do so, the mysteries of their profession would soon be divulged: and, secondly, if these aphorisms were committed to writing, the noviciates, confiding in such artificial aids, would no longer be at the pains of sufficiently exercising their memories. Many of these poetical proverbs are composed in that peculiar kind of metre, which is distinguished by the name of *Englyn Milwr*, and these verses are possessed of such strong internal marks of antiquity, that I may with safety pronounce them to be the genuine productions of the Druids. And, as they are by no means unworthy of being considered as the real effusions of those learned sages and philosophers, it will not, I hope, be deemed a digression, or by any means irrelevant to the object of this introduction, to gratify the reader with a specimen of one of these oracular compositions, together with a close literal Latin version. The first two lines of these poetical triplets seem to contain some of the privileges of the Druids, and the third generally exhibits some maxim of wisdom or axiom of prudence. The following were transcribed from the Red Book of Hergest, in the library of Jesus College, Oxford:—

1.	1.
Marchwiail bedw briglas, A dyn fy nhroed o wanas; Nac addef dy rin i wàs.	Virgulta betulæ viridis Meum pedem e compede solvent; Secretum tuum juveni ne reveles.
2.	**2.**
Marchwiail derw mewn llwyn, A dyn fy nhroed o gadwyn: Nac addef dy rin i forwyn.	Virgulta quercûs de luco Solvent pedem meum e catenâ: Ne reveles secretum tuum virgini.
3.	**3.**
Marchwiail derw deiliar, A dyn fy nhroed o garchar; Nac addef dy rin i lafar.	Virgulta quercûs frondosæ Pedem meum e carcere liberabunt: Ne reveles secretum tuum homini loquaci.

The foregoing stanzas, as well as many others of the same description, are still extant in the above mentioned book, called Llyfr Coch o Hergest, and likewise in several MSS. in the libraries of Llanvorda near Oswestry, and Hengwrt near Dolgellau; and, on account of their having accidentally been discovered among the compositions of that ancient bard Llywarch Hen, Dr. Davies and Edw. Llwyd have hastily and inconsiderately pronounced them to be some of his productions; but the frequent recurrence of the oak, their favourite tree, and the dark allusions to the druidical rites and privileges, most evidently and convincingly, (in my opinion,) denote their origin to be from that source. But here it may be objected, that the Druids could not, (as Cæsar declares it was not their usual practice,) have committed these verses to writing. Granted it was so in his time; yet it is manifest from the poems of our celebrated bard Taliesin, that, in subsequent times, they did not strictly adhere to this resolution; for many of their pretended mysteries are divulged in his compositions. It is also evident, that, in these early ages, the Druids were not the only persons, who were thus cautious of revealing their secrets to the vulgar; but the Bards also endeavoured to conceal their poetical rules and metres, from the public; for their book of prosody, containing the intricacies of the art, is distinguished by the name of *Cyfrinach y Beirdd*, (i. e. The Secret of the Bards,) and they were strictly prohibited from explaining these, except to their own noviciate disciples, which continued to be their practice nearly to our own times. But, notwithstanding these strict prohibitions, it is well known, that the poetical compositions of the bards were publicly recited; and it is evident that, after the commencement of the Christian æra, the Druids were not so scrupulously cautious with respect to these rules of secrecy, which may be proved from some stanzas, which I have seen in an ancient MS., denominated *Englynion Duad*, probably from a bard or druid of that name. Some few of the lines I shall here subjoin, for the inspection of the reader.

Bid gogor gan iâr,
Bid gan lew drydar,
Bid oval ar a'i câr;
Bid tôn calon gan alar.

These lines have been introduced into our Welsh proverbs; and the following remark is made on them at the end of Dr. Davies's MS. copy.

"Gwyl y rhagor y sydd rhwng y rhai hyn ar rhai sydd yn Llyfr Coch, a hen gopiau eraill; a gwybydd fod y gerdd hon yn hen iawn; gan fod cymmaint o ymrafael rhwng yr hen gopiau." i. e. Advertat lector quàm variant inter se exemplar Hergestianum et alia exemplaria in hoc cantico, et sciat, hoc carmen ob differentias prædictas esse vetustissimum.

Those learned men are, therefore, mistaken, who suppose, that the Druids never committed any of their compositions to writing; when it is evident, that these and others of their productions have been conveyed down to us. Taliesin, as I have before hinted, informs us, that be was instructed by them in many of their mysteries, particularly in that of the μετεμψυχωσις, and in many other rudiments of their philosophy. And hence it is, that his works are more obscure than those of any other of the ancient bards.

There is also a certain degree of obscurity in the very words and language of Taliesin; and the same may be observed of the compositions of Aneurin Gwawdrydd and other bards of the same age, a catalogue of whose works may be found in the learned Edward Llwyd's Archæology, collected from the notes of William Maurice, Esq., of Cefn y Braich. But Mr. E. Llwyd never saw any of the poetical compositions of Taliesin, Aneurin, and other early bards, except those of Llywarch Hen, which he found in *Llyfr Coch o Hergest:* and the works of these ancient authors will afford us very material assistance, not only in the investigation of our ancient British language, but also in examining historical facts, and in tracing the origin of the various tribes, who inhabited this island during that early period. Taliesin, in a poem, of which the following is the title, "*Cerdd am Feibion Llyr ap Brychwel Powys,*" mentions three separate nations, who had taken possession of different parts of Britain, previous to his time, viz., *Gwyddyl* (Celts or Gauls,) *Brython*, and *Romani*, (Romans.)

Gwyddyl, a Brython, a Romani,
A wna hon dyhedd, a dyfysci;
Ac am derfyn Prydein, cain ei threfl.

And they are represented as exciting war and tumult on the borders of this fair isle, and its beautiful towns and cities; and it appears evidently from this poem, that the first inhabitants were *Gwyddyl* or Celts, which circumstance Mr. Llwyd and others have proved most satisfactorily, from the names of mountains, rivers, &c. But by the word *Gwyddyl* Taliesin must, by no means, be understood to mean the modern Irish; for their language at present contains a very considerable mixture of Cantobrian and Spanish, and differs very materially from the ancient genuine Celtic and British, which clearly appears from the writings of the old bards, and the ancient British Proverbs. For, if any person were vain enough to suppose, that he could discover the meaning of some of our obsolete British words, by consulting an Irish Dictionary, he would soon find himself woefully disappointed, and I am clearly of opinion, that the ancient genuine Celtic dialect had a very near affinity to the old Welsh or British. I believe, that the persons, denominated *Gwyddyl* by Taliesin, were genuine Celtæ, and inhabited this island previous to the arrival of the Britons, and probably soon after the general deluge, and that these Celtæ were the progeny of the Titans; for the Curetes and Corybantes, who were their princes and nobles, are clearly identified with the *Cowri* of the British history, written by Tyssilio (the bishop), which Geoffrey of Monmouth has very improperly translated *Giants*. And this blunder of his has been the source of endless mistakes; for the word *Cowri* evidently means princes, generals, nobles, or persons of great eminence. The Curetes are therefore our *Cowri;* and the Corybantes (i. e. *Cowri-Bann*) were princes or persons of great eminence, as the expression denotes; and, what is still more to our purpose, the word gwyddyl also implies any thing conspicuous, and is nearly synonymous with *Cowri*, which is the usual term, even to the present day, to designate persons of uncommon stature or great bodily strength. The Curetes, therefore, were evidently our *Cowri*, and the Corybantes (i. e. *Cowri-Bann*) imply princes or leaders, or persons of the most eminent rank and consequence: and, in order to corroborate this assertion, it may be observed here, that there is a very high mountain near Towyn, in the county of Merioneth, which, to this day, bears the name of *Gwyddyl Fynydd;* and the highest peak or summit of Snowdon, is denominated *Yr Wyddfa*, (i. e. the highest eminence or the most conspicuous,) and by the common people, even at this time, is known by no other name. And *Gwydd Grug* means a high hill, or eminence; *Gwydd Fryniau*, high banks; and *Trum Gwydd*, the ridge of a mountain; and many others, which it would be tedious and useless to enumerate. And it may also be observed here, that the Κελται and Γαλαται of the Greeks, and the *Celtæ* and *Galli*, of the Latins, appear to me to bear no other import. For *Gallt* and *Allt* are clearly synonymous with *Gwyddel*, and denote any thing high or eminent, though the word *Gallt* is, at present, restricted to designate the steep ascent of a hill, or a declivity; but, that the word *Gallt* was anciently used to denominate high mountains may be justly inferred from the word *Alps*, which is evidently composed of two Celtic words, Gallt-ban, or pen, i. e. Allt-ban, Al-pen, or Alpine, which commutation or change of initial letters will appear easy to any person acquainted with the British language, and perfectly justified by the rules of grammar, as the mutations of radical letters in Welsh are well known to be nearly endless. It would not be difficult to prove, that the ancient Britons are descendants of the Celtæ, and a close connection and affinity may be traced between their language not with the ancient Celtic only but also with the Greek; and, it is at the same time very evident, that their dialect differed materially from that of the aboriginal inhabitants of this island, and whom on that account they denominated *Gaillt* and *Gwyddyl*. The British language retains to this day many words purely Greek, such as *Haul*, Ηλιος, the sun, *Dwfr*, Υδωρ, water, and many others, which have been pointed out some time by the learned *Pezron*. But, that the Britons had other words of the same import purely Celtic may be proved from the works of the ancient bards; for *huan* is made use of by Iorweith Vychan, and many other bards, to signify the *sun*,—

Llewyrch ebyr myr, morfeydd dylan;
Pan lewych *huan* ar fann fynydd.
Iorwerth Vychan.

Coruscatio portuum aquarum, et paludum marinarum;
Cum sol splendet ab excelso monte.

And the old bard, *Avan Verddig*, in his elegy on the death of Cadwallon, the son of Cadvan, makes use of *bêr* for water, instead of *dwr* or *dwfr*.

"Goluchav glew, hael, hilig Nâv Nêr,
Aded gynt, ettiynt, hyd yn *irfer* hallt."
Avan Verddig.

Exorabo potentem et liberalem Dominum Creatorem,
Iverunt ad madidam aquam salsam.

And from hence it is manifest, that *huan* and *bêr* are two ancient Celtic words; but, if any one were to consult an Irish lexicon in hopes of finding the expressions, he would be disappointed; yet he may discover *bir* among the obsolete words in that language. The names of moors, meadows, and rivers, in different parts of Wales, may also be produced as an additional evidence that *ber* and *mer* originally signified water,—for instance, *Bereu Derwenydd*, near Snowdon, *Castell y Berau*, in Llanfihangel y Pennant, in Merionethshire, where many mountain torrents meet. *Aber*, a confluence, seems also to justify this opinion, and *inver*, in the Erse dialect.

A TRANSLATION OF

CYWYDD MARWNAD LLEUCU LLWYD,

BY LLEWELYN GOCH AP MEIRIG HEN. (A BARD OF THE FOURTEENTH CENTURY.)

AN ELEGY,

TO THE MEMORY OF LLEUCU LLWYD, THE FAIR NYMPH OF PENNAL.

Lleucu Llwyd, a great beauty, was a native of Pennal, in Comit. Meirion; she was greatly beloved by Llewelyn Goch ap Meirig Hen o Nannau, and died when he was gone on a journey to South Wales; upon his return, he composed this Elegy; which is a master-piece in its kind.

"*Llyma haf llwm i hoew-fardd,*
A llyma fyd llwm i fardd;" *&c.*

LO, to the jocund Bard, here's a barren summer; to the Bard the world is desolate.

How is Venedotia bereft of its bright luminary? How its heaven is enveloped with darkness, ever since the full moon of beauty has been laid in the silent tomb! Mournful deed! a lovely Fair, in the oaken chest; my speech can find no utterance since thou art gone, O thou of shape divine! Lamp of Venedotia; how long hast thou been confined in the gloomy grave! Arise, thou that art dearer to me than life; open the dismal door of thine earthly cell! Leave, O fair one, thy sandy bed; shine upon the face of thy lover. Here by the tomb, generous maid of noble descent, stands one whose mirthful days are past, whose countenance is pale with the loss of thee; even Llewelyn Goch, the celebrater of thy praise, pining for the love of thee, helpless and forlorn, unequal to the task of song.

I heard, O thou that art confined in the deep and dismal grave, nought out of thy lips but truth, my speechless Fair! Nought, O thou of stately growth, fairest of virgins fair! But thou hadst promised, now unfeeling to the pangs of love, to stay till I came from South Wales; lovely silk-shrouded maid! The false Destinies snatched thee out of my sight; it nought concerns me to be exposed to the stormy winds, since the agreement between thee and pensive me is void! Thou! thou! lovely maid, wert true; I, even I was false; and now fruitlessly bemoan! From henceforth I will bid adieu to fair Venedotia. It concerns me not whither I go. I must forego my native soil for a virtuous maid, where it were my happiness to live, were she alive! O thou whose angelic face was become a proverb; thy beauty is laid low in the lonesome tomb! The whole world without thee is nothing, such anguish do I suffer! I, thy pensive Bard, ramble in distress, bewailing the loss of thee, illustrious maid! Where, O where shall I see thee, thou of form divine, bright as the full moon! Is it on the Mount of Olives, loveliest of women? Ovid's love was nothing in comparison of mine, lovely Lleucu; thy form was worthy of heaven, and my voice hath failed in invoking thy name. Alas! woe is me, fair maid of Pennal. It sounded as a dream to me, to hear that thy charms were laid in the dust; and those lips which I oft have praised, excelled the utmost efforts of my Muse. O my soul, whiter than the foam of the rapid streams, my love, I have now the heavy task of composing thy Elegy.

Lovely virgin! How are thy bright shining eyes closed in everlasting sleep in the stony tomb! Arise to thy pensive Bard, who can smile no more, were he possessed of a kingdom; arise in thy silken vest, lift up thy countenance from the dismal grave!

I tell no untruth, my feet are benumbed by walking around thy dwelling place, O Lleucu Llwyd, where heretofore, bright lamp of Venedotia, I was wont to celebrate thy beauty in fine flowing verse, where I was wont to be merry in praising thy delicate hand and tapering fingers, ornamented with rings of gold, lovely Lleucu, delicate sweet-tempered Lleucu! Thou wert far more precious than reliques to me! The soul of the darling of Meirionydd is gone up to God, its original Author, and her fair corpse is deposited in the sanctuary of holy ground, far, far from me in the silent tomb! The treasure of the world is left in the custody of a haughty black man. Longing and melancholy dirges are the portion of my lot. I lament with faltering accents over the lovely Lleucu! whiter than the flakes of riven snow. Yesterday I poured down my cheeks showers of tears over thy tomb. The fountains of my head are dry, my eyes are strangers to sleep, since thou art gone; thou fair-formed speechless maid hast not deigned to answer thy weeping Bard. How I lament, alas, that earth and stones should cover thy lovely face; alas that the tomb should be made so fast, that dust should ever cover the paragon of beauty, that stony walls and coffin should separate thee and me, that the earth should lock thee fast in her bosom, that a shroud should enclose a beauty that rivalled the dawn of the morn; alas that strong doors, bolts, and stately locks should divide us for ever!

EVAN EVANS, alias IEUAN PRYDYDD HIR.

CYWYDD MARWNAD LLEUCU LLWYD.

LLEUCU LLWYD ydoedd rian rinweddol, nodedig am ei glendid a'i phrydferthwch, yn byw yn Mhennal, ar lan yr afon Dyfi, oddeutu pedair milltir o Aberdyfi, ar ffordd Machynllath, yn y 14eg canrif. Cerid hi â chariad pur gan LLEWELYN GOCH AP MEIRIG HEN, o'r Nannau, gerllaw Dolgellau. Ond nid oedd ei thad mewn un modd yn foddlawn i'r garwriaeth, ac achubai bob cyfle i yru anngbariad rhwng Lleucu a Llewelyn. Un tro, dygwyddodd i Lewelyn Goch fyned ar daith i'r Deheubarth, a daeth ei thad at Lleucu, a dywedodd wrthi, er mwyn diddyfnu ei serch oddiar y bardd, fod Llewelyn wedi ymbriodi yno â merch arall. Pan glywodd Leucu yr ymadrodd hyn, hi a syrthiodd mewn llewyg, ac a drengodd yn y fan! Dychwelodd Llewelyn adref; ac ofer ceisio darlunio ei deimladau pan ddeallodd fod hyfrydwch ei lygaid wedi huno yn yr angau; a than ei deimladau cyffröus ar yr achlysur, efe a gyfansoddodd yr alarnad ganlynol, am yr hon, er holl gloffrwymau'r gynghanedd gaeth, y gellir dywedyd, megys y dywedodd Daniel Ddu am alargwyn Burns ar farwolaeth ei *Highland Mary*, mai cerdd ydyw a fydd byw nes bo i holl dyrau dawn syrthio i lynclyn annghof tragwyddol.

Yr oedd yr anffodus Lewelyn Goch yn fardd penigamp yn ei ddydd; a chyfrifir ei fod yn ei flodau o'r flwyddyn 1330 i 1370. Argraffwyd chwech o'i gyfansoddiadau yn y gyfrol gyntaf o'r *Myfyrian Archaiology of Wales;* ac y mae amryw o honynt yn aros hyd yn hyn mewn llawysgrifen heb weled goleuni dydd. Nid ydys yn gwybod fod yr alarnad a ganlyn wedi ei hargraffu erioed o'r blaen. Y mae yn ein meddiant gyfieithiad Saesonig o honi mewn rhyddiaeth, o waith Ieuan Brydydd Hir; ac efelychiad o fesur cerdd, yn yr un iaith, o waith y diweddar Risiart Llwyd, Bardd Eryri. Ysgrifenwyd marwnad Llewelyn Goch ei hun gan Iolo Goch.

Y mae, neu o leiaf yr oedd, caead arch un Lleucu Llwyd, yr hon a fu farw yn y flwyddyn 1402, i'w weled yn Eglwys Llaneurgain, yn sir Fflint; ond nid ymddengys mai Lleucu Llwyd o Bennal yw y rhian a gofféir yno. Yr oedd Lleucu Llwyd Llaneurgain yn ferch i Rys ab Rhobert, o'r Cinmael, ac yn wraig i Hywel ab Tudur, o'r Llys, ynmhlwyf Llaneurgain, ac yn nith i'r bardd Dafydd Ddu o Hiraddug. Hywel ab Tudur ydoedd un o henafiaid y teuluoedd presenol sy'n dwyn yr enw *Mostyn*

Y mae *Llewelyn a Lleucu*, yn gystal testyn cerdd a *Romeo and Juliet;* ond pa le mae'r Shacspear Cymraeg i ysgrifenu trychwawd arno?—*Y Brython.*

LLYMA haf llwm i hoew-fardd,
A llyma fyd llwm i fardd!
Nid oes yng Ngwynedd heddiw,
Na lloer, na llewyrch, na lliw,
Er pan rodded—trwydded trwch—
Dan lawr dygn dyn loer degwch.
Y ferch wen o'r dderw brenol,
Arfaeth ddig yw'r fau o'th ol!

Cain ei llun, canwyll Wynedd,
Cyd bych o fewn caead bedd!
F' enaid! cyfod i fynu,
Agor y ddaiar-ddor ddu!
Gwrthod wely tyfod hir,
A gwrtheb f' wyneb, feinir!
Mae yma, hoewdra hydraul,
Uwch dy fedd, hoew annedd haul,
Wr llwm ei wyneb hebod,
Llewelyn Goch, gloch dy glod;
Yn cynnal, hyd tra canwyf,
Cariad amddifad ydd wyf;—
Ud-fardd yn rhodio adfyd
O Dduw gwyn! hyd hyn o hyd.
Myfi, fun fwyfwy fonedd,
Echdoe a fûm uwch dy fedd,
Yn gollwng deigr lled eigr-braff
Ar hyd fy wyneb yn rhaff:
Tithau, harddlun y fun fud,
O'r tew-bwll ni'm hatebud!
Tawedawg ddwysawg ddiserch,
Ti addawsud, y fud ferch,
Fwyn dy sud fando sidan,
Fy aros, ddyn loew-dlos lân,
Oni ddelwn, gwn y gwir,
Er dy hud, o'r Deheudir,
Ni chigle, sythle saeth-lud,
Air na bai wir, feinir fud,
Iawn-dwf rhïanaidd Indeg,
Onid hyn o'th eneu teg.
Trais mawr! ac ni'm tawr i ti!
Toraist ammod, trist imi,
Tydi sydd yn y gwŷdd gwan
Ar y gwir, ddyn deg eirian!
Minnau sydd uthrydd athrist
Ar y celwydd—tramgwydd trist!

Celwyddawg iawn, cul weddi,
Celwydd lais a soniais i.
Mi af o Wynedd heddyw,
Ni'm dawr ba faenawr i fyw:
Fy myn foneddig ddigawn,
Duw'n fach, petid iach nid awn!
P'le caf, ni'm doraf dioer,
Dy weled, wendw' wiw-loer?
Ar fynydd—sathr Ofydd serch—
Olifer, yn oleu-ferch.
F' enaid yno ä'n fynych,
O'th wela', ddyn wiwdda wych.
Lleucu dêg waneg wiwnef!
Llwyr y dyhaeraist fy llef;
A genais, llygorn Gwynedd!
Eiriau gwawd i eiry 'i gwedd,
O'r geneu yn organawl,
A ganaf, tra fyddaf, fawl.
F' enaid hoen geirw afonydd!
Fy nghaniad dy farwnad fydd.
Lliw-galch rian oleugain,
Rhy gysgadur o'r mur main!
Rhiain fain, rhy anfynych
Y'th wela', ddyn wiwdda wych.
Cyfod i orphen cyfedd,
I edrych a fynych fedd;
At dy fardd ni chwardd ychwaith,
Erot, dal euraid dalaith!
Dyred, ffion ei deurudd,
I fyny o'r pridd-dŷ prudd!
Anial yw f' ol, canmoleg,
Nid twym yw fy neudroed têg,
Yn bwhwman gan annwyd
Cylch drws dy dŷ, Lleucu Llwyd!
A genais, lygorn Gwynedd,
O eiriau gwawd i eiry 'i gwedd,

Llef dri-och, llaw fodrwy-aur,
Lleucu! llawenu lliw aur.
Cymhenaidd, groew, loew Leucu!
Ei chymmyn, f' anwyl-fun, fu
Ei henaid, graïr gwlad Feiriawn,
I Dduw Dad—addewid iawn;
A'i mein-gorff, eiliw'r mangant,
Meinir, i gyssegr-dir sant:
Dyn pell-gwyn doniau peill-galch,
A da byd i'r gwr du balch;
A'r hiraeth, cywyddiaeth cawdd,
I minnau a'i cymmynawdd.
Lleddf ddeddf ddeuddaint ogyfuwch,
Lleucu Llwyd, lliw cawod lluwch!
Pridd a main, glain galar chwerw,
A gudd ei deurudd, a derw.
Gwae fi drymder y gweryd
A'r pridd ar feistres y pryd!
Gwae fi fod arch yn gwarchae,
A thy main rhof a thi mae!
Gwae fi, ferch wen o Bennal,
Brudded yw briddo dy dal!
Clo du derw—galar chwerw gael—
A daiar, deg ei dwyael!
A throm-goed ddor, a thrym-gae,
A llawer maes, rhof a'i lliw mae;
A chlyd fur, a chlo dur du,
A chlicied—yn iach, LEUCU!

LLEWELYN GOCH AP MEIRIG HEN.

THE FEUDAL SYSTEM.

BY

JOHN JENKINS, Esq.

[As much of the preceeding Work relates to Feudal times and usages, the following able Paper from the pen of a modern writer cannot be otherwise than acceptable to the reader.—Ed.]

A CLEAR idea of the Feudal System is in the highest degree interesting to the inhabitants of modern Europe, as it was the first form of society which succeeded ancient civilization, and is the foundation of most of our modern laws, systems, and institutions. Without a definite idea of this system, much or most of the present regulations of civilized life would be unintelligible.

But I have spoken of ancient civilization. What did this term mean? What does it comprise? I believe, it means that progressive or advancing state of human society, which existed among the various nations and empires of the world previous to the dissolution of the Roman Empire. The countries where this civilization reached its highest stage are well-known. History presents them in bold relief on its pages. They were Persia, Assyria, Chaldea, Egypt, Greece, and Rome; and, in an inferior degree, China and Hindoostan. In these countries the inhabitants had substituted a stationary for a wandering life, had acquired the notions and defined the limits and rights of property, had entered the bonds and enjoyed the benefits of society, had extended their ideas beyond supplying the rude necessities of life, had acquired a taste for the comforts and even luxuries of social life, had begun to cultivate the arts and sciences, had built vessels whereby they could traffic by sea, and had erected towns and cities (some of costly magnificence) on land. The bulk of the people had forsaken the sword for the plough, and exchanged the spear for the pruning-hook. They dwelt peaceably and securely in their villages, towns, and rural homes. They divided their employments The land was cultivated, the stock of living animals was fed, and commerce carried on. A parliament or congress of the chief inhabitants assembled, and deliberated on the affairs of State. Laws were enacted, and justice administered in the public courts. The spiritual interests of the people were also provided for, and magnificent temples, churches, and cathedrals were built and adorned the land. A regular gradation of nobles or chiefs was established, to whom the people at large looked up, while a King, Sovereign, or Emperor governed the whole. These are the leading ideas connected with ancient civilization. These elements flourished largely in the last of the old empires, or that of Rome, which before its fall had transcended all that went before in commerce, civilization, learning, réfinement, science, art, as well as in grandeur and extent of territory.

We have spoken of the fall of the Roman Empire. This occurred in the beginning of the fifth century. We will just glance at the state of Europe immediately before the dissolution of that vast empire. The Roman Empire (which comprised Italy and the adjacent territories) was at that time and had been for centuries the only kingdom in Europe where the arts of peace and civilization reigned. All the vast countries north of the Alps, west of the Mediterranean, and east and north of the Adriatic seas, were in a state of comparative, if not complete barbarism. Among the people who inhabited these countries we may name the Franks, who occupied Gallia or modern France;

the Goths, Vandals, and Germanic tribes, who occupied modern Germany; the Scythians and other Sclavonic races, who occupied modern Russia; the Visigoths, who occupied Spain; the Celts, who dwelt in Great Britain and Ireland; and the Scandinavians, who occupied the north of Europe, or Lapland, Sweden, and Norway. These various populations were, during the zenith, and down to the fall of the Roman Empire, in a state of semi if not perfect barbarism. A great portion of them were nomadic or roving tribes, and had in their career of devastation and conquest traversed the vast plains of Asia and eastern Europe, before taking up a more settled though not permanent abode in the broad plains and forests of Germany, Spain, and Russia. The Goths, Scythians, and Sclavonic tribes who thus poured into Europe, were emigrants from Asia. The native races who inhabited eastern Europe were unequal to repel the savage invasions of these formidable marauders, who inundated Europe with their fierce and unsettled bands. If we may credit the account given of these tribes by the Roman writers of the period, their manners were savage, their habits of life simple, but of a roving and predatory character. By the Roman historians they are invariably styled—the Barbarians. They cultivated not commerce, they built not cities, they dwelt not in luxurious towns. Their abode was the vast forest or plain, their occupation hunting and war, their food the produce of the chase or the plunder of war, their dress the skins of beasts and articles of the rudest manufacture. Yet in their spirit was energy, in their hearts a love of conquest and aggrandisement. After having for ages in vain withstood the conquering arms of Julius Cæsar and other Roman commanders, they in turn became the assailants. After the reign of Augustus Cæsar the military spirit of the Romans decayed, their energy declined, their ambition was lost. The chief people surrendered themselves to all the enervating effects of pleasure and luxury. No valorous chief led the army in the field, no Cato or Tully thundered alarm in the Capitol, to summon the inhabitants to glory or even defence:—they were rather found revelling in riot and debauchery at home. No Pompey governed in Spain; no Sallust was Prætor in Numidia. The race of the wise and mighty had departed. The infection had reached the common people, who were equally given up to indolence, license, riot, debauchery, and sloth. In this state was Rome and the Romans, when the barbarians rose in the north under Alaric, King or Chief of the Goths, descended the Alps with the rapidity and force of the avalanche, overthrew the empire, and possessed Rome. Then was presented a scene the most unexampled the world ever beheld. The chief or warrior who a few months before held his counsels in a hut or wigwam on the banks of the Danube or Rhine, was seated on the throne of the Cæsars —the herdsman of the forest inhabited the palaces of Rome. The savage hid himself in the fine linen of the Roman citizen—the barbarian covered himself with patrician gold. The effeminate luxury of the Empire had yielded all to the insatiate energy and ambition of the North.

But even the nomadic tribes of central Europe found the miseries and inconveniences of a wandering and predatory life. The Saxons, Goths, and Scythians experienced the comforts and enjoyments of a settled and stationary life. They even grew weary of conquest, and knew the hazard of warlike achievements. They therefore wished to settle down upon some fixed and definite territory. They determined to appropriate a place which they could call their home, and to inhabit a country which they could call their own. They saw the precarious subsistence which awaited those who depended on the spontaneous produce of the earth, and the greater riches which would accrue from a cultivation of the soil. They therefore resolved on a stationary life. But this new life must have order and laws. There must be a Head to whom they should look up, a law or rule which they should obey. The warrior or chief under whose guidance the tribe had conquered and become powerful, was chosen Head of the community, and Lord paramount of the soil. The lesser warriors or captains were placed next in degree and power. The people at large were in a state of vassalage and dependence upon the Lord paramount and his Esquires and Deputies. The Lord paramount built and fortified a castle on some eligible spot in the domain. This castle was used for the residence of the Lord and his family in time of peace, and for the hospitable reception of his retainers and dependents. But in time of war the castle was the refuge and resort of all the inhabitants of the domain. There they retired before the superior number or power of the enemy, and were generally safe. Thence arose the rights and duties of chief and people. The chief owed to the people protection and security from foreign enemies, as well as arbitration and counsel. The people on the other hand owed the Lord suit and service in time of war to repel the common enemy, and allegiance at all times. For these purposes in time of peace the vassals or people farmed and cultivated the domain for their own benefit, paying to the Lord rent, suit, and service. The Lord reserved for his own use a large tract in the vicinity of his castle. Should any dispute arise between the tenants or vassals respecting the ownership or cultivation of their respective tracts of the domain, or otherwise, the Lord was arbiter or judge. Afterwards and in process of time the Lord called his chief dependents or vassals to assist him in the arbitrament of his subjects' disputes. These tribunals were subsequently called the Baron's Court, or Court of the Manor, and were the only tribunals of justice in the earlier period of the feudal society. The

Lord presided, and was assisted by his principal tenants or vassals. The Baron or Manorial Court was of the utmost importance in those rude times, for there were recorded all the transactions relating to the land within the manor; and there assembled all the tenants who had rent, suit, or service to pay or render, or who had complaint to make of disturbance, injury, or grievance, from a fellow tenant, or vassal. The decision of this court was final, the disobedience of which was punished by heavy fines, forfeitures, and disqualifications.

We thus see that the feudal society arose not more from choice than from the necessity and circumstances of the time. At this unsettled and warlike period, protection was required for the tribe or clan from the enmity or rapacity of neighbouring hordes. The tribe therefore united under one common chief to defend their own territory and people, and when necessary, to make war on a neighbouring or distant community. Rule and internal government were also necessary for the comfort and security of the tribe itself. These were therefore the circumstances which induced, or rather compelled the various tribes or hordes of the barbarian population of mediæval Europe to enter the feudal society. And in this manner sprung up, soon after the dissolution of the Roman Empire, that vast net-work of feudal society, which eventually extended itself from Cape Trafalgar to the Euxine Sea, and from the Gulf of Bothnia to the Pillars of Hercules.

It was among the vast forests and plains of Russia, Hungary, Germany, and France, and by a people just emerging from barbarism, that the feudal system arose, and that about the fifth century of the Christian era; thence it was carried by the Continental invaders into their newly conquered territories. But in no country was the system more predominant, than in Gaul, or France, whence it was carried by their Duke of Normandy, or our William the Conqueror, after the battle of Hastings in the eleventh century into Britain, and was more rigorously established here for the protection of the conquerors and the subjection of the native races than it had ever been in Normandy itself. The Conqueror parcelled out all the richest parts of the territory among seven hundred of his Captains or warlike retainers, and erected each into a Barony. The Barons rented a portion of their domains to their Knights, which were denominated knights' fiefs, and were 60,215 in number;—these again sub-let part of their fiefs to their Esquires. The cultivation of the soil and all kind of manual labor were carried on by the vassals, or villeins, who formed the mass of the people. Each class owed rent, suit, and service to their superiors, and the whole were subject to the Lord paramount, or Sovereign, to whom the right to the soil of all the land in his kingdom was reserved, and the herbage or surface alone was granted to the Barons and their tenants, on condition of yielding suit and service to the King, failing which the land reverted to its original owner—the Lord paramount. The wily Conqueror thus founded a superstructure of government which proved impregnable to all assaults from the vanquished races, and reared a cordon of despotism strong and compact from within, and unassailable from without.

The object of this superstructure being military strength, each Norman Baron erected a stately castle fortified by walls, towers, and, if available, a moat, on the strongest site or position within his manor. Here the Baron dwelt, with his domestics, and a chosen body of his warlike vassals, who always bore arms, and watched and were prepared by day and by night at any alarm to sally forth to any summons of conquest or defence. In times of peace the chief occupation of the Baron and his principal retainers was the chase, and the game on the manor was preserved with the greatest care, and its destruction guarded against by the forest laws, which were the most cruel of any enactments on record, inasmuch as the punishment for killing a deer or even a hare was the taking out the eyes of the delinquent; while at the same time the punishment of homicide, or murder, was only a small pecuniary fine, and when perpetrated by the Baron or any of his retainers on an inferior vassal was seldom enforced. In short, under this system there was then no appeal or redress by an inferior for any crime or wrong perpetrated by his superior in rank; and the vassals, or people at large, were in a state of the greatest subjection and most abject slavery, inasmuch as the will and pleasure of the superior liege formed the only law of the land.

It is certain that the feudal system after the Norman model never existed among the Saxons in this island, or on the continent of Europe, previously to the Norman Conquest. Their Kings were mostly elected to the throne; and the land was possessed principally by their military chieftains, called Thanes. This order was at first confined to military supremacy; but in process of time successful merchants and others who had acquired wealth were admitted into the rank. The Thanes resided in large irregular halls upon their estates, in a coarse but very hospitable manner: their halls were said to be generally filled with their neighbours and tenants, who spent their time in feasting and riot. The great distinction between the Anglo-Saxon nobility and the Norman, according to William of Malmesbury, was, that the latter built magnificent and stately castles; whereas the former dwelt in large but mean houses, and consumed their immense fortunes in riot and hospitality. Nevertheless this social communion, combined with the hearty generosity and manners of the Saxon nobility, made them extremely popular among their tenants and vassals, between whom was established a spontaneous and steady attachment. The next in degree were called Ceorles, and were freemen. These conducted most of the occupations on the land and in trade;—they formed the most numerous class of the Anglo-Saxon population, and enjoyed all the rights of freemen, as these were uuderstood in those times;—they had a voice in the national councils, served on juries in the County and other Courts, and their rights and liberties were protected, and generally enforced by fines against each other, and even against their superiors. The Anglo-Saxons rejoiced in their system of trial by jury, and boasted it as their peculiar institution. It was also a law among them that none should be tried except by his equals in the government. These institutions, with the historical open-heartedness of the Thanes and landed proprietors, secured to the Ceorles or freemen as much of real liberty and justice as those rude times might admit.

But the Saxon government is defaced by the odious vice of slavery. The slaves were those whom they had conquered in battle; and the Anglo-Saxons introduced them into this island. They were household slaves, performing menial duties, and predial or rustic slaves who labored on the soil. The proprietors sold their slaves with their estates, and they were regarded as chattels: yet the master had not unlimited power over his slave, for it was ordained that if he beat out his slave's eye or teeth, he gained his liberty; and if he killed him, he paid a fine to the King. Yet, notwithstanding this protection, and although the slaves were confined to races vanquished in battle, yet the practice formed a dark stain on the Saxon institutions.

The government of the Ancient Britons, or Cymri,

corresponded much with the Anglo-Saxon, except that their King was hereditary, and that they were always free from the odious institution of slavery. Sovereign power was inherited among the Cymri, according to the present rules of descent in England, from whom it was probably derived. The chief people were the Princes or large land-proprietors, who dwelt in magnificent style, and exercised unbounded hospitality in their halls upon their estates. Here they received their retainers and tenants, to whom they dispensed the greatest liberality: here also dwelt the Bards, Priests, and Literati of the period—the Taliesins, Aneurins, and Dafydd ap Gwilyms—in the enjoyment of the most profuse favors and protection from their munificent patrons. Hence also the spontaneous and faithful attachment of the whole to their Princes,—as exemplified in the poems of the Bards, and the warlike records of the Cymric nation. Besides the Princes, were a large number of independent landowners or Esquires distributed over the whole island. The great mass of the people, as in every community, labored on the land, or were employed in domestic and mercantile occupations. Slavery or even abject servitude was unknown among them: every class enjoyed the rights and exercised the privileges of freemen, and seldom failed in obtaining redress for any crime or wrong. In their freedom from slavery, and their full enjoyment of civil rights and immunities, the Cymri of ancient times formed a striking contrast with all the European nations.

The effects of the Norman Conquest varied altogether as it respected the Anglo-Saxons and the Cymri. The former were entirely subjected to the feudal system, and their lands forfeited and parcelled out among the Norman chiefs. The forest laws and other odious parts of the feudal system were executed in all their rigor against the vanquished Saxon: hence the sanguinary feuds and mortal enmity which for several centuries existed between the Saxon and Norman race. The former, repelled by the feudal system from open war, retaliated by private and secret murders and injuries upon their Norman oppressors: no Saxon impeaching, the murder or crime was never discovered, and the perpetrator unpunished. At length the Normans, being decimated by this practice of stealthy revenge, passed a law that every Saxon in the parish should answer for every Norman found killed within its limits. This law, which would have been rigorously executed, at last suppressed the Saxon retaliation; nevertheless the hostility between the two races continued for ages, and was only inflamed by the contempt and oppression of the Norman on all occasions evinced. The Cymri on the other hand remained free in their mountain fastnesses and plains west of the Severn and Dee, and unaffected by the Norman invasion and conquest. They even rejoiced at the change, inasmuch as it supplanted a foreign and adverse race—the Saxon—by a kindred and more congenial people; for the Normans were Celts descended from the same Cimbric origin, and had many qualities of mind and heart in common with the Ancient Britons: whereas the characteristics of the Saxons, and of the Teutonic race in general, were entirely opposite. The Normans celebrated the anniversary feasts and cherished the memory of the Cymric King Arthur of the Round Table, whose chivalric fame they regarded as much their own as the Cymri, for he ruled the Celts of Gaul as well as of Britain. The Cymri therefore looked on with placidity and satisfaction at the mutual enmity and reprisals of Normans and Saxons, for they remained unconquered and unmolested in their upland homes. We find them occasionally under their Princes making inroads into England, and conquering and retaining much border territory. The Norman Kings therefore established on the Welsh borders the Lords-marchers, or Lords authorised to conquer and hold by the sword land in Wales; and erected a chain of castles and fortresses from Chester through Shrewsbury and Gloucester to Pembroke, for the defence of the frontier, and the repression of sorties from Wales. Hence the Grosvenors, De Greys, Cliffords, and Mortimers of border chivalry. Hence also the border wars between them and Gruffydd ap Conan, Owain Gwynedd, Llewelyn, and other Princes of Wales, wherein great courage and chivalry were displayed on both sides, and seldom to the advantage of the Norman. At last, after ages of bloodshed and war, and repeated failures, the subjection of the Principality was accomplished, A.D. 1283, by Edward the First, who, to extinguish the last embers of patriotic fire, massacred upwards of one hundred Welsh Bards, in addition to many Cymric Princes. But the Cymri were still discontented and given to insurrection, until a monarch of their own Tudor blood was placed on the British throne in the person of Henry the Seventh, A.D. 1485. Henceforward they became more reconciled to the larger and dominant race, and at length subsided into peaceful submission and attachment to the British throne and laws.

But to return to the feudal system strictly so called, we find the Lords and Barons were all-powerful within their dominions, and had the power of giving or taking away the life, liberty, and property of their retainers and vassals. They often made war upon each other, the consequences of which were frequently awful in the streams of blood which flowed, and the murder, rapine, and spoliation which ensued. Evidences of these internal wars are seen in the ruined castles and dismantled towers which cover our own country and the continent of Europe. The Barons would frequently league together, and make war upon the King or Sovereign, in which they often triumphed. A remarkable instance of this is found in

English History, when the Barons joined in opposing King John, and wrested from him Magna Charta at Runnymede. The De Veres, Bohuns, Mowbrays, Nevilles, Howards, Percys, and Somersets often overshadowed their sovereign lieges in England; while the powerful families of Douglas and Scott for ages held the Kings of Scotland in awe. The Kings and Sovereigns were more in fear and had greater apprehensions of the feudal Barons, than from the mass of their subjects, and were therefore often completely obsequious to their wills. But ever and anon would arise an Edward or a James, who, defying the enmity of the feudal chiefs, diminished their powers and restrained their excesses. Yet this was never done, or even attempted, without the greatest opposition and danger, and never but by a brave and formidable Prince.

Each of the great Barons kept a Court, and indulged in a style of pageantry corresponding in an inferior degree to that of Royalty, of which he occasionally affected independence. When the great Earl Warrenne was questioned respecting the right to his vast land possessions, he drew his sword, saying that was his title, and that William did not himself conquer England, but that his ancestor with the rest of the Barons were joint adventurers in the enterprise. As the Barons were so powerful, the Sovereign never made war or undertook any other great enterprise without first convoking and consulting them, as their co-operation was necessary to his success. In fact, such was their position in the realm, that no change in the laws or government, nor any great act of administration, could be accomplished without their advice and consent. Hence they formed with the ecclesiastical hierarchy, the sole and supreme legislative council of the Sovereign. Independently of the necessity for their advice and co-operation in national enterprises, the Sovereign was desirous of convoking the Barons to his councils at stated periods, as a badge of fealty, and to remind them of their allegiance to Royalty; which in the autocratic retirement of their castles, and the solitude of their manors, they were prone to forget. Whensoever any of the Barons rebelled against the royal authority, the Sovereign assembled the other Barons to assist him in suppressing the mutiny. If on the other hand any Baron should be unable to repel the encroachments of a neighbor, he appealed to the Sovereign as the supreme liege for help to resist and punish the aggression, which with the aid of other chieftains was generally granted. The Sovereign therefore stood in the same relation to the Barons of the whole realm, as they individually to their vassals, the feudal theory being, that all land was held ultimately from the Sovereign in return for military and other services, failing which it reverted to the Crown.

The Barons, as may be supposed, exercised unlimited power within their domains, as the Sovereign never interposed in questions between the Lord and his vassals, so long as the chief rendered the services required by the Crown. Hence the power of each Baron was absolute within his dominions; and from his acts there was no appeal, much less redress. He even affected Royalty by obliging his principal vassals to give attendance upon him, in like manner as he and the other Barons paid court to the King, and by establishing Courts and Judges of his own to administer justice to his vassals. In short, every Barony was a miniature Kingdom, with an army of retainers, a train of officials, and other insignia of State grandeur corresponding with the wealth and power of the chief. To maintain this condition, the Baron was under the necessity of raising a large revenue from his Barony; and as a great display of power was essential for the chief, his exactions from the vassals and all within his power were consequently heavy. This revenue was obtained from heriots, fines, and tolls; which being arbitrary, the amount depended on the want which called it forth, or on the conscience of the chief. A heriot of the best horse, or certain head of cattle, or a fine of so many marks, were payable to the Baron on the marriage or death of his vassal, and on each fresh succession to the fief. These exactions were not confined to the immediate vassals and villains, but extended to the whole population within the limits of the Barony. The towns were in this era small, consisting principally of villages, which, as they were situate within some Barony, were equally subjected to fiscal burdens. These, in addition to heavy fines demanded for any building, liberty, or encroachment on the manor, consisted of tolls and duties imposed on the exportation or importation of goods, and on the sale of horses, cattle, or stock which, to increase the revenue, were prohibited being sold outside the vills, or except in the fairs and markets there licensed to be held, whereupon the tolls attached. By this means the Baron raised a considerable revenue to support his power and state. But as the Baron was more hostile to the trading community or the population of towns, than to his own military vassals and tenants on the soil, as being less serviceable to his warlike power, and more antagonistic to, and discontented with his seigniotal privileges,—he imposed on the former heavier fiscal burdens, and spared no opportunity of oppressing them with the most odious extortions. The military and mercantile spirits have always been antagonistic and hostile, and the germs of that great conflict which has since existed, and in recent times been so grandly developed between the two elements, are plainly discernible in this era—the cradle of its history.

But as the boroughs increased, the towns multiplied, and commerce extended, an antagonistic principle or element to the powers and privileges of the feudal nobility grew up. The reigning power having so much cause for dread of the Barons, was desirous of conciliating the burgher nobility, or the population of towns, and from time to time made large concessions or grants in their favor. This was done as much to foster a rival power or influence to the feudal nobility, as to win over the towns to the interest of the King. These grants consisted in charters of incorporation, that the towns might be freed from the rule of the landed nobility, and might accomplish their own government; and grants of fairs, and markets, and tolls, as well as the rights of representation in parliament. Thus in times past the Kings of Britain were often in friendlier alliance with the towns and burgher nobility, than with the feudal Barons and landed aristocracy. By this means the power and privileges of the feudal nobility, which up to the fifteenth century were nearly absolute and uncontrollable, were much reduced, and are in the present reign nearly taken away. This result has been owing almost entirely to the growing importance, influence, and intelligence of the burgher or trading population. It is thus that in political society as in nature and the material world, results are accomplished by the antagonistic operation and conflict of rival or opposing principles, elements, or influences.

The other great influence which counteracted the feudal spirit from an earlier period, and mitigated its severities, was religion, or the Church. This was natural and inevitable; for the overwhelming influence of religion over the human mind in all ages and nations is the universal deduction of history. It appears to strike its root even the deeper, in proportion to the strength and ruggedness of the mind on which it operates, as plants are more luxuriant from the rankness of the soil where they grow. The fulminations of Sinai or the dulcet harps of Zion have seldom failed in moving the heart of man, and exciting its tenderest and best emotions. We find this verified even in the darkest times, and among the most ferocious nations. Clovis, Charlemange, and William of Normandy are magnificent illustrations. The first, from being one of the most ruthless and savage warriors and conquerors at the head of the Franks ever known in history, no sooner heard the preaching of the Gospel through the instrumentality of his wife Clotilda, than he immediately embraced its truths, and by the most abject humility and self-denying sacrifices for the remainder of his life endeavored to atone for his past cruelties. His great successor, Charlemange, less barbarous and with higher capabilities, at the head of his Germans vanquished continental Europe after innumerable and ferocious wars; yet succumbed his lofty spirit to the influence of Christianity, and prepared by his sword a way for its missionaries. We also find that William the Conqueror, by the deepest penitence and remorse, and by large munificence to the Church, sought to make recompense for the cruelties and excesses of his reign.

It was therefore inevitable that in the middle ages the influence of the Church should operate on the feudal Barons, and soften the rigors of their power. In the vicinity of the Baronial castle arose a village, whose inhabitants were generally dependent on the Lord. In the village sprung up a church and a pastor. The village Priest generally ministered to the inmates of the castle, as well as to the inhabitants of the hamlet; and as learning, or even the rudiments of scholarship, were then confined to the clergy, the religious minister was also the secretary, teacher, and counsellor of the Baronial family. He thus acquired influence and mastery over the youth and age of the circle, and seldom failed to seize the advantage in imbuing them with his benign creed. Hence the contrast presented in those ages between the chieftain in the camp and field, where he was all vigor and ferocity, and in his own hall, where he displayed many virtues of the christian life. Hence also the generally milder character of the heir apparent and future wielder of the Baronial power, than of the sire. To this source we may also in a great measure ascribe the diminishing severity of each succeeding Baron, and the much more humane and improved conduct and manners of the late than early chieftains.

But this is regarding religion in its private and spontaneous, yet in its best influence, in subduing the rigors of the feudal chiefs. It had a separate, more worldly, but yet powerful influence in the Church. Constantine the Great made the Church (which was previously a voluntary and spontaneous association of christian people) a national and compulsory institution, and a fundamental part of the imperial fabric: he added it to the Roman Empire; succeeding Emperors maintained it; and it became a preponderating influence in the State. It was feared that after the irruption of the Barbarians and their conquest of the Empire, although private belief and individual creeds might remain and be preserved, yet the Church as a political element and fabric would inevitably fall and perish in the imperial ruin. But in this the anticipations of men failed; for we find that the Goths, Vandals, and Scythians were equally susceptible of the influence of the religion of Christ, which many of them and especially their chieftains embraced, and often aided its progress with the sword. We also find that as soon as the barbarian conquest of Rome settled into distinct nationalities and governments, the powers followed the example of the great Constantine, and added religion to the State, and constituted the Church a political fabric. In this manner, before and at the commencement of the middle ages, every European state had its National Church. This polity existed equally in Britain, where the Church became a rich and powerful corporation, often rivalling and occasionally transcending the feudal Barons in wealth, dignities, and influence. The Prelates of the Church were by law Barons of the realm. Anselm, in the reigns of William Rufus and the first Henry,—Thomas à Becket, in that of the second,—both Archbishops of Canterbury, and Cardinal Wolsey, in the reign of Henry the Eighth, are illustrations of the great wealth, power, and dignity which the ecclesiastical hierarchy from time to time enjoyed in this country.

The extensive wealth and influence of the Church excited the jealousy and enmity of the feudal Barons, between whom were continual disputes, which sometimes led to violence and war. In their progress we find the Bishops and dignitaries of the Church occasionally substitute the mitre by the helmet, and the crosier for the sword, and rivalling the feudal chieftains in their military exploits. We also find the Church generally allied with Royalty or the sovereign power in their differences with the feudal Barons; but occasionally with the latter in curbing the royal prerogative and power. The Church generally cast its influence into the scale of either power which might happen to be weakest, and for the purpose of counterbalancing the opposite power from which there was greatest apprehension and dread of usurpation and wrong. The ecclesiastical influence and power were also much courted and cherished in general by the Kings and Queens of Britain, as a support to themselves, and a restraint on the feudal chiefs; and they often, when practicable, seized opportunities of enriching the ecclesiastical order, and adding to their power. The Church also sometimes lent its aid and influence to the popular triumph and cause.

It is, therefore, evident that the feudal system met with much antagonism and counteraction from the Church, and that its rigors were much diminished in consequence. The beneficial effects which followed were not always owing to the purest motives, or the benevolence of the Church; but more frequently from the desire of maintaining its own privileges and wealth. But the results to the nation and its liberties were the same as if the ecclesiastical hierarchy had been actuated by higher motives and a purer spirit; and the well-being of the community, was equally promoted.

The Church and the boroughs, in conjunction with the royal power, therefore served to subdue the feudal spirit, and restrain and diminish the powers and privileges of its chiefs.

The effects of the Commonwealth under Cromwell must also have struck fatally at the rigors of the feudal system, in common with many other oppressions, from which they never revived. The spirit of the Commonwealth was deeply hostile to all kinds of ancient tyrrany; and as the feudal law was one of the greatest, it received a serious check. The genius of Puritanism rebelled against the feudal distinctions, as the spirit of liberty which was then triumphant overcame its oppressions. The Baron could no longer at the sound of his horn assemble his ferocious retinue of vassals and retainers, to march to the conquest of political foes, or the suppression of uprising liberty. The Knight could no more ride abroad in his panoply of steel, feared and unopposed by a rabble of villeins and serfs. The spirit of the nation was aroused to its inmost depths in the great struggle for emancipation, and statesmen and warriors arose from its lowest estates. The popular Fairfax overcame the princely Rupert; while the great Commoner—Cromwell—overthrew Royalty itself.

Chivalry had to surrender its crest at Newbury, Marston Moor, and Naseby, to popular bravery and religious zeal. The ancient order of things was entirely changed, and new institutions everywhere took its place, founded on the democratic power. Brewers and butchers now occupied the seats in the Senate formerly held by Barons and Knights; while Fleetwood and Harrison commanded the army of Manchester and Essex. No greater contrast existed than that of the Puritan captain with his skull cap, buff coat, and leather buskins, and the Cavalier with plumed hat, velvet cloak, and silk hose. Not more opposite were they in character than attire: the former a grave, stern, austere, gloomy, and religious democrat; the latter a gay, lively, free-thinking, licentious, and haughty aristocrat: the first was the impersonation of religious faith and prowess; the last of feudal pride. It was therefore inevitable, that in the course of that great struggle between the two elements which ended in the triumph of the popular cause and the establishment of the Commonwealth, feudal arrogance and oppression received a fatal shock.

The leading principle or idea embodied in the feudal system was that of a head, or chief, with dependence by the vassals and retainers. The same principle pervades our laws and institutions, and is in a great measure the fruit or effect of the feudal polity. Among other instances of its operation we may mention the law of primogeniture, the object being to create a family chief. The property qualifications necessary for parliamentary rights and representation, for the magistracy, and other stations of power and dignity, are illustrations of the same effect. The Peers sit and vote in the Upper House of Parliament as Barons of the Realm; while the Members for counties in the other House are returned as Knights of the Shire; and the Judges of the land are designated Barons of the

Exchequer, or Knights' Justices; and the parliamentary Members for boroughs are styled Burgesses,—thus still retaining their feudal distinctions. The preponderance everywhere given to property in land, over wealth in money, trade, or other moveable goods, is a result of the same policy. Indeed it may be said, that the leading principles which govern property in this Kingdom, have their main origin and foundation in the feudal system; although the legislation of the last half century has done much to abolish the enormities with which it was theretofore disfigured.

But it may be asked, what were the effects of the system which we have briefly sketched? Were they good or evil? Did they advance or retard human society and civilization? These are difficult and important questions, in the solution of which probably few will entirely agree.

That the feudal state was rendered necessary by the circumstances of the period, we have, we think, sufficiently shown. That its influence has been in some respects beneficial is also incontestible. The predominant feature of the feudal dominion was force—physical force; and this was the only one suited and practicable for the barbarian population of Europe in the middle centuries. Reason and right were terms unknown and foreign to the masses then emerging from uncivilized life. Force was their own law, and by this must they themselves have been ruled. The Baron or Lord, in enforcing the severities of the feudal code, therefore instructed his vassals in a vocabulary which they understood; he governed them by the only suitable rod. To have addressed them as citizens, and moral and accountable beings, and to have explained to them their duties and rights from a description of the nature, condition, and destinies of man, would have been to have spoken to them in an unknown tongue—in a language they could not have understood.

Moreover, the very relation in which the vassals stood to their Lord, and the services and duties which they were compelled to perform, taught them obedience—trained them to docility and submission. It induced them to reflect on others than themselves,—to regard the wants and rights of others beside their own. This was a great point gained in subduing and training the barbarian just leaving his roving life in the forest or on the mountain. This was a step to further improvement, and to a milder and more rational rule; by this he was trained for a gentler government, and better laws.

The feudal institutions gave birth to chivalry, which exercised so predominant a sway through the middle ages, and in what light soever it is regarded, was beneficial in its influences. It conjures up to our mind the brilliant scenes and magnificent achievements of the period, whether viewed in the enchanting pages of romance, or the more sober records of history. It brings before our minds the mail-clad warrior dispensing refined hospitality in his armor-hung hall, to a princely retinue of retainers and guests, or mounted on his fiery steed, pressing forward to the mortal encounters of honor. The Knight is equally interesting, whether we look at him armed to avenge in single combat the maiden's dishonor or orphan's wrong, or we follow him into the stately tournament, there to encounter in the perilous and sometimes fatal lists. In either case we see displayed the highest qualities of man—courage, honor, dignity, fidelity, skill, and manly strength. We find the same characteristics accompany him into the tented field, where amidst hills of carnage, and at the close of a doubtful day, the bleeding knight contends bravely under the shadow of the red-cross banner. The crusades were a magnificent effect of the religious aspiration of chivalry, whatsoever opinion may now be formed of the policy of those great contests.

No sight more glorious can be imagined than the chivalry of the West marching triumphantly through the heart of Europe to avenge the wrongs and indignities of the Cross upon the Infidel, and contend against four-fold odds under the walls of Antioch and Jerusalem, to recover the Holy Sepulchre from the pollution of Moslem hands. Whatsoever opinion the sober philosophy of history may now pronounce on these great wars, they were dictated by the highest aspirations, and ennobled by the most heroic actions, and they stand out nobly on the headlands of the past as monuments of human grandeur.

Although we have only viewed the institution of chivalry in its outward and more attractive aspects, yet it inculcated a high code of personal morality, very beneficial in the feudal ages. In this era the law was feeble, and its administration so often fruitless, that the greatest restraint on power, and the best security for the rights of individuals, and more especially of the weak, was personal honor; and this in its highest sense was generally characteristic of the barons and knights. They as frequently armed to redress the wrongs of the weak as to avenge their own personal injuries. The maiden's wail, the orphan's cry, were to them the most potent spring of action for the most fatal rencontres. The faithless knight who might happen to injure virgin purity, or oppress unarmed and defenceless people, roused the resentment of the whole order of chivalry, and was pursued from castle to cloister, and from land to land, till his blood atoned for his lust or cruelty. Chivalry inculcated upon its members the highest honor, fidelity, truth, and justice; and in the absence of strong public law, administered equally with a powerful and impartial hand, formed the best code of law and morals in the feudal times. We find examples of faithless barons and recreant knights, as there are exceptions to every rule, and blots upon every picture; yet in the main the very code in which they were instructed, and the habits which they acquired had a most beneficial influence in the formation of their characters, and furnished many illustrious examples of human virtue, and public renown.

The feudal system was, moreover, fertile of the military spirit, and this in its fullest vigor was necessary for the defence of the nation, as well as of individuals, in the dark ages. The feudal polity was first established by the sagacious Conqueror, as a military structure to overawe the vanquished Saxon; and though its rigor became relaxed in after reigns, yet its very existence rested on military organization, and the education of the soldier was its chief aim; the cultivation of the soil and the pursuits of commerce, being regarded as secondary and inferior occupations, and were treated with disdain by the feudal chiefs. Hence the universal predominance of military power and rank in the middle ages, and their monopoly of distinction and wealth. Hence also the paucity of mercantile greatness in those times.

As the martial discipline and organization of his retainers and vassals was necessary to the supremacy of the Baron, so the co-operative forces of the Barons were necessary for the maintenance of the throne, and the safety of the kingdom. The former was in continual peril from domestic ambition and discord, and the latter from foreign foes. A Montfort and a Neville, a Percy and a Douglas, were only restrained from subverting the royal power, and grasping the sceptre in their own hands, by the support given by the other Barons to the sovereign,—evinced on many a well-fought field. The invasion of the kingdom by continental armies, was only prevented by the confederate array of the King and his Barons.

In the absence of that division of employment which

in modern times produced a standing army, the feudal organization with its martial aspect alone supplied the nation with its defence. No sooner did the Frank or Northman display his banner on the wave, for the conquest of Britain, than hill signalled hill, from Devon to the Orkneys, to summon the united Barons to the defence of the realm. With such alacrity was the alarm obeyed, that before a hostile flag could be planted on the headlands of the island, the enemy was driven into the sea, or to the refuge of his ships; leaving full many behind to attest the folly of the expedition. Not less ready were the feudal chiefs to follow the British ensign into foreign wars, there to sustain the glory of its fame. Poictiers and Azincour, Steinkirk and Landen, Ramilies and Blenheim, witnessed the heroic prowess of English chivalry on their hard-fought fields, while the terrible charge of the British infantry passed into the proverbs of those lands. From this system sprang an Essex and a Raleigh, a Chandos and a Churchill, with other great captains of the British hosts, who, by the military organization and discipline which it afforded to the nation, were enabled during the reigns of the Plantagenets, the Tudors, and the Stuarts to preserve our soil inviolate from a foreign foe, and to force entire Europe into respect and homage of the British name.

It is also true that the Baron, his family, domestics, and retainers, were in this era the only persons who possessed any scholarship, learning, or even good manners. The interior of the castle was graced with beauty, order, and comparative refinement. There letters and learning were sought after, if not largely acquired. Good manners and regularity prevailed. The Baron himself spent much of his time in the bosom of his family, and must have been improved in the gentler circle which there assembled. He for a time lost the bluntness and ferocity of his warlike life. A priest, or minister of religion, was also generally an appendage of the castle; and his profession, being an improving, learned, and pacific one, must have acted beneficially on those with whom he associated. The instruction and example of the inmates of the castle must therefore have been beneficial to the whole feudal society around: to which may be added the historical fact that after the introduction of the feudal system, and by the sanction and encouragement of the Barons, were compiled the only literary works of the period of which we have any account. In the solitudes of the baronial castle were composed the only chronicles of that era which have descended to us. Within the walls of the castellated abode generally dwelt the priests, bards, and other literati of the time; where they had leisure and encouragement to pursue their avocations; and thence issued forth their chronicles, poems, and productions. These influences must, therefore, have tended greatly to the civilization and improvement of the whole feudal society.

On the other hand, we must not overlook the fact that the feudal state was decidedly hostile to general freedom —its very nature militated against general liberty—its existence was inconsistent with progress and the spread of freedom and intelligence. The continuance and influence of the feudal dominion depended on the passive submission of all the inhabitants of the domain. Every manifestation of discontent or uneasiness on the part of the latter was, therefore, watched by the chief with a jealous eye; every attempt at disobedience was punished with severity. The chief warded off all principles dangerous to his own monopoly of power. All struggles for general liberty were crushed with an unrelenting hand. The great and only desire of the Baron was to perpetuate the then existing system. Every attempt at amelioration was alike inimical to his wishes and power.

The feudal dominion was also extremely prejudicial to the nation in the inveterate hostility which it manifested to commerce, agriculture, and productive industry. Military power and strength being its chief aim, all pursuits which tended to divert the people from martial exercises and display were discouraged by the feudal chiefs. Hence the cultivation and improvement of the soil was but feebly prosecuted, while the pursuits of commerce and mercantile enterprise were opposed and repressed, from a suspicion of their antagonism to the feudal dominion. The Baron delighted in extensive chases, and parks studded with trees, and covered with brushwood, where game might take refuge; and in vast forests and barren uplands, where the deer and the hare might wander undisturbed; while the furrow of the corn-field and the hedge-row were restricted to the smallest dimensions consistent with the necessities of the population of the manor. The hound was more valued than the sheep-dog; the fowling-piece than the sickle; while herds of wild deer browsing the slopes were more estimated than the oxen on the plain. The huntsman and gamekeeper held higher rank than the ploughman and reaper; while all the prizes of ambition lay open to martial enterprise alone.

But to none was the hostility of the feudal chiefs more rancorous than to the pursuits of commerce. The most odious of sights was the tall chimney of a manufactory peering through the oak and elm of the chase; while the pollution of mills and workshops on the banks of pellucid streams was not to be borne. The mines of the mountain were closed, lest their produce might destroy the salmon and trout of the rivers; while houses and ships were left unbuilt, that the forests be not denuded of their stately timber.

The hostility of the feudal chiefs to mercantile progress

was the more inveterate, from a feeling and knowlege of its antagonism to their own irresponsible power. Every manufactory which was set up bore a brow of hostility to the castle; while every town was in feud with the manor. In every war or tumult the towns and commercial villages ranged their forces in opposition to the Baron and his clan; and whensoever an opportunity offered for suppressing and subverting the feudal dominion and privileges, the mercantile community never failed to raise the axe and strike at their root.

The Barons, therefore, manifested the utmost dislike and hostility to the progress of manufactures and towns. Seldom could a fitting site for a village or manufactory be found except within the limits of a manor; and the lord, if he even conceded the liberty for the erection, never failed to burden the grant with exorbitant rents and exactions, and to fetter it with the most oppressive restrictions. These grants would never have been made, only for the temptation of gold. The feudal chiefs were, from their ostentatious power and display, mostly poor; and in exchange for a high rent or large purchase money, they were induced to grant tracts of land to the manufacturer and merchant, whose money capital was the only bait for the cupidity of the proprietor. Hence, from the reign of Edward the First onwards, the conflict of capital representing commerce, and territorial interest representing the lords of the soil. The former power, feeble at first, grew steadily under the more favorable reigns of succeeding monarchs, and in modern times has made such strides, as to equal, if not surpass, the ancient dominion of the fief.

Moreover, the excessive power of the Barons was full of danger to the peace and security of the realm. Where the dominion and government of the mass of the people were in so few hands, the peril of the nation was great from the discontent or ambition of one or more of the chiefs. A Mowbray, Bohun, Mortimer, or Clifford, could at the head of his clan disarrange the affairs of the entire kingdom, and plunge the nation into war. This danger was also increased from the turbulent disposition of the Barons. The feudal chiefs dwelt apart in the strongholds of their castles, and the solitude of their manors, and exercised unlimited dominion and sovereignty over the inhabitants of their domains. Their mode of life and irresponsible power generated an independence and insubordination which could ill brook restraint or abridgment even from the sovereign, setting aside from another chieftain, and which often broke out in open rebellion, defying even the power of the crown. Hence the insurrection of a Leicester, a Warwick, and a Northumberland, which required the utmost force of the sovereign and his confederate Barons to subdue. Hence also the intestine commotions and civil wars which were so prevalent in the feudal ages, and which from time to time paralysed the progress of the nation, and occasioned the sacrifice of innumerable lives.

The feudal dominion was, in the last place, very unfavorable to art, science, and discovery. Its chiefs had little leisure from foreign wars and domestic tumult for their prosecution, and had less inclination to encourage their promotion by others. Their attention was absorbed in schemes of territorial aggrandisement and political intrigue, as to devote little time to the improvement of the mind. The only learning which they patronised was the mummeries of monkish superstition and priestly adulation. True science was neglected, or even discouraged. We do not find one name throughout the dark and stormy reigns of the Plantagenets which may rank in the first class of scientific merit. We must descend to the Tudors before we meet with any light to dispel the Egyptian darkness which enveloped science. It was the reign of the virgin

Queen Elizabeth which was embellished by that galaxy of illustrious stars in the firmament of discovery, which mapped out new and more useful paths for investigation, and will shed everlasting light upon science. It was in this epoch when the feudal dominion had been shorn of much or most of its pristine glory, and when commerce and manufactures were encouraged, and the liberty of the subject was more secure—that a Bacon, a Raleigh, a Camden, and a Davis, arose to delight and bless mankind with their magnificent discoveries. The paths shadowed out by these great names were afterwards pursued under still more auspicious reigns, throughout which we find a joint alliance and equal progress between mercantile grandeur and civil freedom, and their hand-maiden science. In these latter times we meet with a Newton, a Davy, a Watt, and a Stephenson, whose discoveries and works have yoked matter to accomplish the purposes of man, and made the elements tributary to his designs. It is likewise more than probable that had the human mind in modern times not emancipated itself from feudal servility and thraldom, Britain and the world would have been deprived of these universal blessings, and our own glorious island would at present hold little or no higher rank in Europe than benighted Spain, or the Italian peninsula.

Now that the pomp, glory, and circumstance of the feudal state have passed away, we may leisurely look back on its history, contemplate its features, and observe its effects and tendencies. In this retrospect we are encouraged by the better condition of the age in which we live, and the brightening prospects of the future. But in all our inquiries and wanderings let us never forget that man has in all ages been inconstant, and human nature imperfect, and that the best of all institutions are probably those which approximate the laws that Solon gave to the Athenians; who said, "My laws are not the best ones possible, but they are the best which the Athenians can bear."

PRINTED BY OWEN MILLS, LLANIDLOES.

A LIST OF SUBSCRIBERS.

Printed in the order in which they were registered during the years 1860 and 1861.

Rev. David Evans, Penarth, Llanfair.
W. Llewelyn, Esq., F. G. S., Glanwern, Pontypool.
Miss Davies, 12, Harper Street, Bloomsbury, London.
Rev. James Rhys Kilsby Jones, 10, Priory Street, Camdentown, London.
Mr. R. Peregrine, Llanelly.
— Thomas Hamer, Llanidloes.
— T. G. Jones, Llansaintffraid, Oswestry.
— W. Jones, (a descendant of the author) Yspytty Ystwith, Cardiganshire.
Andrew Jones Brereton, Esq., (*Andreas o Fôn,*) Mold.
Rev. D. Rowlands, M.A., Llanidloes.
— J. Edwards, M.A., Rector of Newtown.
Bernard Quaritch, Esq., 15, Piccadilly, London, 12 copies.
R. Richardson, Esq., Maes Cottage, Rhayader.
T. Richardson, Esq., Dolgroes, Yspytty Ystwith, Cardiganshire.
Rev. J. B. Evans, B.D., Vicar of St. Harmon, Radnorshire.
Mr. James Evans, Postmaster, Lampeter.
T. T. Griffiths, Esq., Wrexham.
Messrs. R. Hughes, & Son, Wrexham.
Mr. John Meedus Jones, Llanidloes.
Rev. D. Davies, Incumbent of Dylife, Montgomeryshire.
N. Bennet, Esq., Glanyrafon, Trefeglwys.
Rev. Thomas Williams, (a descendant of the author) Curate of Llanwrin, Montgomeryshire.
Mr. David Williams, Dyfngwm Mines, Dylife.
John Jenkins, Esq., Llanidloes, 2 copies.
Frederick J. Beeston, Esq., Glandwr, Llanidloes, and 16, St. George's Place, Hyde Park, London, 2 copies.
W. Chambers, Esq., Hafod, Cardiganshire.
Rev. W. Jones, Crescent Street, Newtown.
Rev. Owen Wynne Jones, (*Glasynys,*) Curate of Llangristiolus, Bangor.
Mr. W. Walter, Mount Pleasant, Trallwn, Pontypridd, Glamorganshire.
John Biddulph, Esq., Dderw, Swansea.
Mr. W. Lloyd, Warrington.
Arthur James Johnes, Esq., Garthmill, Welshpool, 3 copies.
Robert Edwards, Esq., Mayor of Aberystwith.
W. H. Thomas, Esq., South Place, Aberystwith.
Rev. C. D. Rees, M.A., Rhayader.
John Jones, Esq., (*Talhaiarn,*) Battlesden, Woburn Beds.
Mr. Robert Isaac Jones, Tremadoc.
——— Wynne, Esq., Coed Coch, Abergele.
Mr. C. D. Bynner, Llangadvan.
Rev. T. James, (*Llallawg,*) Netherthong, Huddersfield.
Rev. John Mills, 40, Lonsdale Square, Islington, London.
John Jesse, Esq., F. R. S., Llanbedr Hall, Ruthin.
Rev. John Davies, Walsoken Rectory, Wisbeach.
The Right Honourable the Earl of Powis, Powis Castle, Welshpool.
The Right Honourable Lord Llanover, Llanover Park, Abergavenny, 2 copies.
George Hammond Whalley, Esq., M. P., Plâs Madoc, Ruabon.
Mr. Thomas Benbow, New York.
John Maurice Davies, Esq., Barrister at Law, Crygie, Aberystwith.
Rev. Richard Jenkins, B. A., Abermagwr Cottage, Crosswood Park, Aberystwith.
W. P. R. Powell, Esq., M. P., Nanteos, Aberystwith, 3 Copies.
Rev. David Williams, Llanedwy Rectory, Llanelly, Carmarthenshire.
Lady Augusta E. Marshall, Ruabon, 2 copies
Rev. Charles Williams, D. D., Principal of Jesus College, Oxford.
Rev. D. Silvan Evans, Llangian, Pwllheli.
— J. Williams, (*Ab Ithel,*) Llanymowddwy Rectory.
— Lewis Evans, Head Master of Ystradmeirig School, Cardiganshire, 2 copies.
— Owen Jones, Vicar of Towyn.
Thomas Wright, Esq., F. R. S., 14, Sydney Street, Brompton, London.
William Jones, (*Gwrgant,*) 20, King's Arms Yard, London.
Rev. Robert Williams, M.A., Rhydycroesau, Oswestry.
George Osborne Morgan, Esq., 2, Stone Buildings, Lincoln's Inn, London.
J. W. Szlumper, Esq., C. E. Milford Haven.
James Davies, Esq., Rhosrhydgaled, Aberystwith.
John Jones, Esq, Dinorben, St George's, St Asaph.
Mr. W. W. Jones, (*Gwilym o Fôn,*) Towyn.
— Owen Mills, Llanidloes.
— T. J. Lloyd, Machynlleth.
Rev. James Griffiths, Vicar of Llangynnor, Carmarthen.
John Scott, Esq., Corbet Arms Hotel, Aberdovey.
Rev. Thomas Jones Hughes, Vicar of Llanasa, Holywell.
John Dendy, Esq., B.A., 36, York Street, Manchester.
Rev. D. Parry, B.A., Darowen Rectory, Machynlleth.
William Price, Esq., Llanffwyst, Abergavenny.
John Jones, Esq., 26, North Parade, Aberystwith.
John Evan Thomas, Esq., F. S. A., 7, Lower Belgrave Square, London.
Rev. Henry J. Evans, Curate of Dowlais.
— David Lloyd James, Vicar of Pontrobert, Montgomeryshire.
Mr. Richard Mills, the Green, Llanidloes.
Miss Sarah Mills, Llanidloes.
Thomas Stephens, Esq., Merthyr Tydvil.
W. H. Reece, Esq., F. A. S., New Street, Birmingham.
James Rees, Esq., Carnarvon.
Ensign E. Powell, Trewythen, Llandinam.
Mr. Thomas Hughes, 10, Croston Street, Liverpool.
Mr. D. J. Roderic, Llandovery.
— Evan Jones, Machynlleth.
— John Beavan, Newtown.

CONTENTS.

The first figures refer to the Translations, the second to the Originals.

CORRESPONDENCE.

THE END.

The Vale of Taff, a Poem, by John Thomas, price 1s.; yr Arweinydd Cerddorol, gan R. Mills, pris 4s. 6d.; The Cambrian Melodist, price 6d.; the Educational State of Wales, by the Rev. J. R. Kilsby Jones, price 2d.; Gwaith Eos Ceiriog, pris 6s.; Testament W. Salisbury, pris 7s.; Williams's Gems of Choral and Sacred Music, price 3s.

A list of other Books gratis, and Post free.

A List of Books Published or Sold by John Pryse, Bookseller, &c., Llanidloes, Montgomery. All post free for their value in stamps; when not to be had from a Bookseller, please send to the Publisher.

THE CAMBRIAN MINSTREL, by John Thomas. (Ieuan Ddu.) Small 4to, (Merthyr Tydfil, 1845,) in 13 Parts, paper covers price 6s. 6d. "The Work is equally interesting to Welsh readers, as nearly all the matter contained is inserted in both languages."

A Melody for Cristmas or New Year's Eve, by R. Lowe, Price 1½d,

Williams's Epitaphs for Grave-stones, Price 9d,

The Inundation of Cardigan Bay, by the Rev, G, Edwards, M,A, Price 9d

Will be published as soon as Subscribers' names are received for 400 copies, price Half-a-crown,

THE HISTORY OF THE ANCIENT BRITONS,

by the late Rev, Theophilus Evans, sometime vicar of Llangammarch, and discoverer of the Llanwrtyd Mineral Waters, &c, Translated from the Welsh, with notes from the works of modern writers, The book will be printed on good paper, and stitched in paper covers,

Will be published as soon as Subscribers' names are received for 250 copies, price 5s,

THE HISTORY OF WALES,

by Caradoc of Llancarvan, translated from the Welsh, The publisher has long noticed the want of a re-print of this most interesting History; it having become very scarce, he ventures to hope to have at once sufficient Subscribers to enable him to issue the book forthwith

DRYCH Y PRIF OESOEDD,

yn ddwy ran, Rhan I, sy'n traethu am hen Ach y Cymry, o ba le ydaethant allan; y Rhyfeloedd a fu rhyngddynt a'r Rhufeinwyr, y Brithwyr, a'r Saeson; a'u Moesau cyn troi yn Gristionogion, Rhan II, sy'n traethu am Bregethiad a Chynydd yr Efengyl yn Mhrydain, Athrawiaeth y Brif Eglwys, a Moesau y Prif Gristionogion, Gan y Parch, Theophilus Evans, gynt vicar Llangammarch, yn ngwlad Fuellt a Dewi, yn Mrycheiniog, Yn nghyda Rhagarweiniad a nodau eglurhaol, gan y Parch, Rhys Gwesyn Jones, un o awdwyr y "Gwyddoniadur Cymreig," &c, Adargraffiad o'r argraffiad a gyhoeddwyd gan yr awdwr yn 1740, Pris mewn papur (i Danysgrifwyr) 2s, Cloth Gilt, 3s

The Love Songs and War Songs of the Ancient Britons,

BREEZES FROM THE WELSH MOUNTAINS,

A Scrap Book of Cambrian Prose and Poetry, compiled by John Pryse, The book contains translated specimens of the works of the most eminent Welsh Bards, Warriors, and Philosophers, Price 1s, 6d

YLlyfr Rhataf yn Nghymru!! Newydd ei Gyhoeddi, Pris 6c. Y CYFAILL I BAWB, Yn cynwys yr "Almanac Tragwyddol," y dull newydd i olchi dillad, wrth yr hwn y gellir cwblhau golchiad chwech wythnos cyn boreufwyd, Hefyd, yn agos i 300 o gyfarwyddiadau ereill yn dangos y ffordd oreu i drin anifeiliaid, ac i wneyd llawer iawn o bethau gwerthadwy, yn nghyda *chatalogues* am filoedd o lyfrau, a hysbysiadau am lawer iawn o bethau nas gellir eu henwi yma, Y ffordd i gael y llyfr—rhowch 6 o stamps llythyran (yn nghydag enw eich trigfa) mewn llythyr, wedi ei gyfeirio at John Pryse, Bookseller, Llanidloes, Montgomery, a chyda throad y post fe anfonir y llyfr yn rhydd

IF YOU WISH TO RESTORE YOUR HEALTH AND INVIGORATE YOUR SPIRITS, you cannot do better than take a trip to one or other of the Welsh Mineral Springs. Before you leave home, send for a copy of Pryse's Handbook to the Breconshire and Radnorshire Mineral Springs, which contains the History of *Llandrindod, Llandegley, Llanwrtyd, and Builth Wells,* with full directions for using the *waters* by a thoroughly qualified medical Gentleman; topographical, antiquarian, and geological notes and exerpts from the writings of the most eminent authors; an Hotel and Lodging-house directory; and descriptive journeys from nearly all the principal towns within a circle of 50 miles. The reader will also find in its pages much amusing and interesting reading for odd leisure hours, all of which is calculated to add to the enjoyment and amusement of the visitor and tourist. The book is neatly bound in cloth, and although it contains above 200 pages, it is not too bulky for the Lady's reticule or the Gentleman's pocket. *How to obtain it,*—Send 24 penny stamps to JOHN PRYSE, BOOKSELLER, LLANIDLOES, MONTGOMERY, and it will be sent Post free to any address.

A Short Familiar Catechism, by the late Rev. T. Charles, of Bala, Price 2d, or thirteen for 2s

Everett's Catechism, translated into English by the Rev, R, Thomas. Price 1d, or one hundred for 6s

The Mother's Gift, (Welsh or English,) 1d, or one hundred for 6s

English and Welsh Letter Writer, Price 6d, and 9d, in cloth, 3d, extra

The Welsh Interpreter, Price 6d, and 9d, bound in cloth, 3d, extra

Everybody's Friend; containing a valnable collection of Receipts, Proverbs, &c, Price 6d,

Gweledigaethau y Bardd Cwsg, (The Visions of the Sleeping Bard,) by E, Wynne, with Life, Price 1s,

Pughe's Beauties of English Poetry, with a literal translation of each piece into Welsh, Price 14 pence

Motives for Progression, by the late D, L, Pughe, with Life, Price 6d

The Unity of the Christian Church, by the Rev. R. G Jones, Price 6d

The Good Old Time is come at last, (Song & Music) by H, Jones, 2d

J. Jenkins, Esq, (Solicitor) on the Nature, &c, of Friendly Societies, 2d

The following Books are preparing for publication, subscribers' names for which will oblige. CANIADAU SEION A'R ATTODIAD, gan R. Mills, pris 12s.; GWAITH BARDDONAWL DAVYDD AP GWILYM, gan Dr. Owen Pughe, pris 6s. 6d.; the CAMBRIAN TRAVELLER'S COMPANION—Biographical and Topographical Sketches, collected by John Pryse; price 1s. 6d., the ENGLISH POETICAL WORKS OF IOLO MORGANWG, price 5s.

www.ingramcontent.com/pod-product-compliance
Lightning Source LLC
Chambersburg PA
CBHW031955060726
47497CB00016B/2204

* 9 7 8 3 3 3 7 3 2 8 0 2 3 *